SHATTERED CRYSTAL

WRITTEN BY
M.T. SYLER

Shattered Crystal

Written by M. T. Syler

Book One of the Crystal Fae

Telaria
Unseelie
Yule
Mabon
Celetrix
Litha
Ostara
Seelie
N
W

Copyright

Shattered Crystal

Book One of the Crystal Fae

Copyright © M.T. Syler 2023

All rights reserved.

No part of this book may be produced in any form or by any electronic or mechanical means, including information storage and retrieval systems, without written permission from the author.

Cover and header artwork by M.T. Syler

2024 Alternate Cover Art by Koti Komori

Trigger warnings

This book has some dark themes as well as some explicit scenes. There is mention of abuse as well as murder and assault.

Also, trigger warnings for foster care and child abuse.

The main character is an escort, which is a SW.

Remember your mental health matters!

Prologue

All my life, I've always tried to roll with the punches—learning to keep myself calm when everything around me was going to shit. I'd learned a long time ago that fighting against your fate only made things worse. Sometimes, you just had to take what life gave you and make a shitty lemonade out of it, even if the lemons it gave you were moldy and full of worms.

This past month, I had only gotten a taste of a happy life, and I wanted more. Too bad things don't always go the way you plan. You know what they say, "Life sucks, and then you die." Or in my case, then it sucks some more.

Laying on the ground, unable to move my body, I wanted to scream but found my voice lost. This was it. The end. How fucking cruel. Someone was talking to me, but it was hard to make out the words. My mind couldn't focus because something else was speaking over my thoughts. The voice was strange, ethereal, insisting it was time for me to move on to my next journey. I try to resist, I really fucking try, but it doesn't matter.

"It's time...destiny awaits."

Destiny? What destiny? The only thing I want to do is stay here. I'm going to wake up, and this will have only been a bad dream.

Please, let this all have been a dream.

A few months ago, I would have welcomed this new adventure with open arms. But now, I questioned whether my desires and choices had any weight in what would happen next. I hated the things I had to do to survive; I hated myself. I just wanted to be happy. Was that too much to ask?

My consciousness was being ripped from my body, and there was not a damn thing I can do about it. Bitter tears streamed down my face. I worked so hard to turn my life around, and for what? For it all to be taken away?

It wasn't fair. Why do I have to be the one to go? Don't I get any say in what happens to me? Does what I want matter at all?

It wasn't perfect, but this life was mine.

The push and pull make me feel like I'm being ripped apart at the seams. My eyes drift to the feminine hands that beckon me closer. I felt a snap as my spirit was torn from my body, and I let out a silent scream. Of course, this would be how it went—a shitty end for a shitty beginning.

I don't want this! I don't want to go!

Fate doesn't care about what you want, though.

Chapter 1

Two months ago

Hair? Check. Makeup? Check. Charming personality… that one I still needed to work on. Everything else seemed to be in order, though, except for this feeling I had in my chest. A lead weight had fallen in my gut and was pulling me down, down, down. Something was different about tonight. Nothing looked different, but there was a spark in the air that made me think that things were about to change.

My nose filled with the usual scent of spilled alcohol and a heady mix of unwashed bodies. You could almost forget about it if your body lotion was strong enough. I spritzed my perfume over my neck and chest to cover any lingering smells. The scent was one of my favorites: rose and honey.

The club was dimly lit, bathed in a red, pulsing light that seemed to heighten the energy in the room. The sultry beats of the music thumped through my chest, making my heart race an erratic beat.

Baby Dolls was far from perfect, but then again, so was I. At one time, this club might have been beautiful, but not anymore. I eyed the dirty red carpet and the stripped wallpaper that was smudged with black. In the low light, the stains were hard to make out, but I knew they were there. I've been working here for five years, and it never gets any better. Despite the smile I plaster to my made-up face, my reality was far from happy. It's a mockery of a grin that feels fake even to me.

As I waited for my turn to take the stage, I took a moment to survey the small dressing room. The owners had made an effort to treat us dancers with a table set up with glasses of sparkling wine—a supposed splurge to celebrate the night. But looking closer, I noticed it was most likely left over from the clients and had been sitting out for hours. The bubbles were long gone, leaving it flat and devoid of taste. I shouldn't drink it. I know that, and yet I found myself picking up a glass and taking a sip. It's bitter and hot as it goes down my throat. Still, I couldn't deny the feeling of appreciation for the gesture. Better then nothing.

Quickly, I drank it down to settle my nerves, needing the liquid courage before my performance. Like every night, I tell myself,

'This is a normal night, and my monsters won't find me here,' this stupid mantra came to me one night and stuck with me. It calms my racing heart as I repeat it again and again.

The drink helps me to relax a little but does nothing to alleviate the dark feeling I have about tonight. *Pull yourself together, Mel! Nothing is going to be different about tonight.* The sudden stress I feel has me reaching for another glass. As I drank it, I took a moment to check my appearance in the cracked mirror. My makeup was still flawless, and my hair was perfect. Men liked to say they preferred a no-makeup look, but if the years have taught me anything, it was that men are full of shit.

My delicate makeup accentuates my natural beauty, and my strawberry blonde hair was styled in bouncy curls that cascade down my back—catching the dim light and glistening in a coppery radiance. I give my reflection a sly smile. *Come on, gorgeous, let's make those men hand over all their cold, hard cash.*

The song playing over the loudspeakers was almost over, and then it will be my turn. I consider having another drink, as alcohol has become a welcome crutch. But too many glasses will have me swaying and not in a seductive way, so I decided against it.

Drinking was my vice of choice. At least I could take comfort in the fact that I hadn't turned to drugs but fuck if sometimes it wasn't tempting. Luckily for me, I knew release was coming soon. When my head hit that pillow tonight, I would escape to a fantasy only I could see. That world belonged to me and only me, and even when things were going wrong, my dreams were always there to comfort me.

As the light flashed above the red velvet curtains, signaling my turn to perform, I took a deep breath and tried to clear my mind. I kept my expression bland, neutral. *Only a few hours of this, then you get to go to sleep.*

Walking through the curtains and onto the stage, I could hear the familiar opening notes of my chosen song begin to play through the speakers. I took another deep breath and focused on the rhythm, letting my body move and sway to the beat. The crowd fell silent as I began to dance, my hips swinging and my body undulating to the music. In the dim light, I could feel the eyes of the men fixed on me, their gazes burning with desire as they watched me move. As the tempo increased, I let go of my inhibitions and granted their wish to see my naked flesh.

I drew out the striptease as long as possible, slowly revealing more of my body as the song progressed. My pushup bra was hidden under a sheer blue nightie that was tied at the front, and my barely-there panties were covered with lacy thigh-highs that accentuated my legs. The fabric of my outfit leaves little to the imagination, but I keep my movements sensual and alluring, allowing the audience to feel the heat of the performance.

Removing the nightie by undoing the bow but not taking it off completely, I open it to show off my cleavage. I caress my breasts through the fabric. Sliding my hands down my body, I reach for my toes. It gives the crowd a good view of my round ass while I look over my shoulder coyly and begin unrolling my socks. I slid myself to the ground, falling in a split, then flipped myself to my back, tossing the white lacy thigh-highs away. Money was placed on the edges of the stage, but I didn't go to grab it. It takes work to get this good at stripping. If you've ever been to an amateur night at a club, you know what I mean.

We kept some of the cash for stripping, but that wasn't our primary source of income. The real money comes afterward, in the rooms upstairs. In a place like Baby Dolls, everything can be purchased for a price, including the staff. And if you were interested in a different sort of entertainment, the barkeeper sold alcohol and a variety of drugs.

My bra fell to the floor, the cool air causing my nipples to harden as goosebumps blossom over my skin. While the crowd watched my strip tease, the owner, Micheal, took bids for a night with me.

Micheal was a small, weaselly-looking man with thinning black hair, which he often wore pulled back in a low ponytail. He seemed to think wearing his hair long made him look younger—as if that could work. Besides his horrible lack of style, Micheal wasn't a horrible boss. He paid us fairly, or at least better than most other clubs. But don't get me wrong, he's an asshole. Seriously, some days, the way he talked to me made me want to take some scissors and chop that greasy ponytail right off his head—but things could be worse. Tonight, he's wearing a tacky blue Hawaiian button-down, sticking out like a sore thumb in the crowd of suits.

Observing the crowd as I danced, I saw Micheal sitting at the bar, sipping cheap beer and exchanging money with clients. He must have felt me looking at him because he turned his beady black eyes to the stage and smirked at me—I wanted to flip him the finger. With all that money he made from my body and the others, the man still wouldn't invest in better clothes—*Cheap Ass.*

When I first came here, I knew I would be stripping, *obviously*—but I was surprised to find that it's basically a modern brothel. At first, I wasn't comfortable with the idea of selling myself for a place to live. But after doing it the first time, I found I could mostly block out what I was doing to survive. And being homeless again was not an option.

When I turned eighteen, a bad boyfriend convinced me to run away with him. That obviously didn't pan out, and after going through the foster care system with no family, I suddenly found myself broke and alone.

A friend from the same group home as me worked at Baby Dolls. She told me she got to sleep all day, and the cash just kept on coming. The owners even had an apartment building across the street and offered the girls low rent. How could I pass up a job *and* a place to live?

That *friend* of mine, well, she didn't last here long, and I haven't heard from her since. I bet she found herself a boyfriend or sugar daddy willing to put up with her shit. *Stupid bitch*. Whatever, I don't need a man to rescue me. I'll find a way out of this place on my own. At least, that's what I kept telling myself.

My eyes look out to the crowd as I dance, but It's hard to see the faces of the men who watched me. Not that I want to see them. The lights were set up in a way that left the guests in the shadows and the dancers in the spotlight. I caught a glimpse of myself in the wall-length mirror and froze. Staring back wasn't me, but someone who can only exist in my dreams. She smiles slowly and beckons me forward.

This girl looks just like me, with the same strawberry blond hair and mismatched eyes—one blue and the other hazel brown. The obvious difference was our ears: mine are rounded, while hers are pointed. Also, her smile was warm and inviting—nothing like my lifeless expression. The girl was there and gone in an instant, making me question what I saw. *The light must be playing tricks on me. Or maybe the wine was bad?*

I start dancing again, running the tips of my fingers up and down my breasts. My hips moved side-to-side, guided by the rhythm, slowing down as the song ended. When it came to dancing, I shined. My talent made me one of the most sought-after escorts by clients. Through the years of back-breaking practice, blood, sweat, and tears, I had become pretty good at what I did. And due to that dedication, I had no shortage of men looking to spend their money on me.

Time's up.

Quickly, I gathered the money and clothes from the ground, making sure to keep my moves sensual. The men are still watching. I continued to keep my face blank, unbothered by my nakedness, as I pulled back the curtain and returned to the back room. It was cluttered with an overflowing clothing and footwear collection, crammed haphazardly into racks and piles. Amidst the tangle of fabrics and footwear, a few wigs were tucked away—if you wanted to change your look. Although, I found it super awkward if your client was into hair pulling.

    Becky was waiting for me when I went into the dressing room. She was older, I'm guessing in her late fifties, with graying hair and a smoker's cough. Becky was what you would call a 'house mom,' basically, the woman who keeps us in line and makes sure we're where we're supposed to be at any given time. She was probably in the trade when she was my age, but it was kind of rude to ask.

    "Get ready, Mel. You have a gentleman waiting," she said.

    "A gentleman?" I responded, my tone laced with skepticism. "And here I thought we only served pigs."

    I touched up my makeup in the mirror and had another glass of champagne, trying not to think about what came next.

    Becky stood with her hands on her hips, her impatience clear as she watched me finish getting ready. "Watch your tongue with this one. He looks like the type who wouldn't hesitate to hurt you if you step out of line," she warned.

    "Just what I needed," I said, trying to hide my frustration.

    Once I was back in my outfit—a blue, gauzy thing meant to give off an air of innocence—Becky said, "He's waiting for you in room eight. Put on a smile, Mel. You don't want to give him the impression that you're ungrateful." After that *lovely* speech, she handed me the room key, and I headed off to meet my client.

My full name was Melancholy Brown, not that we used last names around here. Also, who names a kid Melancholy? It was as if my parents knew my life would be filled with hardship and suffering. Thanks for that, Dad, whoever you are.

I could feel the glares from the other girls waiting to dance. As one of the most highly requested workers, I had made a few friends. Not playing into their games, I ignored the looks I was given and tried not to think about what I was going to do. Putting mental walls around my memories to keep myself safe, I started my walk to the elevator. If you compartmentalized your brain enough, like separating memories in locked boxes, it was as if none of it happened. Keeping a part of myself locked up so tight that this place wouldn't break me. Nothing would break me. *Never again.*

Baby Dolls was located in the South—one of those border towns where people went missing all the time, and no one gave a shit. The buildings in the area were dilapidated, their exteriors weathered and worn from years of exposure to the elements. The club where I worked was housed in a particularly decrepit structure, a two-story building divided into a club on the first floor and a hotel on the second. The brick exterior was stained and cracked, and the windows were smudged and in dire need of a cleaning. The entrance was marked by a neon sign that flickered and buzzed, casting a garish light on the grimy pavement below. Despite its appearance, the club was a popular destination for those looking for a night of entertainment and excess.

Walking down the dimly lit hallway with my head held high, I couldn't help but notice the state of my surroundings. The wallpaper was peeling away from the walls, revealing patches of moldy drywall underneath. The flickering lights overhead cast an eerie shadow on the threadbare carpet beneath my feet. I tried not to cringe at the assortment of unknown fluids, giving off a musty smell that made me want to hold my breath. Generic paintings hung on the walls, their frames chipped and cracked, a poor attempt to make the space appear more upscale. The overall effect was one of neglect and decay, making me feel as if I were in a haunted hotel rather than a high-end establishment. *Fucking Micheal.*

I put on a new persona like a mask, and with a deep breath, I slide the keycard to enter the room. The man that was waiting for me was one I've never met before. A glance around the room revealed all I need to know about how this night was going to go. My eyes catch sight of the leather toys and whips lined up on the bedside table, and I try to keep my expression neutral. Becky was right; this was a man you don't want to cross. Unfortunately, I've dealt with his type before, more than I'd care to admit. I steel myself for what's to come.

The man sitting on the bed was probably in his late forties, balding, yet he carried himself in such a way that he exuded power. The suit he was wearing screams wealth, and I bet it cost him more money than I make in a week. The look in his eyes was cold and unyielding. In his hands, I noticed a set of metal handcuffs waiting for my wrists. If I'm scared, I don't let myself know it—locking my emotions away.

He's clearly a man who's used to getting what he wants, and I know that there will be no room for negotiation or refusal. I studied him carefully, taking in all the details in order to prepare myself for what was to come.

"Let's get started, shall we?" He said in a firm voice, his grin widening as excitement shone in his eyes. I took a deep breath and put on a mask of composure, shutting the door behind me as I prepared to fulfill his desires. This was what he came here for, after all.

Chapter 2

After that *enlightening* evening, I found myself alone in the dimly lit hotel room, the only source of light coming from the small lamp on the bedside table. The room was sparsely furnished, with a queen-sized bed, a small dresser, and a window that looked out onto the city's dark and deserted streets. My apartment is across the road, and I wasn't looking forward to the cold walk back. Hopefully, one of the girls would still be there, and we could walk back together. A glance at the clock told me it was two in the morning, still early by club standards.

My head was still fuzzy from the wine, but it didn't stop me from remembering my time with my client. If I had to describe my night, I would say it was one of the worst experiences I've had in this line of work. I've had rough clients before, but nothing like this. Memories of the encounter flash before my eyes, causing me to shake with disgust. I quickly shut those thoughts down, not wanting to give in to those feelings—it was time to lock up that box and move on. *This is a normal night, and my monsters won't find me here.*

Before I left, I took advantage of the private shower the hotel provided the clients. Sighing, I let the hot water soothe some of the aches I've gained from my client's rough treatment of me. The steaming water fell over me, enveloping my skin in a cocoon of warmth. The heat seeped into my tired muscles, loosening the knots of tension. I closed my eyes, letting the water wash away the evidence of the pain and misery I felt inside. The suds and grime of the evening swirled down the drain. I took my time in the shower, relishing the sensation of the water cleansing my body and mind.

Scanning over my pale skin, I saw fingerprints starting to bruise and grimaced. I would be sore tomorrow and probably the next day after, too. But at least right now, the shower was relaxing. Unlike my apartment's group bathroom, these rooms were stocked with various body washes, shampoo, and conditioner as if the men would ever use any of them. Choosing the oatmeal and almond body wash, I lathered myself up and felt *so* much better afterward. There wasn't much that a hot shower couldn't fix.

After that, I put on a fluffy robe and stepped out, careful not to slip on the wet floor. Wiping the condensation from the mirror, I winced as I noticed the other bruises on my neck that would be difficult to cover up. *Damn,* I knew the client had been choking me, but the bruises looked purple and blue. They're going to be impossibly hard to hide with concealer. I should have told him to stop. I'm not sure he would have listened, though. They never listen when you ask them to stop.

A heavy sigh left me as I thought about having to work like this. Hopefully, Becky will understand and give me tomorrow night off. I deserved a break after this night, and the business could afford to let me have some time off. Plus, it's not like we would be super busy anyway.

Tomorrow was Christmas Day, or technically, today was. Honestly, I was surprised we were going to be open. It's the same thought I had every year, and every year, I was shocked by how many men showed up.

Who would want to come to a strip club on Christmas? I thought to myself as I started to get dressed in my lingerie. The blue nightie luckily managed to survive my client's rough handling— *thank God*. These skimpy outfits weren't cheap, and I didn't want to waste money replacing them. At least it kept me somewhat covered, and it wouldn't leave me completely naked on my way back downstairs. I'd have to get my regular clothes from the dressing room; no way I was walking home in this.

The apartment building across the street was a rundown structure divided into small rooms for the dancers. Despite the cramped quarters and high cost of rent, most of the dancers— including myself—had no choice but to live there. My roommates, who I shared the small space with, were friendly and easygoing, but the apartment had its fair share of problems. The most pressing issue was the bathrooms. Unlike the *luxurious* private shower provided by the hotel, the bathrooms in our apartment were communal and located on the ground floor. They were small, dirty, and lacked privacy, with only curtained-off stalls separating one person from the next. The bathrooms reminded me of my high school locker room, and I couldn't help but feel a sense of discomfort every time I had to use them.

The cleaning staff never seemed to make their way to the bathrooms, and with twenty-some-odd girls living there at a time, things got pretty nasty. Trying to look on the bright side, I remembered that at least they kept the hotel rooms clean. They always made sure all the sheets were washed and stain-free. We also had access to a large laundry room, and I found that clean clothes were a luxury everyone deserved. *See, it was practically a five-star hotel!* Or at least as close to one as I'd ever get in my pathetic life. This was all that I deserved and all that I would ever be—a worthless girl with no money and no family. If only I were strong like the characters in my fantasy, I would have found a way to overcome my problems by now.

Making my way down to the elevator, I headed towards the dressing room, trying to shake off the feeling of hopelessness. There were a few girls getting dressed, but none of them were ones I wanted to walk with. Some of them, like Anna, were more likely to stab me in the back than keep me safe. Quietly, I got my clothes from the locker, not paying them any attention as I changed. Still not seeing either of my roommates, I decided to walk back by myself.

Giving the club one last look, I started my walk outside. As I headed out, I couldn't help but feel a sense of dread. The cold night air bit at my skin, and I pulled my jacket tighter around me, trying to stay warm. I knew that I needed to stay alert, as there was always a chance someone may be waiting for me in the shadows. But the streets were deserted, and I made it safely to the apartment building.

I used my access keycard to enter. All the girls have one, and you didn't dare lose it. Besides the owners giving you hell, keeping access to the building limited was the only thing keeping us safe. After getting inside and hearing the door auto-lock behind me, it was only a short distance to my room.

The hallway is narrow, and the ceiling feels low, making me feel as though the walls are closing in. The smell of stale cigarette smoke and cheap perfume lingers in the air. I make my way to my room, the sound of my shoes clicking on the linoleum floor adding to the eerie silence.

As I approached my door, I couldn't help but feel a sense of relief wash over me as I saw that my roommates, Jess and Amber, were not there. Their absence gave me a chance to unwind and relax before I went to sleep. The studio apartment was cramped and tight, set up like a dorm room with three twin-sized beds and small dressers. With everything so close together, it was hard to have any personal space or privacy.

Since my roommates weren't back yet, it must mean that it was a rough night for them, too. Some weeks were like that, and as we got closer to the holidays, it seemed to bring out the angrier clientele. It could be the stress of seeing family or the rising costs of gifts. In any case, it was a horrible time to be working for anyone.

Everything was increasingly expensive, making it impossible to live alone. Houses had become unaffordable for the average person. Not that I'd know anything about that. I'd been poor for as long as I could even understand what money was. Money was food, money was power, and I was in serious need of some cash. I've been saving for years to get out of here, and if I'm honest, I could have already. I just didn't really see the point. Everywhere was the same, so I'd just be miserable somewhere else.

When I was small, I used to wish for Christmas magic—for Santa to give me *anything* I wanted. A loving family. A home that I could call my own. Of course, I never got those things. So no, Christmas time didn't hold a lot of good memories for me.

The only Christmas I could sort of remember fondly was one back when I was six years old. It was my first foster home after my mom left me. That Christmas, I'd been living with the Evans family, and my social worker told me they had plans to adopt me. I had high hopes for that—thinking I would finally get to have a normal childhood. And for a few weeks, I did. Turns out, I was wrong to hope for more than that. All it took was one false accusation to get sent back into the system. Closing my eyes, I fall back into the memory of that day.

The Christmas tree stood tall and proud, adorned with sparkling lights that danced and glimmered in the room. The presents underneath were piled high, each one wrapped in a shiny golden paper that glinted under the tree's warm glow. Some of the presents even had my name written in neat cursive script on a tag. My foster mother, Mrs.Evans, had gone the extra mile and purchased a special outfit for me to wear on this special day. The red velvet dress was soft, with delicate white trim that rustled as I twirled and spun around. The aroma of delicious food wafted through the air, with an abundance of cookies and desserts that I had never been allowed to indulge in before. I remember thinking, this is going to be my new life, my new family, and things are finally going to be better. It was the happiest I've been in my whole life.

Things were going well for a time. I had been living with the Evans for over a month, and they introduced me to so many people—calling me their new daughter. Everyone I met seemed so happy to meet me, greeting me like I'd been a part of the family my whole life—everyone, with the exception of one person, Aunt Lilly.

She was a large woman, swallowing all the space from a room. Her layers of clothes, which I can only assume were made by a personal seamstress, were gaudy and bright. She wore stacks of necklaces and rings on all of her fingers. The perpetual sneer on her squashed-in face made her look like an angry pug—I take that back. Pugs are cute and sweet. Aunt Lilly was neither of those things.

When she met me, she took one look at me, saw my mismatched eyes, then turned to my foster mom and shouted, "That girl's a devil! I wouldn't keep her in my home if I were you. Send her back to where she came from."

Me, a devil? I was just a little girl looking for a new family.

The next morning, I descended the staircase with eager anticipation, my heart pounding with excitement as I imagined the pile of presents waiting for me underneath the tree. But as I reached the bottom of the stairs, my excitement was met with cold, accusing stares from my new family. I was accused of stealing a precious necklace from Aunt Lilly's room. And at six years old, I couldn't understand why they would think such a thing of me. My mind raced with confusion and fear as I tried to plead my innocence, but my words fell on deaf ears. My new family was convinced of my guilt, no matter how much I protested. Even when the necklace was found, they were convinced that I had put it back, guiltily, to cover up my crime. The betrayal and hurt of that morning still lingered in my mind, casting a shadow over what was supposed to be a joyful holiday celebration.

"I told you that girl was no good. You should call and have her arrested!"

"Dirty thief!"

"Worthless child!"

The words echoed in my skull—I'd been called all these things and much, much worse in my life. That day was definitely the first day I started to believe those words. Despite being kicked out of my new home, it was still the first time I got to experience the magic of Christmas, at least for a little while. To be honest, the time I spent there wasn't bad, especially compared to many of the homes I'd been in. At least no one touched me, and I had food every day.

Putting the memory in the box, along with the darker ones I keep hidden from myself, I start getting ready for bed.

My small dresser is filled with comfy clothes, preferring soft materials compared to the outfits I had to wear for the club. Dressing in something comfortable and familiar, I feel more like myself again. The matching top and bottom, adorned with cute little bunnies, were a welcome change from the tight and revealing outfits I was forced to wear for work. I had always had a fondness for rabbits; something about their gentle and timid nature resonated with me. If I was into spirituality or believed any of that stuff, I might hope to be reborn as a rabbit—frolicking in the flowers, living in a little bunny den. Surely, that was better than being a whore in a crowded apartment.

The room was furnished with only the bare essentials. None of us living here had a lot of possessions, and money was tight. You'd think for all the hours I put in, I'd have a little more money to spare. But, they charge rent at this dump. Granted, it was still cheaper than most apartments, but I'd prefer my own space. Any spare money I made, I'd been storing under the loose floorboards under my bed. My plan was to try and get a flight out of here and move somewhere new. A place where no one knew me or what I'd been through—maybe Italy. I have always been a big fan of pasta, so why not? I'd been thinking about it a lot, but I had no real motivation to do it yet.

My roommates Jess and Amber showed up, busting in the door. They were looking worse for the wear. Jess was a tall redhead with a big ass, her almond-shaped green eyes and full lips always looking a moment away from smiling. Amber was a short girl with dark, velvety skin and midnight curls, which she kept in two puffs most days. We'd been fast friends since they moved in here last year, and after all the roommates I had before, I was extremely grateful it was them now. Tonight, they looked drained and ready to turn in for some much-needed rest.

"How was your night?" I asked them, looking for any marks or bruises. Besides being tired, they appeared fine.

"Better than yours, by the look of you." Amber laughed, her words laced with exhaustion. "Our client wanted the 'double special.' Why do men always think they can handle two women at once when they can't even make one girl come." She giggled, turning to Jess. "Good thing I have you to help me get off." Jess and Amber had been seeing each other for the past couple of months. And though it wasn't against the rules, it was generally frowned upon by the club to have partners.

Jess purred, giving Amber a sultry look. "You know it, baby."

"Well, at least someone here gets to finish." I joked back. "My John just wanted to see someone bound and at his mercy. Why do I always get the rough clients?" I questioned, my voice coming to a whine as I complained about my night.

"It's that sweet face of yours. Makes men want to own and subdue you." Jess guessed, looking me up and down.

I let out a snort and just nodded my head. That was something I had been told before. I had soft features and a smattering of freckles across my cheeks that generally made me appear younger than I was. Why that made men want to hurt me, I'll never know.

"What are your guys' plans for Christmas?" I asked them.

Amber started to get excited, "I bet Becky gives us off tomorrow. We should try and go to the diner. I wanna get a milkshake!"

"I can give you a milkshake." Jess simpered, but Amber just laughed her off.

"We're open tomorrow, so I doubt we will be off. But, we could go before our shifts." I told her. "I could always go for some cheesecake. Chances are good that it will be the only place open tomorrow besides the club."

We all agreed to go together, and I mentally calculated how much money I'd need to bring with me. Jess and Amber start playfully arguing about where to go and what to get.

"…and then, I'll order fifty pancakes!"

"Fifty? But you can barely finish two!"

"Ugh! But I'm starving!"

"Well, come here. I have something you can eat."

Tuning them out, I finished up my nighttime routine. I kept face wipes on hand and brushed my teeth using a water bottle so I didn't have to go to the bathroom. With minty fresh teeth, I turned off my bedside lamp and said my good nights to my roommates. This was my favorite part of the day—sleeping. Ever since I was a little girl, I would sleep whenever I had the opportunity. The excitement of going to sleep now has me thinking about my dream world.

While other kids dreaded nap time, I was keen to enter the realm of dreams. It had been my escape for as long as I could remember, and in my dreams, I was essentially a fly on the wall, watching a story play out before me. It was the same characters, always on new adventures. I felt like we grew up together, and I watched as their struggles mirrored my own. In my dreams, I would follow an elf male named Kleptis Klein, along with his sister, Mystic. They were the closest friends I had ever had, and they didn't even know me. Living in a world called Jelaria, they thieved and killed their way to the top.

Their world had a complex court system hierarchy and laws I hardly understood. It was a magic world filled with creatures I'd only read about in fairy tales but must have subconsciously added to their world. Elves could transform at will and use various kinds of magic. Klein and Mystic are gifted with the powers of ice and wind, respectively. I may not have understood everything completely, but what I did understand was that I loved dreaming about it.

Klein was a beautiful male with glistening snow-white hair and piercing silver eyes. His physique was a work of art, with chiseled muscles and a face that could have been sculpted by the masters. I couldn't help but feel drawn to him, and his beauty was mesmerizing. Though his body bore the marks of battle, with scars crisscrossing his tan skin, they only added to his rugged charm. They were a testament to his strength and resilience, and they only served to make him more alluring in my eyes.

Klein's sister, Mystic, was just as beautiful, with a striking half-black, half-white mane that was divided down the center. Her silver eyes were adorned with a ring of gold at the edge of her iris, giving them a unique and otherworldly appearance. They were not related by blood, as far as I knew, but the bond they shared was undeniable. To me, they were more important than anyone else in the world, with Klein feeling like a part of my soul and Mystic like a sister to me.

I've been watching their story play out for as long as I could dream, and it seemed more real to me than my own life. What I wanted, more than anything, was just to be able to walk into their world and stay. I wish I were strong and resilient like them. Instead, all of my scars are on the inside, where only I can see.

Closing my eyes, I did my best to get comfortable on my old mattress. I start counting backward from one hundred. With practiced breaths, I begin to drift off. I wonder what my friends will be up to tonight. A gamble gone wrong? An assassination? Or perhaps they would be planning some great heist? I never knew what would happen, and often, they would never be where I'd left off last.

Three... Two... One... There you are.

Chapter 3

Jelaria

The soft glow of the early morning sun filtered into the room from the east-facing window, illuminating Klein as he sat at his worn but reliable wooden desk, sorting through a pile of documents. This room, like each one in the Guild's headquarters, was a simple yet luxurious space, complete with its own en suite. A privilege reserved for few outside of the wealthy elite, the availability of modern conveniences such as plumbing and electricity, which had greatly advanced in recent times, provides the Fae with a source of power beyond magic.

The grand mansion of the Thieves Guild was situated in the opulent section of the city under the vigilant gaze of the city guards. Despite the seemingly suspicious location, the influence of money seemed to make any issue vanish, with the guards firmly bribed by Klein's master. This advantageous arrangement allowed Klein to effortlessly carry out his heists, his movements unnoticed by the authorities.

Klein's gaze lingered on the desk, its surface scarred with years of use and neglect, yet it held a sense of familiarity and comfort to him. The desk, much like Klein himself, was out of place in the Thieves Guild headquarters. It was made of rich red oak and stood out in contrast to the pale and elegant furniture surrounding it. But to Klein, it was a symbol of his independence and self-reliance. It was the first thing he ever bought for himself, and it held a special place in his heart.

Despite his lack of control over his life, this old desk made him feel like he had a say in something. It was a source of comfort in his otherwise chaotic world. He often sat at the desk, running his fingers over the smooth and rough surfaces. It may not have fit in with the rest of the elegant furnishings in the room, but it was Klein's, and that was all that mattered to him.

In the back of his mind, he felt a presence—light, like a butterfly's wings brushing against his mind. It was something he had always known. The presence came to him when he felt like giving up. With him his whole life, it felt like a guardian spirit sent to watch over him.

There are times when the presence seems to be sleeping. Here, but also not here, at the same time. Currently, the sensation seemed awake and aware of what was happening. He'd never told anyone about the presence, not even Mystic. He didn't even know how to describe it without sounding crazy.

Shuffling the papers before him, he finds what he's looking for. For weeks, he'd been trying to move money from his various bank accounts to keep the amount he had hidden. Klein sighed as he gazed at the papers. He was so close to reaching his goal, but it felt like it was still far away. He leaned back in his chair and closed his eyes, letting his mind wander to the future he dreamed of. A life without the need to constantly look over his shoulder, without the fear of being caught. A life where he and Mystic could finally be free and live without the shackles of their past. He opened his eyes and took a deep breath, steeling himself for the work ahead. The future he wanted was just within reach, and he was determined to make it happen.

But for now, he had a job to do—a job that could secure their future and that would bring in enough money to finally repay their debts. Klein pushed away the thoughts of revenge, focusing on the task at hand. He needed to be careful; every move needed to be calculated and precise. One slip-up, and they could both end up dead. But, he was confident. He had the skills and the determination to pull it off.

Deep in his heart, Klein knew he wasn't done killing yet. He still needed to make those monsters pay for the crimes they had committed against him and his sister.

Like most in his line of work, his start in life was a shitty one. He'd been born on an island off the coast to the west. They refer to it as Bastards Bay—whatever original name it had been lost to the common Fae. There was probably a map in the royal libraries that held its proper name, not that it mattered. If Klein had his way, the whole place would be destroyed and burned to the ground. That island was a place no child should be, yet it was littered with them. With gambling houses and bars and Fae courtesans on every corner, it was a sinner's paradise. *And boy, did the Fae love to sin.*

The Royals came from their castles to the island to cater to dark desires—children, often being a byproduct, left behind and forgotten. With it being so hard for them to conceive normally, it didn't seem to be a problem when the mother was a whore. Klein guessed it had something to do with the bloodlines of breeding royal families together too long. At any rate, the unclaimed bastards roamed the streets. They were looking to steal any coin they could to gain just enough to survive another day.

If you were unlucky, you might end up sold in the fighting pits, like Klein and Mystic. Though, without those fighting pits, they might not have been picked up by the leader of the Thieves Guild. The other possible fate offered from the Bay was being sold as a servant—a job that Klein and Mystic were not suited to. No. *They were born for this life.*

Klein's existence has been brief. He was only thirty years old, young for a Fae of his renown. Through his hard work, taking on more dangerous jobs, and fighting in the Abyss most weekends, Klein would be the youngest to leave the guild debt-free. At least, he hoped he would be anyway. Every day, that goal seemed further and further out of his reach.

He trained his body to be quick, agile, and strong, ensuring he was always one step ahead of his opponents. He practiced with his swords until they felt like an extension of his body. He learned how to pick locks and disarm traps. He became an expert in hand-to-hand combat and assassination techniques. He also studied the ways of magic, using it to enhance his abilities and gain an advantage over his enemies. All this training and hard work had made him one of the most skilled thieves in the world. But it had come with a price, a price he was willing to pay if it meant that he and Mystic would have a brighter future. His targets called him Kleptis, "god among thieves," but his friends called him Klein. It was the name he was born to—and the only gift his mother ever gave him.

Magic was common in varying degrees, but the amount Klein had been given was beyond the normal. Along with his wolf form, he was a formidable foe. It helped him to endure the pits along with his sister, with whom he shared no blood—but for that of the opponents, they slayed together. As a bastard, Klein's parentage was hard to place. However, with his magic of ice and the color of his hair, it was safe to assume his father was from the Unseelie Kingdom. His mother was still alive and well, living in the Bay—much to his displeasure.

Mystic's family was harder to pin down, and she had very little magic. Instead of strong magic, she had a gift for poisons and a second form of a hooded black snake. What little magic she did have was that of wind—which she used mainly to increase her speed. Her mother was a Fae courtesan who sold her to the Pits when she realized she'd never be able to make her into a suitable whore. She died when she was young and never saw Mystic become the accomplished Fae she was today. Mystic was the name she chose for herself. The name her mother gave her was one she had never told anyone, not even Klein. When he asked her why, she simply stated that her mother didn't deserve a single part of her. Even with her mother long dead, she still held a grudge against her—with good reason.

Shaking himself out of his thoughts, he turned his attention back to his papers. If they wanted to pay off their debt, they would either need one really big job—which was risky—or a bunch of smaller jobs. The issue was the longer it took, the more debt they incurred. Living in the guild wasn't free, and they still needed to figure out where to go after this. The Thieves Guild was located in Celetrix, a large market town between the two major land masses of the hourglass-shaped continent they were on. To the north was the Kingdom Of Unseelie, and to the south was the Kingdom of Seelie.

In the distance to the east, Klein could just make out the shimmering Crystal Cove, where the largest and most sacred temple for the Church of Shining Lights existed. The whole island is covered in large glittering crystals of all colors. The building itself was made entirely of bright gemstones. The entire thing gave Klein a sense of dread. He heard the rumors about that place. Fortunately, they hadn't had much dealings with the church and wanted to keep it that way.

There was a loud crash as Klein's sister busted into his room without a single knock. She wore a hooded black cloak over leathers and a mischievous grin on her face. Today, she had her hair parted to the right—hiding the white half of her hair and showing off the black half. When she's on a job that requires being hidden, she parts her hair that way. White hair was hard for stealth. This was why Klein kept his white hair shorter than most males of Jelaria.

Breathless from excitement, she exclaimed, "Klein, you won't believe the job I found for us!" With a flick of her wrist, she tossed aside the bank papers he was previously working on, revealing a job request from the guild board. The amount of gold written at the bottom of the request immediately caught Klein's eye. Pushing his fingers through his hair, slicking it back—a habit he couldn't seem to help, Klein contemplated the job request.

The job was on a crumbling parchment that he immediately recognized because of the script written on it. There was a reason no one had taken this job yet. It is a classic thieving job, only involving the royal family of Ostara—which was pretty risky in and of itself. But the item requested would be nearly impossible to steal—for anyone else that was. The buyer was looking to purchase the Spring Time Sapphire, a necklace with a large deep blue gem handed down and given to the Ostara Court heir. Klein hadn't felt the risk was worth it, so he never mentioned it to Mystic.

Letting out a sigh, Klein brought a hand to his forehead. "I don't know about this one." He said, a hint of disapproval in his voice. "We'd have to travel all the way to the south. Not to mention, find the current holder of the necklace."

Sighing dramatically, Mystic responded. "Yes, yes. I know all about that. *'The current heir is known as the slumbering princess. They said she had been born asleep, never being awake for more than a few moments.'* But that can't be right. Can it?"

Klein was sure he had heard stories of the heir as a child. Fae used to say she would have the power to bring down mountains when she was older, but that was many years ago.

Mystic continued, "Anyway, some say it was a curse—but as Ostara has no other legitimate heirs, she has to be the current holder of the necklace. We can bet they aren't guarding it that closely, and we know where it is. *See,* I'm not entirely dim-witted!"

"No, not *entirely*." Klein deadpanned. "The history books claim the gemstone was created using the life force of the first and most powerful ruler of Ostara. Also, according to the history books, he was kissed by the gods of old. Most royal families made the same claim. That doesn't make it true, though. Obviously, taking this job would gain us fortune and freedom, but..." he let out a sigh, pinching the bridge of his nose, "a thing *this valuable* is going to be heavily guarded, and we only get our freedom if we don't get caught."

Her eyes squinted as she took in his expression, "I see that look on your face. Trust me. If anyone can pull it off, it's us!" she practically shouted, throwing her hands up. "They'd never catch us!"

"It's too risky. We're so close to getting free. Do you really want to spend your immortal life underground?" he said. Criminals in Jelaria are dealt with swiftly and often painfully. For smaller crimes, you might lose a finger or two. For larger ones, you might be given the option to give your life to the church. For the worst criminals—such as being caught stealing from the Royals, the punishment was unimaginable. "Do you really think it's wise to take on a job so risky?"

"What's *risky* is staying trapped under Lycanthus's thumb forever."

Klein looked at the map on the wall, taking in the distance they would have to travel. The courts joined together and created two large kingdoms—the main castles in the far north and south.

Each Court had its own underground dungeon, with wards in place, preventing you from taking your life if the torture became too much. Elves, specifically, are a long-lived race—and if they lived long enough, they could choose to return to the ether. Some Fae decided to give their lives to the church by turning into crystal, a thought that didn't sound appealing to Klein. The imprisoned Fae spent their time being diced up and healed repeatedly for eternity—or so the rumors claimed. Klein *seriously* hoped he would never have to find out for himself what happened in those chambers of hell.

"It's just a *necklace*. We've stolen way larger stuff. With the right spells, no one will even know we were there." She argued with him. He looked at the amount on the scroll again. That amount of gold would leave them set for life.

"Please, brother, just think about it," she pled.

Sighing, he raised his eyes to hers. "I'll look into it," he promised. "If we're going to attempt this plan, it *must* be foolproof. It's going to take weeks of planning and acquiring the items for the spells needed to pull this job off. We'll definitely need to make charms for the wards, adder stones, and an amulet of invisibility wouldn't hurt, either. We can't just rush in there and get our heads cut off."

Tapping her temple, she said, "I've got plans for that too. Don't worry so much. The Ostara court castle is far from here, *sure*, and travel would be a big hurdle—but not impossible."

"Have you even looked at the map? The terrain is going to be difficult to go through. The sandy dunes of Litha, for instance, and on the main roads, we would need the proper paperwork to enter each city. It's not as easy as you think."

"That's only true if we go through the main gates." She said with a smirk.

"I have to think on it." Klein hoped it would work and that they could avoid *all* of the things he was worried about. If they packed light and dodged the city guards at each transition—then *maybe*.

"What's to think on? This is the job of a lifetime."

He started thinking about the pitfalls and advantages. "I suppose so. With our animal forms to help, it should be no trouble to get past the guards so long as we stay hidden. The main issue is the castle. It is sure to be heavily warded against intruders." He paused for a moment. "If anything goes wrong, we're out—necklace be damned. I'm not risking an eternity in the dungeons just to be free of debt."

Crashing noises and cursing came from the hall. "Where did that girl run off to?" a voice roared outside the door.

Letting out a frustrated groan, Klein turned to Mystic to ask her what the hell she did this time—but she's already headed for the open window.

"Distract him, will you? I might have gotten into his liquor cabinet and taken one of his 100-year-old whiskeys. Honestly, I didn't think he'd notice this quickly." She waved the bottle at him before jumping out the window with a wink, her body flipping with cat-like grace.

A moment later, Lycanthus—a mountain of the male who was the leader of the Guild, entered Klein's room with a look of white-hot rage on his face. Klein wasn't small, but Lycanthus dwarfed him with his large frame. He was a 7'5" orc with wiry blonde hair—built like he was used to an axe in his hands. The beads of gold braided into his beard clicked together as he walked, his footsteps heavy on the wooden floor.

Seeing who it was, Klein casually moved his papers so nothing of importance showed.

"I know she went this way, Klein, don't lie to me. If that bottle doesn't make it back into my cabinet by the end of the night, I'm adding it to your tab." He growled at Klein—looking ready for blood, his green skin darkening in anger.

Lycanthus had purchased Klein and his sister from Bastards Bay after witnessing them fighting in the pits. After seeing their animal forms, he deemed them too valuable to waste their lives in there. The debt he held over them was large, and it only seemed to grow.

Not falling for his intimidation tactic, Klein leaned back in his chair, "Can you prove it was her? I mean, without proof, you can't very well charge her for something you're not sure she even took. Maybe you drank it and just forgot?" He said cockily. This is the way of the Thieves Guild. They were taught to leave no trace behind. Klein had no doubts Mystic wouldn't fail at something so simple.

Lycanthus looked down at Klein with a darkened expression, showing off too many teeth. He was known to be unpredictable in his reactions, and both Klein and Mystic bore scars to prove it. But as suddenly as his expression changed, it turned into a smile, and he let out a booming laugh that shook the lights hanging from the ceiling. Today, it seemed, Lycanthus was in a good mood.

"Guess all my lessons to you two didn't go to waste, huh? Very well, *seeing as I have no proof,* I'll let you off this time. But if I catch her in there again, it'll cost you double the next time!"

"Sure, sure." Klein shrugged. "I'll let her know."

"Be sure that you do, boy."

As Lycanthus left Klein's room, he took a look at the clock hanging on the wall. It's eight in the morning and time for his first training session of the day. Getting up to leave, he piles his papers neatly, placing them in a locked drawer—away from prying eyes.

The rooftop training area covered the whole expanse of the mansion with high walls that were spelled to keep in any noise that might escape. A running path went around the perimeter of the space. There are a few other members taking advantage of the training area. Jogging at a steady pace, Klein warmed up his muscles, feeling the blood moving in and out of his heart.

Klein noticed Stella, a guild member who had been trying to get in with his group for years, running on the trail. Picking up the pace, he works his way up to his top speed—to the outside, he looks like a blur of motion. He was showing off a little, *but hey*, it was good practice. Speed had become an essential part of staying alive. He wasn't as fast as Mystic, but he could run his way out of most situations.

After working up a sweat on his sun-warmed skin, he moves on to the weapons rack. Stella caught up to him, leaning on the wall next to him—in a way meant to be sexy. Born as a half-elf, Stella had round ears, which she hid in her black hair by keeping it down or braided. She had darker skin and eyes and would have been attractive if it wasn't for her personality.

"So Kleptis, I hear you're going after the Sapphire. Are you truly going to risk it?" Stella purred, pushing up her meager breasts with her arms. "With just the two of you? Maybe it's time you let me come with you. I could be useful in *all kinds* of ways." She licked her lips suggestively.

A flash of irritation came from the presence in his mind—or was it coming from him? The emotions he felt from it were usually so light he could barely decipher them. But for a moment, it felt like someone was standing beside him.

"How did you even hear about that? I haven't even confirmed all the details." Klein asked, his hands brushing against the familiar weapons.

She rolled her eyes, "Mystic has been bragging about it all morning to anyone who'll listen. She keeps saying you're both going to be the most famous thieves in Jelaria."

Shaking off the strange feeling, Klein turned to Stella. "I don't think I'll be needing any help from you. Now, why don't you run off and find someone willing to take you up on your offer? I'm sure there *might be* one or two males left you haven't tried yet."

"Come on, we could be real good—you and I," she said in a whine. "Why does Mystic get you all to herself?" Pouting, she lifted off the wall to get closer and moved to place a hand on Klein's chest.

Brushing her off, Klein picked up a set of double daggers. "I don't have time for this, Stella; some of us have training to do. Maybe if you trained a little more, you could pull better jobs." Moving with practiced motions, Klein let the blades become an extension of his arms—effectively forcing an end to the conversation.

Stella, however, was relentless in her attempts to get his attention. She continued to make small talk, trying to draw him into conversation. But Klein was focused on his training and didn't give her the satisfaction of a response.

Eventually, she got the hint and moved on to training with the staff. Klein continued with his daggers, moving on to more advanced techniques and practicing different combinations. There was a reason he was the best at the Guild, and you didn't get this good by luck alone. Sure, you could kill someone with magic, but it could cost you precious time. It is much more efficient to use a blade—or teeth.

Putting the blades back on the rack, he went to the water fountain to take a long drink. Mystic really needed to come to more training sessions with him, but she insisted she was good enough without it. If they took on this job—which Klein was pretty confident they would—it was going to be obvious if that was true.

It was summer at Celetrix, and the sun was already beating down on him, causing him to blink at its brightness. Using his power, he coats his skin in a thin layer of ice to cool down. Being right in the middle of the continent, the city had the most moderate temperatures of all. To the north, the Unseelie Court was almost perpetually covered in snow. And to the far south, the land was sweltering most of the year.

Taking a moment to rest, Klein looked out over the city. The waterways divided the city into quarters—the east side, where the guild was located, held the rich housing and a large bustling market, where goods from all the courts could be purchased. Also, to the east, the church had a small temple that was always recruiting members. It wasn't made of crystal like their main church, but out of gray stones with crystals inlaid between. The west side held the fishing docks and slums. If you were fortunate enough to leave the island of Bastards Bay, you often ended up in that part of the city—assuming someone didn't purchase you first.

Returning to his room to shower, Klein thought about the job request still on his desk. Maybe Mystic was right, and they could pull it off. They were the best thieves in all of Jelaria, after all. After his shower, he pulled out a large map of Ostara, making a decision that would be the best or worst one in his short life. Should he take the risk of stealing something so illustrious as the Ostara Sapphire? *Why the hell not?*

Chapter 4

Mel

Waking up with a groggy yawn, I stretched my arms and legs, trying to shake off the disorientation. I must have slept in later than I intended. My dreams kept me captivated for hours. I thought about Klein and his sister's exciting journey, and I couldn't help but feel a little envious. Checking my phone, I saw that it was already past noon. My roommates had long since risen, leaving me alone in the room. My bed was warm and inviting, with its soft down comforter covering my body. The lack of windows in my room made it easy to sleep the day away. If only my mattress weren't so uncomfortable, then everything would be perfect.

Wishing I had someone to discuss my dreams with, I roll over, burrowing deeper under the covers. On days like this, I wanted to share my dreams with my friends in this world, but I never found the courage to. When I was ten, I tried to tell one of my foster moms about my dreams. I explained how Klein and Mystic were having to fight for their lives every night in the pits and that I wished there was some way I could help them. They felt so real to me, and—she just shut me down. She claimed it was just an overactive imagination. After a talk with my social worker, they both decided I needed counseling. They sent me to have a few sessions with Dr. Kilper, the school's psychiatrist. He determined I had anxiety and depression. *No shit.* He also told me my dreams were just a coping mechanism.

Even knowing that I wouldn't stop myself from trying to spend all my time dreaming. When my foster mother started getting complaints from my teachers about me sleeping through school, she sent me away. After that, I decided I was better off not telling people and started to keep the fantasy all to myself. What was the point of telling someone if they were just going to say I was making it all up anyway?

Turning my attention back to the present, I thought about what plans I had for the day and how quickly I needed to be ready. We had decided last night that we would meet up to head to the diner at around four o'clock. That way, if Becky had us work, we would have time before our shifts at the club. Looking at my phone again, I saw that I still had a few hours to kill before I had to get dressed. Rolling over to snuggle under the covers and sighing in a puff of breath, I closed my eyes. I tried to will my body to grant me some extra sleep time. It doesn't listen to me.

After a few moments of tossing and turning, I realized I couldn't go back to sleep. *Damn*. Seeing as that was the case, I decided it was time to wake up fully. I could still stay in bed, of course. I took one of the books from under my bed and began reading for a few hours. The book was just a cheap romance novel that I'd gotten in the clearance bin of a thrift store for a quarter. The crinkled cover had a muscled shirtless man with long, flowing blonde locks of hair, a classic princess romance I'd read a million times. It wasn't nearly as good as my dream world. The characters were bland and predictable, but if I couldn't sleep, it was the next best thing.

The heroine is saved by a handsome prince, who then takes her home to his Kingdom. He ravages her and makes her his queen. Like I said—predictable—but it distracts me for a few hours. The book sucks me in even though I know exactly what's going to happen. Lost between the pages, I hardly noticed when Jess and Amber walked into the room. The sound of their chatter slowly pulls my attention. I looked up, my eyes a little blurry from reading so long.

"Girl, you're not even ready yet?" Amber gasped, pulling me out of my stupor.

Walking in behind her, Jess teases me. "Did you even brush your hair?"

My fingers snagged on a few knots as I tried to make it look less disheveled. "Well, you said we weren't leaving until four. It's only..." I looked at my phone. "3:55."

"Exactly, unless you're planning on going in your pajamas!" Jess laughed, gesturing to my outfit. They are both dressed for warmth, jackets already covering them and boots on their feet.

Apologizing, I said, "No, I just got caught up reading. I suck. Sorry, I'll change right now." Yawning widely, I gathered my covers as I rolled out of bed, folding them lightly.

Deciding to dress for comfort, I threw on an oversized sweater and leggings combo. Slipping on some fuzzy socks and boots to match, I should be toasty warm. Braiding my long hair back to save time, I gave myself a quick once-over in the mirror. *To put on makeup or not? That is the question.* Fuck it, I'll go bare-faced. It's winter right now, so I also grabbed my matching pink scarf and hat.

It only took me about ten minutes to get ready, and the whole time I was getting dressed, Amber was watching me, tapping her foot impatiently. Trying not to roll my eyes, I tugged on my hat, wrapping the scarf around my throat, and I was ready to get out the door.

Jess opened the door, holding it for us. "Come on, Sleeping Beauty, let's get out of here. Don't want you turning into a pumpkin!" She had come up with the nickname when we became roommates, referring to how much sleeping I tended to do. Not very original, but it stuck.

"Wasn't that Cinderella?" I corrected her, "And I'm pretty sure it was her carriage that turned into a pumpkin."

"Yeah, well, tomato tomahto."

We headed out the door, the chilly air outside making our breaths come out in soft white clouds. The diner isn't too far away, but it's freezing outside, and I know the girls won't want to walk. So, instead, we go to the bus stop around the corner. When we get there, I don't see anyone else waiting, and I start to panic. I couldn't remember if the bus was running today, and I didn't think to check online.

"If it doesn't show up soon, do you guys wanna walk?" I offered.

They both gave me blank stares like I just asked them if they wanted to cut off a foot for fun. "You can't be serious!" Amber said as she pulled out her phone. "The website says the bus will be here any minute."

One minute goes by, then another, until we are waiting there in the icy wind for fifteen minutes. Right when I was about to tell them that we should just go home, I saw the bus in the distance. I could just make out the foggy headlights, and I was relieved to see the big monstrosity pulling up. The brakes of the bus screech as it comes to a stop, leaving my ears ringing.

"Thank fuck, it's colder than a witch's tits out here!" complained Jess, visibly shivering and rubbing her hands together.

We climbed on the bus and waved the bus driver our passes. Bus passes are a necessary expense when you don't have another way of transportation. Most people in this town used the bus, as car theft was a major problem living this close to the border. The owner of the club even had a deal with some of the major chop shops and would report any car worth stealing to them for some extra cash—not that I could afford a car worth stealing. And since I didn't plan on staying here, I didn't see the point in wasting my money like that.

The bus driver nodded as he pulled the long handle, causing the door to slam behind us. We found three stain-covered seats together in the back. I wrinkled my nose. They smelled like piss, but what city bus seats didn't.

Rocking up and down the road, the bus rattled, causing me to become nauseous. I turned to Amber, who was sitting in the middle. "I'm glad I haven't eaten anything yet."

"Ugh, I know. And it's cold as shit in here. Hey, driver, can you turn up the heat?" Amber raised her voice to get his attention. "The inside of this bus doesn't seem any warmer than it is outside!"

The bus driver grunted. "Heater's broken."

"Of fucking course it is." I cursed under my breath. We huddled together in our seats to stay warm. Thankfully, the bus ride was quick, only taking twenty minutes to get to the diner. With our shared body heat, we made it there without getting frost-bite—*but it's a close thing*. When I saw the diner coming up at the next light, I pulled the bell to let the driver know it was our stop.

"I'm starving and ready to get me a milkshake!" I said, happy to see the restaurant was open—the neon sign flashing red.

"Me too. Do you think they could make mine hot?" Jess laughed as we entered the building. "Like a coffee milkshake?"

The waiter, who was working today, surprisingly looked cheerful and excited to see us. He smiled at us as we came inside, directing us to take a seat. His name is Alejandro, and he was an attractive hispanic man with black hair and earthy brown eyes. He's around my age, and he'd been working here at the diner for—forever. I was pretty sure his dad owned the restaurant.

The diner is themed to look like it's from the fifties—either that or it hadn't been remodeled in the last seventy years. Pictures of Elvis were hanging on the walls, along with old movie stars and news articles. This place always felt like home. The cracked vinyl booths were mint green and pink and made crunching noises when you sat in them. The square-shaped tables all had cute little jute boxes on them filled with oldies. None of them actually worked anymore but were just kept up for decoration. The quiet Christmas music was filtering in from the ceiling speakers, making me want to hum along. We picked a table that was near a window looking out the parking lot. The only car that I could see was Alejandro's, an old beat-up Toyota Corolla—no chance of someone wanting to steal that.

It was one of my favorite places to eat, and talking to Alejandro was always a nice addition to my day. The club didn't have a full kitchen, only a couple of fryers filled with old oil. Unless you wanted to eat greasy bar food all day, you didn't have a choice but to eat out. I tried it a few times when I was desperate, and it always made me sick. Mostly, I just tried my best to avoid the nausea-inducing 'food' they served at Baby Dolls.

"Hi Alejandro, I see your dad has you working on Christmas," I said, greeting him with a warm smile.

"Like usual! And please call me Alex. Only my dad calls me Alejandro." He laughed with a slight intonation to his voice. It's obvious that Spanish was his first language—his English was pretty good, though. "Someone has to keep this place open!" Taking a closer look at me, he gasped, "Ay, dios mío! What happened to you?"

Avoiding his eyes, I looked everywhere but his face. Alex was wearing a Christmas hat over his short hair and a t-shirt with a cartoon character on the front that I didn't recognize. Over his clothes, he had a black serving apron that was tied around his waist. I could see a notebook and a pen peeking out of the pocket.

Looking around, embarrassed, I checked if anyone was listening. Luckily, the diner was empty of customers—which didn't surprise me on Christmas. I took a moment to collect myself before I answered, my eyes going to the lights hanging on the ceiling. I pulled my scarf tighter around my neck and whispered, "It really isn't that bad, and I'm sure it'll be better in a day or two. When I looked at them this morning, they didn't seem terrible. Some spots were already starting to yellow." I mumbled, all of my words coming together in some sort of word soup.

"Well, I hope the other guy looks worse." He winced, "Have you thought about taking self-defense classes? The streets around here aren't safe."

Amber was the one to answer him. "He's right about that. Women go missing in this city all the time."

Alex kept his eyes on me. "There are some small gyms nearby here. The classes tend to start pretty early, but if you need someone to go with you, I wouldn't mind."

Do I really want to take time away from sleeping to go to the gym? "I'll think about it," I told him, not sure if I'd ever really want to go.

"I could always give you a few pointers on fighting. Or, if you need me to beat someone up, I could do that too." He added.

"Don't worry about him. Besides, he tipped really well, so…" My face felt warm as all my blood rushed to my cheeks. *Why did I have to say that?* Brushing off the concerned look he gave me, I glanced at the menu. "I would like to get the New York Cheesecake, some fries, and the biggest strawberry milkshake you have." *Please take the hint, Alex.*

His eye softened, but he didn't make any more comments. "You got it, chica. What about for you two?" He pulled out a notepad from his apron to take down our order. "Milkshake? Fries? I'm the only one working right now, but I'm sure I could learn to turn on the stove if you want a burger," he joked.

"Do you think I could get a stack of pancakes? Oh, and a coffee?" Jess said with a hopeful smile.

"Yeah, pancakes, I can manage. And for you?" He said, turning to Amber.

"Just a coffee for me."

"Just coffee? Don't tell me you're on a diet again?" I asked her.

She gave me a look, telling me to back off. "Not everyone is as naturally skinny as you, okay?"

Jess offered her a pat on the back. "Sorry, she's feeling a little sensitive. One of the guys last night told her she was looking chunky," she said sympathetically.

Alex took the menus from us. "Got it. Pancakes and a coffee." Not giving Amber time to change the order, he turned on his heel. "I'll be right back with that!" He said as he walked to the kitchen through silver double doors, causing them to swing back and forth.

"I'm not eating them." Amber pouted.

"But you're hungry, love. You shouldn't starve yourself over one stupid comment. Besides, did you see that guy? If anyone needs to lose weight, it's him!" Jess said seriously. After comforting Amber for a while, Jess got her to agree to a few bites.

It didn't take long for us to get our food, as we're the only customers in today. Alex put the food in front of me, and I immediately began to devour it. "It's so good!" I mumbled around a big bite. "You guys seriously have the best cheesecake!"

"I'm glad you like it so much. I always order extra to be sure we have it for you when you come in." He had a happy smile on his face and continued to awkwardly stand by our table while I ate. He put his hand on the back of his neck before he said, "You know Mel, I miss you when you don't come in here, and I get a little worried…" he paused. "Maybe I can get your number so we can keep in touch?"

I began coughing and almost choked on my cheesecake. Jess lurched out of the way, so I didn't cover her in food.

His face started to redden. Getting flustered, he stammered, "Sorry, I mean, if you don't want to, that's okay."

"No, I'm sorry. You just caught me off guard. Are you sure you want my number? I mean, you know what I do for a living." Trying to recover from spitting cheesecake on the table, I wiped my face with my sleeve. *An amulet of invisibility would be really great right about now.*

"Yeah, I know you work at Baby Dolls," he said, not batting an eye. "That's what worries me. The men that go there, they aren't good." He looked down and noticed the cheesecake I spit all over the table. "Let me run to get some napkins real quick for you." He practically sprinted away from me, making me want to crawl into my sweater to hide. *Great job, Mel.*

Jess giggled, "Why don't you just give that man your number? He's been pining after you ever since we've been coming here! Anyone with eyes can see that he wants you!" She took a finger and dipped it in her milkshake, offering it to Amber and giving her a look that's all sex. Amber slowly licked it off. They had really gotten into public displays of affection lately. I'm not a prude, but licking fingers in public was a little much if you ask me.

"You like that, baby?" Jess purred.

Amber slapped her hand away with a laugh. Then she turned to me, "Is he not your style? I thought he was pretty cute, in a puppy dog sort of way."

"You just know that boy would try so hard in bed," Amber joked.

"He seems nice. I just don't want to hurt him with my lifestyle." I argued.

Amber rolled her big brown eyes at me, but jealous boyfriends were a big issue when working as an escort. More than one man had gone crazy over their girlfriend working at Baby Dolls. Some even went as far as bringing weapons to the club—no one got hurt, but the whole thing was still terrifying. Alex didn't seem like the violent type, but you could never really tell. Men with sweet smiles were twice as likely to act aggressively when they found out—in my experience, anyway.

"It's just a phone number. Not a marriage proposal." Jess said.

I considered her, "Maybe you're right. We have been coming here a long time, and Alex has always been respectful and kind. It is just my phone number. The chances of him texting me are slim at best. He is probably just concerned about me."

Alex came back with napkins, quickly wiping up my mess. Before I could get the nerve to say anything, he rushed off, looking a little sad at my perceived rejection.

Sighing, I kept my voice low, telling Jess and Amber. "I didn't mean to hurt his feelings. I just didn't expect him to ask me that."

We stayed there, eating and chatting. Jess was cracking jokes about the men she'd been with recently. She could make anybody laugh with her crude jokes, her full lips stretching into a wide grin. I almost felt bad for the men she was making fun of. Almost.

"…. And then, he says, 'Well, it's because I'm an alpha male.' Like that's an excuse for telling me that my hips were made to bear children." Her voice came out in a mocking tone.

"I hate men like that! It's always preference this and preference that. Like, get a grip. You're not exactly winning man of the year here." I groaned, taking another bite of the cheesecake. It's creamy and rich; the cherry topping dripped down the side. They seriously had the best cheesecake in town.

As I dipped a fry into my milkshake, careful not to drip any on the table, I took a bite. The salty, sweet mixture made my taste buds light up. *Delicious!* A happy noise escaped from my lips. Hearing my moan of pleasure, Jess raised her eyebrows, "That good, huh?".

Mumbling my agreement, I took another bite. "So good! Thanks for forcing me to get out of bed. Now, I can die happy!"

We finished most of our food and stayed talking when I noticed the sky had started to darken. It got dark so early in the winter. Taking a deep breath, I complained, "I really hope Becky lets us just relax. Who'd come to the club on Christmas?"

"Is it like this every year?" Amber asked. This was her first Christmas at Baby Dolls.

At the same time as me, Jess said, "Yes." Both of us sounded really put out by it.

"Unfortunately, men would indeed show up tonight. No matter how we wished they wouldn't," I told her. "We better leave before our phones start blowing up, with Becky trying to find out why we're not back yet."

Alex noticed us preparing to go and rushed to give us the check. "Feliz Navidad, girls. Be safe on your way home."

We split the bill. The total wasn't too high, and evidently, Alex gave us his employee discount. I took some cash from my bunny-themed wallet, leaving a generous Christmas tip for Alex. Piling up our glasses and plates, we tried to make it a little easier for him to clean up. I finished the last drink of my shake as I made the decision to give Alex my number. I wrote it on the back of the receipt and handed it to him. "If you're ever free, maybe we could hang out?"

"Yeah, I'd like that!" He blurted out, taking the paper. The smile he gave me was so sweet I could melt. "I'll text you."

Waving goodbye, we left the diner in a lighter mood and with fuller bellies. I wasn't sure if Alex was going to text me, but I found myself hoping he would.

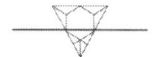

This time, the bus was full of people—all trying to get somewhere fast, and the ride took longer on the way back. By the time we got to the club, it was already around eight pm. We stayed out longer than we should have, and Becky was waiting for us inside when we arrived. She looked grumpy and had a cigarette hanging from her lips—a thick cloud of smoke hovered around her.

"Girls, I know it's a holiday. But, there are requests coming in, and we have work to do." *Who would be making a request on Christmas? Oh, right, lonely men. The kind with no girlfriends or family.* "A gent called and asked for you, specifically, Mel. So get your ass ready!" She let out a large puff of smoke. "He'll be here in one hour."

"Of all the girls working here, someone requested me. Of course, they did. Look at me, Becky. There's no way I can cover these up." I pulled down my scarf to reveal my neck, then pulled up my sleeves. "The man from last night left me with finger-print bruises everywhere. He was into choking, which normally I don't mind, but he was too aggressive."

"Oh, I don't think he'll mind seeing you like this. It's the same client from last night. Seems to have taken a liking to you." She winked at me. "Now, be a good girl and show him a good time." Giving me another look, she added. "I'm sure if you ask nicely, he will be more gentle with you."

Behind Becky was one of the other escorts, Annalise, giving me a look that could cut glass. We have never gotten along. Her obvious jealousy put a damper on any friendship we might have developed. "*A request for her?* Who'd want in that used-up hole?" She hissed at me.

I looked her up and down, keeping my voice steady as I said, "And how are your requests going, Anna, or are you still just working for tips?"

Anna had been here longer than most of us, and her clients seemed to be growing further and further in between. Yellowing teeth filled her thin lips—the chain-smoking and over-tanning she did were certainly doing a number on her. If she didn't turn it around, she was well on her way to being out of work. She twisted a finger in her bottle blonde hair. "Let me take her place, Becky, she looks like shit. I'll show him a real good time."

"Yeah, Becky, let her take it. It's Christmas, and all I want to do is sleep." My whining only seemed to irritate Becky more.

Her rough voice rang out as she started to yell, "He already paid extra for the exclusive rights to Mel tonight, so that's who he's getting! Anna, why don't you get your ass on stage and try to earn some tips." She snapped her fingers. "I don't have time for you. Get moving." Anna narrowed her blue eyes while pursing her lips but didn't say anything else as she left towards the bar.

Before I could leave, Becky stopped me, "Oh and Mel. He wants you to wear something specific. I left it in the dressing room. He's expecting you in Room 8 by nine. Don't be late." She handed me the card key and ushered the girls with another snap of her fingers. "Come on, girls, it's time to make some money!"

Becky wasn't giving me much of a choice, as they already had taken his money. To be honest, I was a little leery of seeing him again. But he did pay really well, and I needed the cash.

When I got to the changing room, I found the outfit laid out just where Becky said it was. It's a black, faux leather onesie with complicated straps all over. There was also a pair of matching black heeled boots, new in the box. Under the outfit, I found a collar with a heart-shaped tag, the inscription saying *'Princess.'* The sight of it made me cringe. I was nobody's princess, certainly not his.

Taking a small bottle from my locker I knock back a few shots of vodka. I was going to need it.

I got myself dressed and pulled up the boots that go all the way to my thighs and over fishnet stockings. Everything I needed to get ready was in this room. The lotion I used had a luminescent powder that made my skin glitter. It smelled like roses and honey. My makeup was dark and smoky. To match the outfit, I paired it with a bold red lip. The combo made me look powerful, even as I felt anything but.

As I checked myself in the mirror, I heard a crackling noise. The lights flickered off, and I saw the girl again—her hands reaching out to me, trying to draw me closer. I touched the mirror, and I felt like if I just pushed hard enough, I could reach her. As the lights turn back on, the girl is gone, and my normal reflection is staring back at me, eyes wide. The girl in the mirror had never reached out to me before, and it was a little unnerving.

Am I going crazy? I attempted to dismiss the vision of the girl and focused on getting ready. Dressing in the outfit was a struggle, taking longer than I thought. Before I knew it, it was 8:55, and I was running late. It didn't seem like it took me that long, and I had to wonder where the time went. *Was I zoned out looking in the mirror?* I jolted out of my trance and quickly made my way upstairs.

Arriving at the room a few minutes after nine, I adjusted the straps that started to dig into my skin. The boots were tall and squeaked as I walked. The outfit was uncomfortable—not something I'd pick out for myself, and I really hoped this was the last time I'd have to deal with this client. Taking a deep breath, I summoned a fake personality—one who is happy to be here—as I open the door.

The man from last night was waiting for me. He was sitting on a chair next to the little side table, an air of entitlement hanging around him. He was wearing another expensive suit tailored to fit his body and made his round figure more shapely.

"You're late, my princess." His voice was rough and gravelly as he spoke, getting up to meet me. Inspecting my skin, he saw the bruises marking it everywhere. "I need to be more careful with my things. You bruise so easily. So delicate." He brushed my hair away from my neck. "Tsk-tsk, my dear, this just won't do."

"Maybe tonight, you could play a little softer?" I asked sweetly as I looked at him through my eyelashes.

He sat back down and gestured towards his lap as he said, "Of course, precious. I can't have my princess looking like she's been in a brawl. I promise to be more gentle tonight."

I moved to sit on his lap, and his stubby hands roamed freely over my body. "You look so beautiful in this, like my own personal dark fantasy." He smacked my thigh and grabbed my arm possessively. "This could be a regular thing, you and me," he grinned.

"My name is Harvey, by the way. But, you can just call me your new Master."

The words sent a chill down my spine and had me wishing I finished off the bottle in the dressing room.

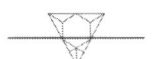

Surprisingly, Harvey was more gentle during our time together, as promised. He took care to leave no new bruises as he spanked my ass over and over again—I was sore, but I'd live. He left the club around midnight, seeming satisfied with my performance and his own. He gave me a broad smile with way too many teeth, and he told me, "I'll see you real again soon, Princess."

The thought made me tremble, not in a good way. In the morning, I was going to talk to Becky and tell her I won't do this again. Something about this man triggered something deep within me, telling me to run—the primal need to get away from a predator.

With the man finally gone, I eagerly headed for the shower, desperate to rinse away the remnants of the night's events. The warm water cascaded over me as I rubbed soap and shampoo into my skin, trying to erase the memory of his touch. No matter how hard I scrubbed, the sensation lingered, making me feel unclean. The feeling of his hands on my body seemed to cling to me, leaving me with a sense of violation and disgust. I washed myself repeatedly, but the memory of his touch lingered, tainting the experience and making it difficult to relax and feel calm.

At least I didn't have to worry about diseases or pregnancy, and I made sure he wore a condom the entire time. Becky always made sure the rooms were always stocked with a variety of options to choose from. Even with that added measure, she had all the girls at the club tested every two weeks to ensure everyone was clean—but things happen, and people slip up.

There was one girl last year who got too comfortable with a client and ended up pregnant. Not the worst thing that could happen, but he was married and wouldn't take responsibility. I wondered what had become of her if she had chosen to keep the baby and if she was doing okay. One day, she disappeared from work, and I never heard from her again.

Needless to say, having kids was a mistake I didn't want to make. To be absolutely sure, I doubled up on contraceptives. The implant in my arm, plus condoms, guaranteed I didn't have any accidents.

Dressed in a fluffy white hotel robe, I walked back to the dressing room—not wanting to go through the trouble of getting back into the outfit. When I was fully dressed, I pulled my phone out of my locker and noticed it had a message notification.

Hey! It was really great seeing you today. I'm glad you gave me your number.

This is Alex, BTW.

Smiling as I read the text, I flopped down onto the chair and thought about what to say back. It was pretty late, and he was probably not awake. Looking back at my phone, I saw the time— *already past one o'clock!* Harvey certainly liked to take his time with me. Deciding it was too late for any reasonable person to be awake, I chose to wait to text Alex back in the morning.

Chapter 5

Jelaria

The excitement of the weekend had finally arrived, bringing with it the much-anticipated fight night at the Abyss. This event was a release from the daily grind and a chance to relieve some of the tension built up from the week. Klein and Mystic are going to be fighting tonight like they did most Saturdays when they weren't on the job. Known for their impressive fighting abilities, the siblings were ready to take on the arena and earn some gold for their efforts. With a winning streak that was almost unrivaled, the only time they ever lost was when they went head-to-head against each other—and even then, it was a close match.

The Abyss was located in the heart of Celetrix, within the walls of the renowned pub, The Golden Chalice. Owned by Lycanthus, who operated under a pseudonym, the pub was known as the most popular bar in town and was also used as a front for the money-laundering operations of the Thieves Guild. To the public,

Lycanthus was known as the Golden Knight, and the true power behind the pub was kept hidden from the patrons. However, the guards were well aware of the real authority in Celetrix and enjoyed the benefits of their loyalty, such as free drinks—as long as they kept quiet about the true nature of the establishment.

All the Fae participants and employees at the Abyss were required to don hoods and masks to conceal their identities, a requirement imposed by the Guild Master, Lycanthus, who had a fondness for the dramatic. He wore a magnificent golden dragon mask with diamond-encrusted teeth that shone in the light, symbolizing his wealth and status. He could be spotted in the crowd, his hulking form towering over the patrons.

The arena had established a set of guidelines that all contenders had to follow. The primary rule was that magic and animal forms were strictly prohibited in an attempt to level the playing field. As if that would help the contestants against Klein or Mystic was laughable.

Although magic was prohibited in the arena, some fighters found ways to use it discreetly and avoid detection. Blade-less weapons such as staffs and training blades were permitted, with the goal being to render the opponent unconscious rather than causing fatal or permanent harm. Despite the rules, accidents were not uncommon, and the Courts did not officially endorse the fights. But as long as the number of fatalities was kept low, they looked the other way. Only in the case of a high-profile death would they take action and conduct an investigation.

Adjusting his hood, Klein made sure his hair was hidden, and his mask was sitting comfortably as he walked around the pub. His mask was a white wolf, very similar to his animal form, with a vicious snarl on its face. Made of white bone instead of gold, the jaw was articulated to open and close while speaking, so wearing it for hours was more bearable. Through the narrow eye slits, his silver eyes shone. A black cloak covered his shirt and black pants that were tucked into his supple leather boots. In his boots, he had hidden a blade, which he never left without. You never knew what might happen, so it was always best to be prepared. You know what they say: *you should never leave home unarmed.* As long as he didn't use it in the fight, having it on him wouldn't count against him.

Mystic was garbed in a similar manner to Klein, and her fighting leathers was encased in a rich, vibrant red cloak that shimmered under the light of the pub's lanterns. Her mask was a chilling representation of a smiling face, with jagged teeth that were meant to instill fear in her opponents. The red paint running down the sides of her mouth created the illusion of blood, heightening the ominous appearance of her mask. Her eyes, with their striking golden ring, were a mirror of Klein's own, and she regarded him intently as he walked around the pub. The oval eye holes of her mask only served to accentuate her piercing gaze.

"Ready to break the bones of tonight's opponents?" Mystic asked Klein with a raspy voice, distorted by her mask. "Fight nights are always more fun when we're together. I can't wait to spill some blood and maybe have a glass or two of sweet wine. Can't you feel the anticipation of the crowd tonight? They want blood as much as I do."

Klein deadpanned in response, "Sometimes I wonder if you're truly sadistic or if you just enjoy making jokes about killing everyone around you."

Mystic chuckled, "Probably the first one."

"I will remind you, sister, that you only have to render your opponent unconscious. Surely you can do that without breaking bones?" Klein stated flatly. Despite her sometimes dark humor, he enjoyed spending time with his sister and even found himself being drawn into her excitement.

"I could," she said with a grin, "but where's the fun in that?" She turned to scan the gathering of Fae. "I'm going to go check out the crowd and see if I can get my hands on something good." She wiggled her fingers in a wave as she walked, bumping into other Fae on purpose.

Klein sighed and shouted after her, "Just don't get caught!"

Mystic laughed over her shoulder as she disappeared into the crowd. "I never do," she said, her pockets likely already filled with the gold of other Fae.

Klein approached the bartender, his boots making a slight suction sound against the wooden floor as he walked. The bar served a wide range of drinks made from various spirits from across Jelaria. Janubis, the barkeep, was a seasoned member of the Guild and had been a part of it since its inception. He no longer took on any jobs, instead focusing on running the Golden Chalice and keeping an eye on the money flow. His black jackal mask concealed his deep ruby-red hair and eyes, a characteristic shared by many Fae of Mabon. Janubis was known for his charm, which seemed to attract females, and he was rumored to have multiple lovers of both genders at any given time.

"Can I get a mug of ale? And none of that watered-down piss you serve the masses." Klein said, his deep voice grumbling as he took a seat on a bar stool.

Janubis flashed a mocking bow as he reached for a mug. "Of course, anything for the esteemed Kleptis." He began to pour the ale from a large keg, his red hair and eyes shining from underneath his black jackal mask.

"How are my victims looking tonight? Anyone who might pose a challenge?" Klein asked, eyeing the mug warily.

"Ha! They look like they'll wet their pants when they go against you," Janubis replied with a laugh. "If you're looking for a challenge, why not fight Mystic again? The two of you always get the crowd riled up."

"No one wants to see that again. Besides, I can't keep letting her win," Klein groaned, taking another sip of his ale. The ale was good, with a light flavor of berries from Ostara, and brewed in a spelled wooden keg. It must have been a fresh delivery this week.

As Klein was about to say something else, Mystic's chuckles interrupted him from the bar stool beside him. "Who's letting who win?" she asked, seeming to have appeared out of thin air. Her ability to disappear and reappear with magic was a common occurrence, but it would still unsettle those who weren't used to it.

Janubis simpered and winked at Mystic. "Mystic, my sweet flower, have you finally seen the error of your ways and are ready to let me take you out?"

Mystic could see the wink through his mask, causing her to giggle girlishly while she waved him off. "A glass of Winter Red." She tossed a ring and a few coins on the table. "That should cover my tab, right Jauni?"

Janubis scooped up the fare into his waiting palm, counting it out as he purred, "Not nearly enough, my dear. You still owe me for last week and the week before that. If you let me take you dancing, I suppose we could call it even." He flexed his arms on the bar counter, clearly trying to show off, as he placed a glass of wine in front of her.

Unimpressed with his display, Mystic quickly took the glass. "Hmm, I don't know. Will you be wearing the mask? If so, I might be persuaded," she chuckled, taking a long swallow of her drink. "A few bottles of this would probably help too."

The two of them flirted back and forth, constantly engaging in this type of playful banter. Although Mystic acted like Janubis's attention bothered her, Klein knew that if it really did, she wouldn't let it slide. He had seen her smash in the teeth of males for much less.

"I didn't know you had a thing for role-play. I'm down if you are," Janubis flirted back with a grin.

Klein noticed Lycanthus approaching the bar with powerful strides, his voice a low growl as he barked out, "What are you two still doing here? The fights are about to start!" Klein downed the last of his ale and stood up, ready to follow Lycanthus to the arena. Klein nodded respectfully to Janubis before setting off into the depths of the earth, taking two hundred steps down a narrow passage that led to the old cave system that housed the arena. Known as the Abyss, the arena was once created by a powerful earth-mover but had since been repurposed by the Guild for hosting fights. The spacious room was circular, with a raised, ringed arena taking center stage. Wooden weapons lined the walls, and iron doors blocked off any branching caves to keep their secrets hidden from the public. Only guild members knew what happened in those caves, and it was not a pretty picture.

Lycanthus strode towards the ring, his voice booming like thunder as he welcomed the crowd. "Ladies and Gentlemen, welcome to the Abyss! We have a thrilling night ahead of us. First up, we have the return of Silver Fang, who will face off against a newcomer, Black Spider. Let's show them both our support!" The crowd erupted into cheers.

The names for the bouts were improvised on the spot—just Lycanthus having some fun. Klein doubted anyone would choose the moniker "Black Spider" for themselves, but he knew better than to make assumptions.

From the other side of the ring, Klein's opponent, a male Fae wearing the standard blank white mask, approached. As they sized each other up, Klein could see the confidence in his opponent's medium build and swaggering step. The cloak draped over his shoulders was made of luxurious fabric, adorned with silver threads, marking him as a Fae of means. However, Klein was undeterred and resolute in his mission to humble this opponent and demonstrate his superior skills in the arena.

The crowd's cheers only grew louder as bets were placed and gold exchanged, gold that Klein was determined to win.

Black Spider, his taunts and beckoning gestures directed at Klein stood in the center of the ring. With a deep breath, Klein relaxed his muscles and raised his hands, palms facing outwards, towards his face. His eyes were fixed on the weapons that were arranged along the edges of the ring.

In the pile of weapons, Klein spotted several short staffs that he quickly set his sights on. While swords were formidable weapons, they lacked the reach of a staff, and with wooden swords being heavier, he didn't want to risk accidentally knocking out his opponent with too much force. So, he made the decision to go for a staff as soon as he saw an opening.

"Begin!" Lycanthus' voice boomed as he signaled the start of the match. The roar of the crowd filled Klein's ears.

Klein's opponent didn't waste any time and swung at him with a closed fist. However, his movements were slow and predictable, making it easy for Klein to dodge. Klein quickly ducked low, taking advantage of the opportunity to strike at Black Spider's ribs. Black Spider hissed in pain and tried to back away from Klein's reach, but in doing so, he exposed the back of his legs. Without hesitation, Klein kicked his leg out from under him, causing Black Spider to fall to the ground with a loud thud.

"This is going to be quick." Klein taunted him. "After only a few moves, you're already down on the ground. Pathetic." Taking advantage of the moment, he reached for the staff, paying Black Spider little attention and not worried in the slightest. This was a mistake, as he was feeling cocky, and his guard slipped—leaving his back exposed.

Suddenly, he felt the hot breath of his opponent on the back of his neck, and before he could react, a brutal force impacted his spine. Despite the warning signals ringing in his mind from the butterfly-like presence, it was too late. The blow left Klein wincing in pain, a sharp grunt escaping his lips as the bruise spread across his back.

"Guess you're quicker than I thought," Klein rasped. He swung his staff, striking Black Spider across the face and causing his mask to come askew. At that moment, Klein caught a glimpse of blonde hair, but Black Spider quickly adjusted his mask back in place, avoiding any further blows from Klein's staff. Despite Klein's efforts, Black Spider seemed to be picking up speed, dodging each strike with ease. *How the fuck is he moving so fast?*

"Not so cocky now, are you, Silver Fang?" Black Spider spat out, clearly enjoying the turn of events.

Realizing the danger he was in, Klein increased his speed to blinding levels. He executed a series of jumps and flips to cause confusion before striking Black Spider in the chest with the end of his staff. Black Spider exhaled sharply as he was knocked to the ground, quickly rolling towards a wooden sword at the edge of the ring. Klein rushed forward, hoping to prevent Black Spider from grabbing the weapon, but he managed to get his hand on it. Swinging the sword at Klein, Black Spider leaped to his feet. Klein was too quick for him. With a graceful twist of his body, Klein avoided the blade and circled around Black Spider, using the end of his staff to strike his wrist. Despite the pain, Black Spider refused to let go of the sword, maintaining a death grip on the weapon.

Black Spider was not half bad at dodging and weaving away from Klein's staff. Klein couldn't help but commend his opponent for his skills, as he must have been trained by a master in one of the Court Castles. He suspected that there was a royal son hiding under the mask, seeking to prove his worth. Unfortunately for him, Klein fought dirty, and Black Spider's noble background wouldn't help him in the ring.

He threw his staff, causing Black Spider to break concentration and look up, trying to avoid the incoming weapon. While he was distracted, Klein grabbed Black Spider's wrist, twisting it until he heard a satisfying crack. The break caused Black Spider's hand to open and the weapon to fall away. Reaching out with his other hand and spinning on his back heel, Klein caught the falling sword before it hit the ground. Using the momentum, he swung the sword upwards, catching Black Spider under the jaw with a crushing blow. Black Spider was sent flying into the air, landing on his back in a cloud of dust. He didn't get back up.

"The match goes to Silver Fang!" Lycanthus announced to the cheering crowd.

A couple of guild members entered the arena to attend to the unconscious Black Spider, hauling him out of the ring. Klein discarded the sword back into the pile and raised his hands in victory, a triumphant smile spreading across his face. The fight had been quick, just as he had anticipated. Klein hoped that Mystic's match would last a bit longer. The longer the fight, the more bets could be placed.

As Klein began to exit the ring, Mystic approached him, her voice taunting his earlier statement. "So, you didn't need to break any bones, did you?" she said with a hint of sarcasm.

"He had a weak wrist, clearly," Klein said with a laugh as he patted Mystic on the shoulder. "Who knew it would break so easily?" Despite the humor in his words, Klein's back was starting to ache, and he knew if he looked at it, he'd see a large, purple bruise starting to form. "You're up next. Try not to hurt yourself," he added. The bruise was his own fault for allowing his opponent to hit him like that.

The crowd erupted in excitement as Lycanthus announced the next fight. "Next in the ring, our returning champion Succubus!" Mystic bowed with a flourish, earning cheers from the crowd. She was known for putting on a good show and stretching out her fights. "And the challenger, Dragon's Bane!"

Klein's hand came to his chin as he tried not to laugh at the name of Mystic's opponent, Dragon's Bane. He watched as the contender entered the ring, facing off against Mystic. The Fae appeared to be male, shrouded in a black cloak and wearing a blank mask, much like the last contender. He moved with a light grace, his hands ready in a fighting stance in front of him and his broad shoulders squared off towards Mystic.

"Begin!" Lycanthus shouted, his voice echoing above the cavern as the crowd erupted with excitement.

Mystic started quickly, throwing blows with a speed that had the crowd going wild. She made sure to put on a good show, slowing down her punches to give Dragon's Bane a chance to dodge. The male tried to hit her back, but she twisted away, avoiding every shot he took. Realizing that she was toying with him, Dragon's Bane dropped and rolled to the edge of the ring, coming back up with a staff in hand.

Mystic's opponent swung the staff at her legs, but she was too quick, back-flipping and coming up with a staff of her own. Klein could tell the male was getting frustrated as his swings became erratic. He had yet to land a single blow on Mystic. She was dragging the fight out, and he knew it. Mystic flipped and twirled in a dance only she could perform.

A sudden breeze flew through the cave, and Mystic's speed doubled as she went for the finishing strike, moving so fast that it was hard to follow. But, she surprisingly missed the male, who had moved out of the way—his feet seeming to glide across the floor.

That's when Klein saw it, a sparkle coming from the ground that he recognized. Before he could shout a warning to Mystic, her boots hit the ground and slid out from under her. She crashed to the floor, her head bouncing on the ice once, then twice. The crowd fell silent and started talking in hushed whispers.

"Did you see that.."

"Ice magic… isn't that against the rules?"

Mystic flipped her body up, blood spraying behind her, as she pulled out a hidden knife in the same motion. She slashed toward her opponent and landed a blow, slicing his arm in a quick move that caused him to drop the staff. She let out a roar of anger. "You fucking cheated!" She screamed.

He gripped his arm to stop the wound from bleeding. "You bitch!"

With a dagger in hand, Klein jumped into the arena, ready to defend his sister. "No magic!" Klein growled. The male raised his hands in front of him defensively as if that would stop Klein from doing what needed to be done.

"She used it first! Using the wind to increase her speed. No way someone is that fast." He yelled.

He wasn't wrong, but Klein didn't point that out. Mystic was slow to make another move against him, and Klein could see blood leaking out from under her mask. "Don't you have any honor!" Klein yelled, his voice filled with anger as he pressed forward, ready to claim the male's head.

"Honor?" He huffed. "Who knew there was honor amongst thieves?" He ripped the mask and cloak off, throwing them away from him. The face that greeted them was filled with rage, his features scrunched up in a scowl. Klein recognized him immediately. The male was the newly appointed Guardian of Celetrix. Every twenty-five years, two new Guardians were chosen to be an envoy from the Courts, one from each kingdom, to keep the Fae of the city in line.

This one's name was Ferguson, hailing from the Unseelie Court, a Royal Elf of Yule. His ash-gray hair and piercing blue eyes made it obvious. Ever since he had been appointed, he had been trying to "save" the Fae of the city, trying to weed out any wrongdoers and the filth—a truly impossible task. Lycanthus had already approached him about working out the same deal he had with the old Guardians, but he was proving difficult to be persuaded.

Not wanting to end up in a prison cell, Klein lowered his blade, putting it back in his boot. He rushed to Mystic and checked her for injuries; she seemed a little shaken but otherwise fine. Not many had tried to outmaneuver her using magic.

"What kind of place are you running? Cheaters and fixed fights!" Ferguson's question was directed at Lycanthus, who had just joined them in the ring.

"Sorry, my lord, surely this is a misunderstanding?" He apologized, groveling in a way that Klein had never seen before.

"Misunderstanding? No, I think I see things just as they are." Ferguson sneered.

The crowd had started to disperse, not wanting to be caught in the fallout if things ended badly.

"Let's go back to my office," Lycanthus pleaded in a hushed tone, "I believe we can work this out amicably, as the honorable gentlefae that we are." Ferguson's eyes flickered with anger, but eventually, he nodded in agreement. As they descended the stairs, Lycanthus led the way while Ferguson followed closely behind. Klein and Mystic were left behind in the cavern.

With the commotion from the crowd now having dissipated, Mystic removed her mask, allowing Klein to inspect the damage to her head. A one-inch gash was visible at the back, oozing with blood. Although it was bleeding profusely, Klein was certain it would heal cleanly within a few days. He carefully checked her pupils for signs of a concussion and was relieved to see that they were reacting normally.

"Is it serious?" Mystic asked, her voice filled with concern.

"Not at all," Klein replied with a reassuring smile. "A few stitches and a healing tea should do the trick." He turned to face her, his expression turning stern. "What were you thinking, using your magic like that? You were only supposed to use enough wind to win the competition, not show off to the point that it was noticeable."

Mystic rolled her eyes, "How was I supposed to know it was that Guardian? No one has ever noticed me using magic before."

Klein grumbled as he helped her put her mask back in place. "We'll be lucky if Lycanthus doesn't add the cost of the bribe money needed to cover this up to our debt," he said, a worrying thought. If

Lycanthus did add the cost, they would be left with no choice but to steal the necklace in order to get out of the situation. Depending on the cost, it could have wiped out most of their savings. They were so close to paying off their entire debt to Lycanthus, and Klein had hoped that this situation wouldn't cost them more, even if it were partially Mystic's fault.

    The two of them made their way back to the guild house, where Klein tended to Mystic's wound, stitching it up and brewing her a healing tea. The cut was small, and with proper care, it was unlikely to leave a scar, as it took a lot to scar the body of an elf—a fact that Klein was well aware of. They were in dire need of a proper healer at the guild house. Sadly, those with healing magic were both rare and expensive to keep around.

Chapter 6

Mel

Stretching my arms above my head with a contented sigh, I rose from the bed. My dreams had been vivid and intriguing lately, and I was loath to let them slip away—but I knew I couldn't stay in bed forever. I hugged the blanket tight around me, relishing in its warmth and softness. It was a Monday, my day off, and I had the freedom to do as I pleased—provided my finances permitted. Remembering Alex's message, I retrieved my phone from the charger and quickly typed out a response.

Me: Good morning! Sorry, I didn't get back to you. I was working late.

What I wouldn't have given to stay in my dream world and never come back to reality. Unfortunately, I was stuck in the real world. Up and ready for the day, I grabbed my bag of toiletries and headed to the bathroom. There were several other girls getting ready in there, so I had to wait for a sink to become available. Group bathrooms were a nightmare, and the smell inside made me want to vomit. Someone in here was clearly having a rough start to their day.

Jess was waiting in line for her turn in the shower stall. She looked sleepy, rubbing her eyes. "Good morning!" She greeted me with a smile. "How was your night with Mr. Big Spender?"

Rubbing my neck unconsciously, I answered, "Not too bad, actually. It went way better than the last time. I think he felt bad for the bruises he left me with the night before."

Jess pouted with concern, "Well, good! He should be sorry! I know he was more gentle this last time, but men like that give me the creeps. If he ever treats you that roughly again, you should ask Becky to ban him from booking you."

"Becky will ban him if I ask her to, but he did pay really well, and I'd hate to miss out on it. Besides, he seemed a lot better the second time," I admitted, though I had promised myself the night before that I wouldn't deal with Harvey again. Sadly, that was a lie I told myself, and I wasn't strong enough to say no to that kind of money.

Jess shook her head, "I don't know, girl…"

I tried to reassure her, "I'll be fine, don't worry about it. I can handle myself." The sink opened up, and I washed my face and brushed my teeth. "I really don't think he'll hurt me like that first time. Besides, he might never book me again anyway. There are a lot of other girls who work here."

In the mirror, I could see that Jess was still lost in her thoughts. "It'll be okay, Jess," I told her again.

"Yeah... okay," she still sounded concerned for me, as if she was trying to think of something to say that would make me change my mind about telling Becky.

Not sure how to stop her from worrying, I washed my face and ended the conversation. A shower stall opened up, and she headed for it after giving me one more look, mouth turned down. The bathroom, with its four shower stalls and four toilets, was designed in a practical manner, lacking any of the creature comforts one might expect. The utilitarian design, combined with the stained floor tiles and limited cleaning schedule, gave it the appearance of a prison shower. Wearing flip-flops was always a good idea since it was never clear when the floor was last mopped.

The club had a small cleaning staff that worked across the street. They came every morning to change out the upstairs rooms and stock the bathroom there. Sometimes, if we were lucky, they'd clean this bathroom too, but it hadn't happened in a while. I was sure Michael felt cleaning was our duty since we lived here, but how were we supposed to delegate that? Becky certainly never helped clean anything.

Not wanting to linger in the bathroom any longer, I made my way back to my room. I could feel Jess's eyes on me as I left, but I chose not to engage in any more conversation about Harvey. He was just a client, a means to an end for me. I knew I could handle seeing him a few more times. Then I could escape from this place.

As I dressed for the day, I decided to go for a comfortable and casual look. I put on a pair of black jogger sweats and a lavender crop top, giving off the impression that I was heading to the gym. But as I checked my phone, I saw a message from Alex that made me smile. The thought of talking to him lightened my mood, and I was eager to see what he had to say.

*Alex: Buenos días! I actually stay up really late, so it wouldn't have bothered me. *smile emoji**

Me: Well, I guess I know that for next time

Alex: Are you busy today?

*Me: No, the only plans I have are those with my bed *laughing emoji**
OMG, I just realized how that sounded. I meant sleeping…

*Alex: Jess and Amber have might have mentioned how much you like to sleep once.. or twice *laughing emoji**

Well, if you aren't busy, maybe you could come by the diner for my lunch break. We could hang out, and the coffee or milkshakes would be on me.

Taking a moment to text back, I try to decide if I should accept Alex's invitation. Talking with Alex was always effortless and enjoyable, and I needed to eat. Just then, I caught a flash of vibrant red hair in my peripheral vision. Jess had sidled up behind me and was now peering over my shoulder, studying the contents of my text messages. She was still wrapped in her towel, her wet hair cascading down her back. We always did our hair in our room rather than in the crowded bathroom. There was a blow dryer and other styling tools on a vanity in our room that we all shared.

"Oh, texting already? If you want my advice, I say you go for it!" Jess said. Of course, she would advise that.

"I'm considering it, but I really just wanted to take it easy today, maybe catch up on some reading," I replied, sounding a bit grumpy. "And I need to run to the store for some groceries. My snack stash is running low."

Jess's gaze followed my pointing finger to the empty snack boxes stacked on our mini fridge. "You can read on the bus and stop at the store on the way home. Besides, you look fantastic in that outfit. Why not show it off?"

I shrugged, glancing down at my outfit. My trim stomach was on display, giving me an hourglass silhouette, and even though the outfit was comfortable, it still managed to make me look stylish and put together. "I guess I don't have a good reason not to go, so why not spend some more time with a friend?"

"*Friend,* sure, Mel." Jess teased as she started getting dressed in a pair of jeans and a long-sleeved shirt. Her jeans emphasized her curvy ass even more. For a moment, I considered changing into jeans as well but quickly dismissed the idea. Jeans were the devil's fabric; I was sure of it. I would never subject my bare skin to the rough and unforgiving material. Chuckling to myself, I quickly texted Alex back.

Me: What time is your lunch break?

Alex: 12:30 It's only thirty minutes, but we aren't busy so I can still talk in between helping people.

Me: Ok I'll see you there.

"There, I did it! I'm going to have lunch with Alex." I laughed, tossing my phone aside so as not to change my mind.

"Good for you, girl. Don't do anything I wouldn't do!" Jess purred as she began to walk out the door. "Now, I have to find out where my girlfriend has run off to. Bye!"

As I finished getting ready, I brushed my hair, untangling the knots. I decided to wear it loose today, covering it with my pink beanie. My jacket was a black designer pea coat, a thrift store find, with golden buttons set in neat rows. It was amazing what some people considered trash. Their loss was truly my gain. Despite my neck looking better today, I still chose to wear a matching pink scarf to deflect attention from any marks.

After slipping on my gloves, I set off towards the bus stop. This time, I didn't have to wait long for the bus, and there were not as many riders today. Although it was still cold, the bus was faster than walking. As I sat on the bus, staring out the window, my breath fogging the glass, I had a positive feeling about today.

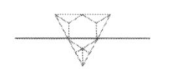

When I arrived at the diner, I could see a few cars in the parking lot, but it didn't seem crowded inside. Hopefully, it would remain that way, and I could have a good visit with Alex. Although I didn't want to take away from his potential tips, I hoped it wouldn't get too busy, and I would be forced to leave early. It didn't seem like that would be the case, however, people were probably still traveling and spending time with their families for the holidays.

The bell jingled as I entered the door, and the warm air from the heater hit my face.

"Welcome! You can have a seat wherever you want!" A voice called out. As I met his eyes, I saw that it was Alex's dad, Manúel, his voice friendly and kind. He looked a lot like Alex, with the same hair and eyes, but age had rounded out his body and thinned the top of his hair. It seemed like he and Alex were the only ones ever there. A few other people worked there on and off, but they were always calling in or not showing up at all.

I gave him my best smile and told him, "I'm actually here to see Alex. Can you tell him Mel is here?"

He looked up from the table he was cleaning, and a wide smile formed on his face. "Mel? Wow, he didn't tell me you were so beautiful. Way out of his league!" He chuckled. "Yeah, I'll go grab him. Have a seat, it won't be long." Tossing the rag into a bucket filled with cleaning solution, he walked to the back.

My hands started to sweat, so I peeled off my gloves and took a seat at a table near the window. It was cloudy that day, and the chances of snow were good, according to my weather app. The diner was mostly empty. An older couple was sitting in a booth at the far corner, and a mom and child were to the left. An oldies station played from the speakers, and "Let It Be" by The Beatles was playing. I started to sing along under my breath.

Before the song was finished, Alex joined me at the table, sliding in on the opposite booth bench. "Thanks for coming to see me. I hope the bus ride wasn't too terrible. Do you want coffee? Toast? It's a little cold for a milkshake, but I can get you one if you want." His words came out a little fast and mumbled.

"Umm, coffee and maybe a side of toast? I have money. You don't have to treat me!" I protested before he could offer.

Alex jumped up, almost knocking over the napkin dispenser. "No! I want to get it for you, so no paying today! I'll be right back!" He left to the back to get our food. He seemed so nervous it was giving me anxiety. I started questioning whether coming here was the right move and wiped the sweat from my palms. This wasn't a date; it was just two friends hanging out for lunch, I reasoned with myself. His paying didn't make it a date, right?

After a few minutes of arguing with myself about what constituted as a date or not, I saw Alex coming back to our table with a tray of food—a plate of toast for me and what looked like a steaming bowl of stew from him. The spicy aroma wafted over me as he placed everything down. His stew smelled really good, a layer of melted cheese covering the contents. He had two mugs of coffee, and I grabbed one of the cups, letting it give my hands something to do.

"Thanks for this, Alex. You didn't have to...." He cut me off.

"Oh, crap! I forgot the milk and sugar for the coffee! How many creamers do you take?" Before I could answer, he rushed back to the kitchen, returning just seconds later with handfuls of creamers and sugar packets.

"That might be a few too many." I giggled, taking two creamers and three sugars from his hands. He placed the rest on the table.

"Yeah, right." His hand went to the back of his neck. "Sorry, I'm just so nervous. I didn't think you'd actually say yes." He sat down across from me, mixing his coffee with a spoon while adding sugar packets—no creamer, just black with sugar.

"Why wouldn't I come? We're friends, right?" I questioned him, taking a sip of my coffee. It was hot but not scalding, so I took a larger drink. *Mmmm, coffee, how did people ever survive without it?*

He blushed a little, "Friends... yeah, of course!"

"That stew smells delicious. What is it?" I asked, pointing to his bowl.

"It's enchilada soup. Have you never tried it before?" He lifted up his spoon, offering it to me.

"Is it spicy? My stomach can't handle it if it's too hot." I eyed the spoon warily. "Jess forced me to try Thai food one time, and my stomach was never the same."

"No, not spicy! It's really cheesy. Here, try it." He offered his spoon again.

Leaning forward, I took the spoon from his grip. We were definitely not at the point of feeding each other. Taking a bite, I let the flavors roll over my tongue, the gooey cheese stretching away from the spoon. A surprised noise left my lips. It was excellent, creamy, with a slight undertone of spice. There were also some crumbled tortilla chips on top that added a little texture to the dish. It's not too hot like I was expecting it to be.

Handing back the spoon to Alex, I smiled, "You're right, it's not that spicy at all! I'm going to have to order me a bowl the next time I'm in!"

He took the spoon back and started eating the stew himself. "You really should! I can get you a bowl now if you want?"

"I'm good. Thank you, though!" I replied honestly. "The toast is enough for me this early."

He looked at me in disbelief. "Early? Are you one of those girls who don't eat breakfast?"

"It's not like I'm on a diet or anything. I'm just not hungry in the morning," I mumbled as I took a bite of my toast. I'd always been this way, not starting my day until the late afternoon.

We ate in comfortable silence. Alex seemed to be enjoying his stew, and I was surprised to find that I liked watching him eat. The food relaxed him, and he seemed to shed the nervous energy he had been carrying. After a while, he began talking about taking self-defense classes.

"You know, there's a gym really close to you that has classes every morning. You should check it out." He sounded hopeful. "I sometimes go there for kickboxing lessons."

As I took the last bite of my buttery toast, I considered his suggestion. "Waking up early really isn't my thing. Why are you so insistent on the whole self-defense thing?"

"It's something every woman should know," he replied. "We could even go together if you're nervous." His face took on a sad expression. "To be honest, I lost my sister a few years ago, and I wish I had made her go to the gym with me. Maybe then..." He trailed off.

I was surprised to hear he had a sister. "I had no idea! I'm so sorry. If you don't mind me asking, what happened to her?"

"She had a falling out with my parents about wanting to be on her own," he said, his voice starting to choke up. "I was younger than her and didn't understand what was going on at the time, but she moved out. She started working at Baby Dolls, and..." He covered his face with his hand. "Sorry, I know you don't like to talk about your work. It's just... my sister was one of those stories you hear—a client gone bad who killed her. I don't want that to happen to you."

I took his hand away from his face. "It's not your fault," I whispered softly. This story made sense to me and explained his passion for me taking the classes. His eyes were red and lined with tears as he looked at me.

"You're right, I know that," he sighed. "It's just hard not to feel guilty, even after all these years. I miss her. I lost my sister, and then I lost my mom too." His shoulders dropped. "It would make me feel better if you came to a couple of classes with me. It would haunt me if I lost someone else when I could have done something about it."

I agreed to try out the kickboxing class, but with a stipulation: "You're buying me coffee!" I put on a forced smile, trying to lighten the mood. "I'm just going to have to suck it up and wake up early. My worst nightmare!"

"Don't worry, I can call you in the morning to wake you up," he offered, finally cracking a smile. "Sleeping beauty."

"Oh no, not you too!" I whined.

"I'll text you the details, and we can plan it. I could even pick you up so you won't have to walk in the cold," Alex said, getting excited.

Mentally, I planned how I would get enough sleep to watch my favorite dream-world friends. Perhaps taking a nap after returning from the gym wouldn't hurt. I asked him, "So, what kind of things are you into besides kickboxing?" As I looked at his toned arms, I realized that I had never noticed before how stacked he was.

Waving his hand towards his shirt, he pointed to the character on the front, a cartoon of an older man in mid-battle on a giant toad. "I'm into anime and manga," he said. "This one is from one of my favorites." That explained the cartoon characters he had on all of his t-shirts.

"I've never tried watching that stuff," I admitted. "It always seemed like it was made for kids." I immediately regretted implying that he was childish for watching it—*bad Mel.*

"Some of it is definitely made for kids," he agreed, nodding. "But there's a lot made for adults too! I have loads of recommendations if you want to try it. Do you use any streaming services?"

"I can watch stuff on my phone. Jess, Amber, and I all split a Netflix account." I lifted my phone to show him the app. "You could always add some stuff to my watch list?" I suggested, offering him the device. He takes it from me, swiping through the options, a look of concentration entering his face.

He spent a few minutes swiping through the options and eventually added a few shows he thought I might enjoy. "They have some good stuff on here. I added a few shows I think you might enjoy. But you really need a Spicy Tuna account to get all the latest shows."

"Spicy Tuna?" I asked, unfamiliar with the name.

"Yeah, it's great! New episodes every week. Here. I'll download it for you and even put in my information so you can start watching." He smiled sweetly and handed back my phone with the new tuna roll icon added to my homepage. "You should totally watch Ramen first. It's a classic. It has ninja wars and epic fight scenes… there are a lot of filler episodes, though, but you can skip those and still get the full story." He talked in an animated way, gesturing his hands as he described the characters.

The story he was describing actually seemed incredibly intriguing, and his passionate delivery was eye-opening. It made me reconsider my previously held beliefs about cartoons. I realized they had evolved significantly since the Sunday morning cartoons I remembered watching as a child.

"Alex! Back to work!" Manúel called out to his son, breaking my concentration. The diner was suddenly bustling with activity as the late lunch crowd started to pour in. I hadn't even noticed their arrival, lost as I was in conversation with Alex.

With a quick nod, Alex gathered the empty plates and coffee cups and left me to enjoy my drink. "I'll go get you a fresh pot of coffee," he said. "Feel free to watch a few episodes here if you like, or if you need to head out, that's fine too."

"I think I'll stick around for a bit," I replied with a smirk, "I'd like to see what all the fuss is about with this Ramen character you're so passionate about." I opened the streaming app on my phone and started playing the first episode, "My Ninja Way."

Alex returned with a fresh pot of coffee, refilling my cup before setting the pot down beside me. "Let me know what you think," he said with a grin before rushing back to help his father keep up with the demand of the growing crowd.

As I watched the episodes, I became engrossed in Ramen's story of rejection and finding his purpose. He encountered a cast of quirky and entertaining characters on his journey, including his eventual best friend, a brooding boy with emo hair. Despite their frequent arguments, it was clear that they would play a significant role in the story. The theme song had me tapping my foot and humming along, even though I couldn't understand the language.

Before I knew it, the clock read past three, and I was shocked at how quickly the time had passed. The story had captured my attention, and I couldn't wait to see what would happen next.

Alex was still bustling around and hadn't gotten a chance to sit down since he had his lunch break. I called him over and said, "I think I should head home now. I don't want to take up valuable space here at the diner." I gestured to the growing line of people waiting for a table. "I'll text you when I get home," I added.

He sent me off with a smile, too busy to give me a proper goodbye. On the way to the bus stop, my thoughts kept drifting back to the anime series that Alex had introduced me to. The artwork was captivating, and the story, while appearing to be aimed at kids, had deeper themes that I was only beginning to uncover. I was grateful to Alex for introducing me to this new obsession. I plugged in my headphones and watched another episode on the bus ride home.

When I arrived at the apartment, Jess and Amber were still out for the day. They had probably gone out to eat or to catch a matinee movie. Since the club was closed on Mondays, everyone was off doing their own thing. I connected my phone to the charger and continued to watch the show. My phone's battery was always a problem; it seemed like it was time for a new one, but they were so expensive.

By the time anyone interrupted me, I was on episode thirty. The show was incredibly emotional, and even the side characters were starting to grow on me. Amber walked in, stumbling a bit, and asked, "What are you watching?"

"Just a show that Alex suggested," I replied. "Where's Jess?" I looked behind Amber but didn't see her.

"She's in the bathroom," Amber laughed. "Those margaritas went right through her!" She stumbled over to their bed. "It was buy one get one free happy hour at the Mexican restaurant, and we couldn't resist!"

Well, Amber's drunken state finally made sense. "It sounds like you two had a lot of fun," I commented, putting my phone away and grabbing a couple of bottles of water from the mini-fridge. I threw one to Amber, who caught it clumsily. "Did you manage to eat anything while you were out?" I asked her, not trying to sound like her mom.

"Food! What a waste of money! They had free chips and salsa, though, so I did eat something!" She giggled before taking a drink of the water.

Just then, Jess entered the room, appearing to be in much better shape than her partner, Amber. "Sorry, Mel," Jess apologized, "Amber had one too many margaritas." She went to assist Amber in standing up and removing her clothes. In our close-knit living arrangement, there was no need for modesty as we had already seen each other in various states of undress. I offered Jess the other bottle of water, which she gratefully accepted and drank down. "I think it's best if we call it an early night. Amber is going to fall asleep any minute," Jess suggested.

Agreeing with her, I changed into my comfortable clothes and turned off the lights. Amber was still giggling on the bed, with Jess trying to calm her down for the night. Before I closed my eyes, I sent a quick text to Alex.

Me: This show is really great. Thanks for suggesting it! Goodnight *Sleeping emoji*

...

Alex: I'm glad you like it! Sleep well, Hermosa.

The reply from him came just a few seconds later, almost as if he had been waiting for me. I couldn't help but wonder if I had been waiting for him as well. My eyes started to feel heavy as I tried to imagine a male elf with shimmering silver hair.

Chapter 7

Jelaria

As anticipated, Lycanthus put the expense of bribing the Guardian on Klein and Mystic. Seated at his desk, Klein ran his fingers through his hair; frustration etched on his face as he gazed at the mountainous pile of paperwork in front of him. The figure on the page was staggering, and Klein's mind raced with thoughts of Lycanthus's insatiable greed. To add insult to injury, Lycanthus had also offered them the opportunity to carry out a few tasks for him, with the details to be revealed at a later time.

Given the nature of their line of work, Klein couldn't shake the suspicion that these tasks would likely involve killing or injuring innocent people. The exorbitant sum required for that single bribe was a hefty price to pay, and Klein couldn't help but question what Lycanthus was trying to hide. The Guardian, Ferguson, was acting peculiar for something as small as a fixed fight, but in the end, he too had been bought off—just like the rest. Guardians were always so quick to consider themselves superior, but in the end, they all buckled to the lure of gold.

It was clear to Klein that if they ever hoped to break free from the shackles of the Guild, they would have to successfully execute the Sapphire Necklace heist. The combined debt he and Mystic owed to Lycanthus was growing at an alarming rate, and Klein was starting to question whether they would ever truly be free, even if they did manage to pay it off. There was more to this situation than meets the eye, and Klein was determined to uncover the truth behind Lycanthus' motives for keeping them trapped within the Guild's grasp.

Klein gazed at the bank papers with a mixture of anger and despair. Despite his and Mystic's hard-earned savings, managed by Klein himself—much to Mystic's displeasure—it still wasn't going to be enough.

Klein's frustration simmered as he meticulously evaluated their finances, counting every gold coin and silver shilling. A deep growl escaped his lips as he grappled with the reality of their situation. The thought of backing out crossed his mind, but the idea quickly dissipated. It was as if fate had a hand in this, driving him and his sister towards this job with purpose. He couldn't help but hope that this was a sign of good things to come and that their endeavors would be rewarded with success. They were due for some good luck.

Today was market day at Celetrix, a monthly event where vendors from all over the continent gathered to sell their wares. As regular shoppers, Klein and Mystic always made a point to attend, searching for rare items or anything they had never seen before. Although they were on a tight budget, they were willing to spend their gold on certain items—if they happened to be worth it.

With a determined pen, Klein jotted down a list of all the items they might need. The charm they required was no ordinary one, and it needed to be undetectable even to the best wards. The ingredients were expensive, and the process was intricate. Firstly, they would need to find two adder stones with naturally occurring holes, small enough to create a necklace. Then, they would need five strands of unicorn hair for each stone, which needed to be wrapped around the stones under the light of the full moon while chanting in ancient Elfish. Finally, the charm had to be soaked in the wearer's blood for at least two days, with a longer soaking period resulting in a stronger charm.

They needed to gather the ingredients while making sure not to attract attention from the law or other parties who might be interested in stopping them. The adder stones could be purchased from vendors at Celetrix, but obtaining the unicorn hair was a different matter altogether. As unicorns were protected creatures, it was illegal to sell any part of them. This had led to a population boost among the species. Klein was determined to obtain the unicorn hair for the charm, even if it meant taking it himself. He didn't plan on hurting the unicorns, just taking a few strands of hair and leaving them be.

As Klein was deeply engrossed in his planning, Mystic abruptly entered the room. "Are you ready to go yet?" she exclaimed, her voice filled with excitement. Market day was always a highlight for Mystic, and the two of them had made it a tradition since their arrival in Celetrix.

"Just about," Klein replied, a hint of irritation in his voice due to the disruption to his planning. "We have a list of items we need to purchase, so try not to waste all our gold on unnecessary things."

Mystic's face lit up with a mischievous grin. "When have I ever bought something we didn't need?"

"Let's see... like the dragon's teeth you were convinced were real or that enchanted blade that only worked when sacrificing pigs," Klein retorted.

"But that blade saved your life, don't you remember?" Mystic countered playfully.

One night, while on a job, Klein and Mystic found themselves under attack by a group of wild boars. The animals rampaged through their camping site, causing destruction and putting Klein's life in grave danger. Fortunately, Mystic sprang into action, brandishing the enchanted blade she had once bought on a market day. To their surprise, the blade suddenly became razor-sharp, effortlessly slicing through the boars and protecting them. After the fight, they made use of the boars as a food source and feasted on a delicious meal of bacon.

"That was the only time it proved useful, but after that, we couldn't even sell the thing," Klein argued, getting up from the desk.

He started gathering the necessary gold and tucked it into a secret pocket of his cloak. They were both dressed as ordinary Fae, blending in with the other market-goers. All weapons were concealed, with Klein wearing a plain brown jerkin over a white shirt and pants and Mystic dressed in a green dress with laces up the side and flowing fabric. Their white hair was visible to all, as they portrayed two siblings from Yule. This was a common disguise they used and what the merchants at the market knew them as. Eagerly, they set off towards the city center and the huge square, which was usually empty but would now be filled with vendors for the monthly market.

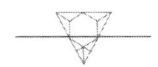

The Market was bustling like usual, with Fae voices ringing out as they haggled over the wares being sold. Stalls were tucked into every corner with fabrics and woven baskets filled with exotic spices—the changing smells tickling their noses as they passed by. Klein and Mystic walked slowly, scanning the stalls as they made their way to a trusted merchant named Mercia. He had been selling goods on market day for as long as they had been shopping there.

Mercia had a smaller build, his body more suited to exchanging gold than blows. His dark blonde hair and watery blue eyes marked him as a Fae from Ostara. Each court had a specific look, and though it varied from Fae to Fae, there were certain markers that were unmistakable. As Klein approached Mercia, he found himself alone. Mystic had run off on her own in search of the stones they needed.

"Good afternoon, Mercia. Did you have anything interesting today?" Klein greeted him.

"Interesting… interesting... Well, I have this new brew of fertility made from the tears of mermaids." Mercia responded with a pinch in his voice as he tried not to laugh at his own joke.

"Very funny, Mercia." Klein deadpanned. "No, what I really need is some information. The kind someone might find difficult to give up." He lowered his voice, coming to a whisper that only Mercia should be able to hear. "I'm in need of unicorn hair, and I would gladly pay the gold for it or for information on where the herd is located."

Mercia tilted his head, his eyes widening with curiosity. "I might know something about that for the right price."

Klein gave him a serious look and jingled the coins in his cloak. "I can pay." He growled menacingly.

Hearing the sound of the gold, Mercia quickly reached for it. "Fifty gold for the information, and you didn't get it from me," he said.

Klein was expecting to pay more, so he quickly agreed. "Done," He had never been let down by Mercia before. He discreetly handed him the gold he needed from under his cloak. "Now tell me where I can find them."

Mercia swept the gold into a hidden box under his table and whispered, "I've heard rumors they rest in the forests of Mabon, frequenting the apple orchards to the east. I've also heard the lord of Mabon watches over them like his own children, so be swift in getting the hair. As long as no harm comes to them, you'll probably be fine... *probably.*"

Comforting.

"Do you have any information on the Ostara Sapphire?" Klein asked, still keeping quiet.

"Unicorn hair and the Spring Sapphire? Naughty, naughty Kleptis, what have you gotten yourself into now?" Mercia shook his head, a little bit of madness creeping into his gaze. "I'm afraid there are some things even I don't know."

Klein knew Mercia was lying about something but couldn't call him out on it. If he had information he wasn't willing to part with, no amount of gold would change his mind. Nodding his head in thanks, Klein left to explore the rest of the market.

Today, vendors from every court have come to the market to sell their wares. Winter wine, berry mead, and other goods were displayed amongst the bustling crowds of Fae. The air was thick with the scent of spices and exotic ingredients, causing Klein's nose to itch, but he couldn't resist the allure of the diverse offerings. He approached a food stand selling savory vegetable pies and grabbed two—one for himself and one for Mystic, who he knew wouldn't be far. His sister had a habit of startling him with sudden appearances, a trick that used to work when they were children. However, Klein was now a grown male and wasn't easily intimidated. As he waited for Mystic, an unnatural breeze brushed the back of his neck, sending shivers down his spine. *Right on time.*

"Are those for me?" Mystic's voice echoed from behind Klein, who handed her one of the vegetable pies without hesitation.

"Here, this one's yours. Did you have any luck finding the stones?" Klein asked, taking a bite of his own pie. The spices were fragrant with a hint of sweetness, and the flaky crust was buttery and warm. Market day was always an excellent opportunity to find something delicious to eat. When they were young and foolish, they used to steal pies like these and hide on the roofs to enjoy their stolen treats. Looking back, Klein now realized that the vendors let them get away with the theft, as they could have easily called the guards to catch them. Out of pity for two poor children trying to survive, they let them be. Now that they had the gold to pay, they made sure to tip generously to repay the vendors' kindness.

After brushing the crumbs from her dress, Mystic said with a conflicted expression, "I did find a couple of stones from a merchant down that way, but..." She tilted her head towards the north.

"But?" Klein prodded.

"Well, she was a bit eccentric," Mystic replied.

They continued walking through the bustling market until they reached the enigmatic merchant Mystic had mentioned. A dark purple tent adorned with stars and moons sewn in gleaming gold stood out amidst the other vendors. As they approached, a potent aroma of incense wafted out from the door flap, filling the air with a rich, exotic fragrance. Klein immediately realized that he had never seen this particular tent before on any of his previous visits to the market.

"A fortune teller?" Klein asked in disbelief. "Maybe we could find the stones somewhere else?" he grumbled. "Fortune tellers are con artists and never truly have the sight. The chances of those stones being adder stones from a tent like this seem unlikely to me." As he turned to tell Mystic that he wouldn't buy them from here, the flap of the tent opened, and a female stepped out. She was shrouded in a hooded cape that was made of the same dark purple fabric as her tent. The cape obscured her features, but Klein could tell she was female from her scent. Multiple layers of clothing obscured her figure, leaving only a mysterious silhouette visible. The fortune teller had already seen Klein and Mystic, and their encounter was now inevitable.

"Welcome! Welcome! Have you come to have your fortunes read? Perhaps to learn about a lover who doesn't return your affections? I have a brew for that!" The fortune teller waved her pale hands, trying to herd them into the tent.

"We're here for the adder stones you have for sale," Klein stated simply, hoping to get away from her as quickly as possible.

"Of course! I have a few. Please, step inside, and I'll get them for you." With no other option, they followed her into the tent. The strong scent of incense was almost overwhelming to Klein's sensitive nose, and he immediately started to sneeze. How could she stand to be in here all day? he wondered. Maybe she had lost her sense of smell along with her wits.

She ushered them to sit on two purple velvet-covered chairs. The chairs were soft and comfortable, and a small table with a large crystal ball sat in front of them. The ball wasn't clear like one would expect, but rather a depthless black that seemed to steal all the light from the candles scattered around the tent. A curtain separated two areas, and the fortune teller went behind it to retrieve the adder stones.

"This was really the only place that had them?" Klein asked Mystic in a low voice.

"Yes, I checked everywhere, and this is the only place," Mystic replied.

Another groan escaped from Klein's lips as he ran his hands through his hair. If they got the adder stones, it would be worth the discomfort, but he wasn't happy about it.

The fortune teller didn't take long to return, pushing aside the curtain. In her hands, she held the two stones, swinging on leather strings. They looked real enough to Klein, and he reached out his hand, palm open, to take a closer look.

However, the fortune teller was smarter than she appeared, and she quickly stuffed the stones into the pocket of her robe. "These aren't cheap. I'll take five hundred gold each," she said with confidence. Mystic's mouth popped open, almost comically.

"A thousand gold for two adder stones?" Klein's voice hissed out. "That's more than we've ever paid for them. Come on, we can find them somewhere else." He stood up, ready to leave the tent, but the merchant grabbed his sleeve.

"They could be discounted?" Her youthful hand yanked him back into his seat with surprising strength.

"We won't pay more than six hundred for both." Klein was firm in his demand. There was no way they were overpaying for these stones. The thought of hunting them down themselves or taking them from the merchant crossed his mind. Then, they'd get the stones and the gold.

"Hmm, six hundred, you say?" The merchant's voice was filled with excitement. "I might be able to do that in exchange for something from you." What could they possibly offer a con artist besides gold, Klein thought to himself.

"And what exactly would you want from us?" Klein asked, his patience waning as he grew tired of dealing with this swindler.

"Simple, just let me do a reading on you both."

Mystic laughed, leaning back in her chair. "Read our fortunes, and you'll give us a discount? That doesn't make sense at all." Klein had to agree. Why would the merchant give them a discount for something like that? Fortune tellers usually charged for readings.

"Let me check if the stones are as real as you say, and then you can do your reading," Klein told her.

"Come on, brother, let's just do it. After all, why be foolish and not accept her offer? It's a forty percent discount! Let her do her reading. What does it matter? It's not like she could tell us something we don't already know." Mystic told Klein under her breath.

"You'd be surprised at what I can tell you, Mystic," the fortune teller said ominously, her white teeth visible beneath her hood as she handed Klein the stones to inspect.

The stones are real alright, and high-quality ones too.

Klein returned the stones to the female, who quickly caught the small leather strings and hid them in the deep pockets of her robe. "Deal," he grunted as he went to retrieve the gold to purchase the stones. He realized it was all the gold he had brought with him, so they wouldn't be able to buy anything more for the day.

"Wonderful! Now, I only read one at a time, my dear," the female said, turning to Mystic. "You'll have to wait outside until it's your turn, and after I've read both of you, you can have the stones." Mystic nodded and left the tent while Klein was left with the female. He was going to be subjected to a fake reading from a fake fortune teller. What could go wrong?

The female smoothed out the black fabric of the tablecloth and placed her hands on the table. "Please place your hands on the black crystal," she purred, her voice taking on an eerie quality. Klein placed his hands on the sides of the ball, which was warm to the touch. "Now close your eyes and think of your future, your hopes, dreams, anything you hope to achieve in this life," the female instructed.

Klein decided to comply and thought about his wants for the future. Freedom, gold, and so many other things crossed his mind. Though he briefly considered the idea of love, he quickly dismissed it. Finding a mate among all the Fae in the world was rare, and Klein had not found anyone he wanted to stay with for more than a night. Mystic would always just be a sister to him, their friendship rooted deeply in survival.

As Klein turned his mind towards his wants, a new scent permeated the room—the light scent of freshly bloomed roses. The candles flickered as the fortune teller placed her hands over his. "I see many things, Kleptis Klein of Bastards Bay. Your life is not an easy one, and it will get harder still. I see choking vines wrapping around your heart like steel bands. Their thorns digging deep and true, you'll never escape them—nor will you want to. A shadow looms over you, crushing everything in its path. Only desolation will be your salvation," she said in a warbling voice.

The ball had become so hot that Klein's hands tingled when he removed them. He felt weak and dizzy for a moment but quickly regained his composure. "Very enlightening. I'll watch out for thorns and shadows," he murmured, feeling uncomfortable. He stood up and left the tent, removing himself from the sickly smell of incense and the female's presence.

Outside, Klein saw Mystic leaning against the tent pole, cleaning her nails with a blade. "Your turn. Make it quick. And make sure you get those stones after!" he growled, feeling a deep migraine starting to form in his head.

"Of course, brother," Mystic replied with a wink before entering the tent. The wait felt extremely long to Klein as he wondered what was being said inside. Despite his heightened senses, the thick fabric of the tent muffled any sounds that might have reached him. After what felt like an eternity, Mystic finally emerged, her face ashen and pale. In her hand was the Adder Stones.

"Didn't take you for a believer," Klein chuckled, trying to lighten the mood. "Did she tell you about the thorns and shadows?"

"Let's just go home," Mystic whispered, her voice barely audible. She handed the stones to Klein, who placed them in his cloak, noticing a slight tremble in her hand as she did. "Let's never talk about this again."

Furrowing his brows, Klein nodded in agreement. "Alright, let's go home. I need to wash the smell of that incense off me," he said, sniffing the fabric of his clothes and wrinkling his nose in distaste. "I might have to burn these clothes."

The two of them made their way back to the guild house, with Mystic remaining silent and reflective for the entire walk. It was strange for her to be so quiet, but Klein respected her need for peace.

Chapter 8

Mel

    It was morning again, and I slowly opened my eyes as the bright light from my phone penetrated my slumber. Realizing that I must have rolled over on it during the night, I groggily reached over to grab it. Checking the time, I saw that it was eleven am, another morning of sleeping in, just the way I liked it.

    Sleeping in this late had another benefit: most everyone would be up already, and the bathroom would likely be empty. Throwing off the covers, I grabbed my toiletries and headed down to the bathroom. It was empty, as I had hoped it would be. As I brushed my teeth, I thought about the previous night's dream. What could the fortune teller have said to them?

Usually, I could remember my dreams pretty well, but inside the star-speckled tent, my memory fogged. My mind only seemed to follow Klein when I walked in the dream world, and although I couldn't know their thoughts or feelings, I had gotten pretty good at reading their expressions. Mystic had seemed so shaken up by whatever that Fae merchant had told her.

You would have thought that being my dream, I would have known what was going on, but that was never been the case.

Sighing deeply, I looked at myself in the mirror, but it was just my normal reflection staring back at me. I was the same empty and worthless girl I had always felt I was. I longed to join my friends in Jelaria, but it seemed like a distant dream. I rinsed out my mouth with water from the sink, trying to shake off these thoughts and not fall into a pit of self-pity. I knew it wouldn't change anything, and I couldn't afford to be sad about my life. I had seen Klein and Mystic overcome impossible odds, and if they could survive the Pits, then I could make it through this.

After getting ready for the day, I went to find Becky. She was upstairs on the club floor, teaching one of the girls how to make her dance more alluring. Interrupting her, I asked, "Hey, I just wanted to figure out the schedule for tonight. What time should I be ready to dance?"

Becky looked me up and down and blew out a puff of smoke. "You won't be dancing tonight," she said curtly.

I was taken aback. "What? I really need the money, Becky. Did I do something wrong? Did someone complain about me? I can do better!" My thoughts became erratic as anxiety took over. I couldn't bear the thought of living on the streets, having seen what that could do to a person.

"It's something you did right," Becky explained. "Harvey, the man who's been booking you, doesn't want you to dance anymore or to take other clients. You must have a magical cunt, because he has paid for you every night this week."

Gasping in shock, I asked, "Every night this week?" I looked around, not seeing Harvey anywhere. "What time will he be here?"

"That's the thing," Becky replied. "He claims to have work obligations and won't be here to see you until New Year's Eve. You'll have to talk to Michael about getting your money."

"Right... okay," I said, trying to wrap my head around it. The thought of not having to work for a week was a relief, even though I would be missing out on a lot of money.

I went to find Michael in his office. It was on the same floor as the club and had a worn, scratched desk surrounded by large gray filing cabinets. A soiled couch sat across from it—I would rather sit on the floor than touch that thing. Michael was typing away at his computer, focused on his work. As I entered the room, he looked up from the screen.

"Just who I wanted to see," he said in a greasy voice that made me feel slimy.

"Yeah, I hear I have a big payday from my client, Harvey," I said, trying to keep my voice strong. Michael had a way of belittling the dancers and keeping most of the profits for himself.

He pointed to an envelope on his desk and pushed it over to me. I opened it to find several hundred dollar bills inside. The money was great, but it wasn't enough for missing four days of work. Before I could say anything, Michael sneered, "You're lucky you're getting that much, so don't be a bitch about it. If it were up to me, I'd have you working all week, despite what that asshole wants. So, in a way, I'm the one losing out here." He turned back to his computer screen and grumbled, "What a waste." And with that, he dismissed me from his office.

Losing out on the money was tough, but at least I had the entire week off. I counted the cash in the envelope, and there were five hundred. I could realistically earn that much in just one good night of dancing. However, I was too afraid to confront Micheal about it. I took three hundred of it and added it to my stash of saved money. It was growing into a substantial sum, and I seriously considered looking into purchasing a one-way plane ticket out of the country. The internet was filled with videos claiming that the American dollar went further overseas, so it had to be true, *right*?

I rummaged through my mini fridge for something to eat, my stomach growling with hunger. There wasn't much left— just an old, wrinkled apple and some milk that had long since passed its expiration date. My coffee jar was empty, and even the breakfast bars I usually kept on hand were gone. When was the last time I went grocery shopping? I figured since I had the day off, I might as well make the most of it and head to the grocery store. Perhaps I'd even find a new book or two at the thrift store while I was out. Grabbing my phone and jacket, I sent a quick text to my friends, Jess and Amber, to let them know where I was going and to see if they wanted anything.

    The grocery store and thrift store were both a short bus ride away and as I didn't have a car, I was limited in what I could bring back with me. I kept several collapsible grocery bags in my jacket, which were thin but could hold more than the plastic ones offered at the store. As I sat on the bus, waiting to arrive at my first destination, I felt my phone vibrate. It was a text from Jess.

Jess: I just heard! Congrats on the sugar daddy lol
Me: Yeah, I guess. I don't plan on keeping him long-term. Just make some money and get out of there.
Jess: Was it the same man as before?
Me: Yeah.
Jess: You better be careful with him, then don't give him your cell number or anything stupid.
Me: I know. I won't. Do you need anything from the store?
Jess: Ummmm let me ask Amber.

...

No, we're good girl! See you later.

    That was convenient for me, as it meant I would have to carry less if they didn't want anything. I placed my phone back in my pocket, but it soon started vibrating again. I wondered if they had changed their minds and needed something after all. When I looked back at the screen, I saw that the message was from Alex, which brought a smile to my face.

Alex: Hey, how's it going? Watch any more of that show?
Me: Hi, yeah I did. It's really good so far. I got the day off again, so I'm just running some errands in town. Wanna join me?
Alex: Sure! Where are you headed and I'll meet you there?
Me: Just the Wally on 4th st.
*Alex: K see you in ten. *wink emoji**

    To be fair, I was inviting Alex to join me for two reasons. First, he had a car, so I wouldn't have to carry all my groceries on the bus, and second, shopping was always better when you have someone to go with. I leaned back in my bus seat, feeling more relaxed than I had in a long time, and before I knew it, the bus came to a stop in front of the grocery store. It was a popular stop, and several people got off the bus with me.

    Alex was waiting outside the store, and before he noticed me, I took a moment to admire him. Today, he was wearing a gray hoodie and black cargo pants, and his wavy black hair was styled in a messy faux hawk that was a few inches long. He looked good. Had he always been this attractive?

    As I approached him, his eyes lit up, and he breathed out a cheerful "Hey!" I noticed he had tucked his hands into his pockets to stay warm.

"Hey yourself, thanks for coming to meet me. I'm sorry if this is a boring request," I mumbled, feeling awkward.

Alex shook his head at me. "I'm so glad you invited me. It gives me an excuse to see you." He looked genuinely happy to be here with me, which was surprising. Had anyone ever looked at me as if I wasn't a burden before? I couldn't remember. My cheeks warmed as I started to blush.

We walked side by side as we entered the store, grabbing shopping baskets just inside. I chose a grocery cart near the entrance, its wheels squeaking but seemed to be in decent shape compared to some of the others.

Trying to start a conversation to ease my awkwardness, I asked him, "So, what would you be doing today if I hadn't invited you?"

His hand came back to touch the back of his neck as his cheeks began turning pink. He always seemed to blush so easily. I was glad to see I wasn't the only nervous one.

"I planned on shopping today anyway, so it's no big deal," he said as he picked up a bag of chips and placed it in the cart. "Really, there's this bookstore-coffee shop combo a few streets north of here that I've been wanting to check out. Plus, I wouldn't miss a chance to hang out with you," he added, his words rushing out and his cheeks turning even more red.

Walking through the grocery store with Alex, I couldn't help but question whether developing a relationship with him was the right choice for both of us. The idea of causing any kind of pain to

Alex, who truly seemed like a wonderful person, made my heart ache.

I grabbed only what I needed, like instant coffee and a few other easy snacks that didn't require cooking—making sure to keep my stuff separate from his in the cart. The store was small, with a limited selection to choose from. Near the front, I turned to the small dust-covered book section. It mostly contained murder mysteries, which were okay, but they always sounded the same to me. The romances I liked all had the same story, too, when you got right down to it.

"Do you like to read?" He asked, noticing where my eyes had gone. Looking at the books with me, he picked up one of the comics scattered towards the bottom shelf before tossing it back down and grabbed another.

Sighing in disappointment, I told him, "I love to read, but mostly just trashy romance novels and fantasy books like that. They don't have a great selection here." Picking up one of the books, I read the description on the back and shook my head. "Definitely not one I want to read."

He nodded, "Yeah, my sister used to love those books too. I'd be lying if I said I hadn't read a couple myself. I bet they have a good selection at the coffee shop if you want to go with me after this." His hands came down to his neck again, and I noticed that he did that a lot when he was nervous.

"Sure, none of this food will go bad in the car, so it should be fine if you don't mind dropping me off after."

"No problem, I'd be happy to." He agreed easily, putting the second comic book back as well.

After completing our shopping, we made our way back to his car. When we got there, he popped the trunk open and offered me a hand with the bags. With ease, he lifted them from my arms and carefully placed them inside. The trunk of his rusty red Toyota was surprisingly spacious, and the bags appeared to take up very little room in it. The groceries I bought consisted of only three bags worth of food, but I knew it could last me a few weeks. My slim figure was more of a result of limited food access rather than an intentional diet.

We chatted on the drive to the shop, talking about random things and all the shows he thought I should watch. There were so many I wasn't sure how one person could watch it all in their lifetime. Some of the shows had hundreds of episodes. Sure, some of it was filler that I could skip, but still, it would take years to watch it all.

Pulling up to the quaint and rustic-looking building, my eyes were immediately drawn to a decal on the window that read "The Book Keepers Coffee Shop." A smaller sign next to it declared "Help Wanted." The thought crossed my mind that perhaps I should inquire about a job, but I quickly dismissed it, feeling as though it was out of reach.

As we searched for a parking spot, we realized that most of them were already occupied. With only street parking available, we had to dig out some change from the ashtray to feed the meter before we could head inside. I felt grateful once again that I didn't have a car—parking was never free.

Stepping inside, I was in awe of the sheer amount of books that filled the shop. Bookshelves overflowed with books, tables were covered with stacks of them, and patrons had them clutched in their hands. The whole place was imbued with the rich scent of freshly brewed coffee and paper, and the sound of baristas hard at work in the background only added to the ambiance. I couldn't help but wonder why I had never visited a real bookstore like this before.

"This is wonderful, Alex," I said, grateful for the experience. "Thank you for bringing me here."

"No need to thank me," he replied, his voice warm and genuine. "I wanted you to come along. In fact, I'm the one who should be thanking you for joining me despite your other plans."

Before I could correct him by pointing out that I had no other plans, my gaze fell upon a book on the table beside me. Its cover was eye-catching and adorned with shimmering golden edges. As I flipped it over to check the price, I couldn't help but wince. The cost was a painful reminder of why I rarely ventured into places like this. If only I had the money, I could fill a library with beautifully bound books and have a rolling ladder to reach them all. But those were just fantasies that I would never be able to fulfill. Sighing, I replaced the book where I had found it.

"Would you like a coffee?" Alex asked, bringing me back to reality.

"Sure, let me give you some cash." I reached for my wallet.

"No need, coffee's on me today," he said with a smile. "Two creams and three sugars, right?"

It felt a little strange to have him pay for me, but I nodded in agreement, surprised that he remembered how I liked my coffee. While Alex went to the coffee counter, I took the opportunity to explore the store. I quickly found the fantasy romance section in the back, where I saw many of my favorite authors. I ran my fingers along their spines, considering buying just one book. Eventually, I picked up a book about a princess locked in a tower saved by a dragon shifter. According to the back, it was a thrilling romance. The cover showed a silhouette of a dragon and a princess embracing. It was a paperback, much more affordable than the gold-edged book I saw earlier. Holding onto it, I went back to find Alex.

The barista caught my attention, her hair a brilliant rainbow hue that seemed to shine under the soft lighting of the coffee shop. She expertly crafted our drinks, every movement precise and graceful. Alex retrieved the cups from the counter, carrying them over to the only vacant table. The Book Keepers Coffee Shop was bustling, with nearly every surface occupied by patrons deep in conversation or buried in books. The hum of activity filled the air. The sweet aroma of freshly brewed coffee and the pages' rustling only added to the cozy atmosphere.

I eagerly took a sip of the coffee as I met Alex at the café, savoring the rich, warm flavor. "Alex, this coffee is amazing! It's so much better than the stuff at the diner."

"I know, right?" Alex replied, taking a sip from his cup. "I've tried to convince my dad to stop buying the cheapest coffee in bulk, but he never listens."

As we sipped our coffee, we chatted about our favorite books. "So, how did you hear about this place?" I asked.

A wide grin spread across Alex's face, his brown eyes sparkling. I noticed there were tiny flecks of green in his eyes. "This store has the largest manga section in the entire city. I've checked them all out, and this one takes the cake."

I was confused. "What's manga? Is it like anime?"

"Sort of," Alex explained. "It's a type of comic book that most anime is based on. Let me show you." He grabbed a book from a nearby shelf and handed it to me. The artwork was stunning, with characters that seemed to leap off the page.

"Wow, these are amazing!" I said, genuinely impressed. "Maybe I should grab a few while we're here." But as I flipped to the back cover to check the price, my excitement faded. "Or maybe not."

"If you want, I have some you can borrow," Alex offered. "I can give them to you next time I see you."

"That would be great," I replied. "Maybe I can pay you back with coffee next time."

It was so nice to have a normal conversation with someone who didn't make inappropriate comments or ask for sexual favors in exchange for a simple gesture. I've learned to be cautious around men after having my trust shattered by past heartbreak. But with Alex, I felt comfortable and safe.

"So, have you thought about the self-defense classes?"

I hesitated, feeling guilty for not having considered it earlier. "Oh, yeah. What day was it again?" I finally answered, trying to hide my lack of interest. *No, I hadn't even thought of it once until you brought it up.* Well, I guess I could have told him that, but it just seemed rude.

"It's on Mondays, Wednesdays, and Fridays," Alex said, giving me big puppy dog eyes. "It starts at six in the morning, and it's only an hour long. I could even drive you if you'd like."

It was a nice offer, and I wouldn't mind spending more time with him even if it did take away from my sleeping time. "This Friday at six?" I mumbled. "I actually have an appointment that morning at ten to get a tattoo. I have been planning this tattoo for years. Sorry, Alex. I know the appointment was a few hours after the self-defense class, but I don't want to risk missing it. I'd have to come back to shower. Get ready all over again. Plus, I can't just expect you to drive me everywhere." I said with an apologetic tone.

The truth was, the tattoo I wanted was designed to match Klein's. I had always admired the moon phases tattoo he had across his shoulder blades, and for my birthday this year, I decided to get the same design tattooed across my collarbones. I had been eagerly counting down the days until my appointment, and I didn't want to miss out on it. It was my early birthday gift to myself, and I hoped that it would look as beautiful in reality as it did in my imagination.

Alex's face fell, but he quickly recovered. "I understand," he said with a shrug. "You're not obligated to do anything you don't want to."

If only that were true.

"Yeah, maybe next time for the self-defense class," I said, feeling a bit guilty for having to turn down his offer.

"Of course, no worries," he replied with a smile. "So, about this tattoo, you're getting... That's pretty cool! I've always wanted to get some tattoos, but my dad is kind of strict about it. He'd probably skin me alive if he found out!" He laughed at his own joke.

"No way, he wouldn't do that," I chuckled.

"Uh, yeah, he would!" he countered, still chuckling.

"Okay, okay, let's just agree to disagree," I playfully shrugged it off. "This will be my first tattoo, and I'm getting it as an early birthday present to myself." I pulled out my phone and showed him the design I had sketched. "It's not exactly a masterpiece, but I think it came out okay."

"It's going to look great on you! Is it your birthday this weekend?" he asked, his eyes lighting up with excitement.

"Nah, my birthday is actually on the 20th. This was just the only day my tattoo artist had an opening," I explained.

"Oh, got it. So, you're a Capricorn, then?" he asked, furrowing his brow in thought. "My sister was really into astrology, and she always used to tell me my horoscope. I'm an Aries, supposedly competitive and ambitious. But that doesn't really sound like me, you know?" he added with a frown.

"Yeah, astrology is all just nonsense if you ask me. All those horoscopes are so generic, they could apply to anyone," I said, waving it off.

"I agree, but for me, those daily horoscopes are a reminder of my sister. We used to talk about them all the time. After she passed away, I didn't realize how much those silly conversations meant to me," he said, his voice taking on a sad note.

"I'm sorry. I didn't mean to imply anything." Pulling out my phone in an attempt to cheer him up, "Do you want me to look ours up for the day? Or is that too weird?"

He took a moment to think about it, then gave me a lopsided smile. "I don't think it would be weird. Honestly, I think my sister would like that. Who knows, maybe she's leaving me secret messages in my horoscope, and I don't even know it because I never read them."

"Okay, here I go." Scrolling through the browser, I found an app that said 'Free Daily Horoscope.' When I opened it, it was a little hard to navigate at first, and it took me a minute, but I found the right thing. "Daily Horoscope for Aries." I read it out loud, "*Aries, today you will have a happy encounter, but don't get too excited, and always remember patience is a virtue.* This seems very vague to me, but I guess the happy encounter could be me."

He looked up with a thoughtful expression and a warm smile on his face. "Thank you for that, Mel. You don't know how much this means to me."

"Should I read mine too?" I asked, meeting his green-flecked eyes.

"If you wouldn't mind."

"It's cool. Okay, Capricorn. Here it is. *Capricorn, your fate is changing swiftly. Be brave. A powerful bond will pull your heart in two directions. As frosted hands take yours, remember the end is sometimes the beginning. Only desolation will be your salvation.*" I laughed and put my phone away. "Well, that's not fucked up at all, is it? Good thing I don't take this shit seriously, or I might be a little worried that something bad was about to happen to me."

Alex didn't look too convinced. "If something happens, I'll do my best to protect you."

Pushing his shoulder back, I giggled, "Going to protect me from a scary horoscope! You worry too much!"

By the time Alex and I finished discussing the merits of horoscope reading, our coffee had gone cold and we were too engaged in conversation to drink it. He purchased a few manga books for himself, and I bought the dragon shifter romance that I had picked out earlier.

Exiting the store, the bells on the door chimed as we made our way back to Alex's car. Conversation with Alex was seamless, and it felt as though we could talk for hours about even the most trivial of topics. The drive back to Baby Dolls was brief, yet my cheeks ached from the constant smiling and laughing.

As I got out of his car, bags in hand, I blurted out, "Thanks for hanging out with me! We should totally do it again!"

"I'll text you, Mel. Maybe the next time we go out, I can take you on a real date," he replied, his face set in a warm smile, leaving me with a stomach full of fluttering butterflies.

The feeling of normalcy was something that was new to me. It was as if my actions didn't define me, but rather that I was simply Mel. When I entered my room and fell onto my bed, I couldn't help but allow myself to sink into the plush mattress, feeling a sense of weightlessness as I bounced. The thought occurred to me that maybe I didn't need to travel to some far-off land to find happiness—it could very well be found right here. Late into the night, Alex and I continued our text conversation, my heart filled with anticipation for what the future held.

Chapter 9

Mel

The past few days had been a whirlwind of texting with Alex and sleeping in late. Every conversation with him felt effortless, and we were getting to know each other better by the day. He was even convincing me that taking self-defense classes would be a wise choice. We made plans to meet up every day starting Monday at six am. SIX AM! The thought of waking up that early made me cringe, but I had already set an alarm on my phone, determined to make it happen.

My dreams had been mostly mundane lately, with Klein and Mystic training and preparing for the heist they were working on.

They were getting close to their goal, and I knew they would pull it off like they always did.

I was in a great mood today, with neither Becky nor Michael bothering me about work. I was starting to feel grateful to Harvey for giving me some space. This was one of the most liberating weeks I have had in a long time, and I usually only got one day off per week. My mind and body felt refreshed like I could finally take a deep breath. The possibilities seemed endless like I could move out, take a normal job, and be just fine. This felt like the perfect time for things to change.

With a deep yawn, I gazed at the clock, trying to fathom how I could possibly wake up early enough for my classes. Waking up at nine in the morning was already a challenge, but today was different. Today was the day I was finally getting my long-awaited dream tattoo—the phases of the moon gracefully etched onto my collarbones. The idea that this art could outlive me and still be visible on my bones even after a thousand of years was nothing short of exhilarating.

The tattoo artist, Larry, was a familiar face at the club where I worked. Although he had a reputation that left much to be desired, he was an exceptional tattoo artist. Thankfully, I had never been one of his clients, which meant I wouldn't have to deal with any awkwardness while getting inked. From what the other girls told me, he had a reputation for his wild and risqué sexual antics. To each their own, but that was well beyond my comfort zone, no matter the compensation.

The tattoo shop, Pins and Needles, was located further away from the club than the diner. It was too cold to make the journey on foot, but I needed to burn off some of my anxiety. By leaving early, I was confident I would arrive just in time for my appointment. Despite my confident exterior, the thought of the needles piercing my skin filled me with apprehension. How could people with so many tattoos endure the pain? Would there be numbing cream available? I was told the process would take anywhere from three to four hours.

As I dressed, my mind was filled with all the things that could go wrong, but I knew I was ready to face this fear. The reason it had taken me so long to get a tattoo was mostly due to my cowardice when it came to pain.

Despite my nerves, I was determined to go through with it. The idea of three to four hours of continuous needlework was daunting, but I hoped the numbing cream would make all the difference. I focused on the end goal—a stunning piece of art permanently adorning my body.

I was wearing a low-cut, cute red sweater dress with black leggings. The swooping neckline of the dress would give the artist plenty of space, so I wouldn't have to remove my top. I was aware that I undressed for a living, but I was paying him, not the other way around. I put on some mascara and lip gloss, doing my hair in a simple ponytail. The bruises on my neck were gone entirely, thank goodness. I really didn't want to explain them anymore. I was almost ready to go.

Throwing on my jacket, I checked my wallet to make sure I had enough money to pay for the tattoo and maybe a coffee afterward. That's when I remembered that I hadn't eaten anything yet. Quickly, I grabbed a granola bar so I would have something in my stomach before the session began. It was dry as I chomped it down, the sugary chocolate chips coating my mouth. It was filling but not exactly healthy. I had to drink some water to wash it down. Jess was lounging on her bed, messing around with her phone, when she noticed I was about to leave.

Looking up, she shrieked in excitement, "Sleeping Beauty's first tattoo! Go get that tattoo cherry popped; you won't ever go back!"

Jess had tattoos, some good and some bad. My favorite tattoos she had were intricate floral pieces on her calves. The soft, curling lines looked feminine as they wrapped around her legs. All her well-done tattoos were done by Larry, which was why I chose him. They had some kind of arrangement where she got tattoos for 'free.' I hoped he wouldn't expect the same arrangement from me. It wasn't that I was ashamed of what I did, but taking clients outside the club was risky because there was no security. Plenty of girls had made that mistake and never came back like Alex's sister.

"I only plan on getting one," I mumbled back to her.

She just laughed, "That's what they all say!" Her full lips painted, a dusty pink, stretched wide. She had been up for hours already, with a full face of makeup, like she had plans to see someone special. It was strange to see her without Amber glued to her hip. Now that I thought about it, Amber had been absent the past few days.

"Hey, where's Amber? Do you two have plans today?"

She looked worried, worry lines etched deeply into her face. "She's avoiding me," she said, her tone tinged with concern. "There's something going on with her, but she won't talk about it." She tried to put on a brave face despite her obvious distress. "Don't worry about us, just go get that birthday tattoo," she added, trying to sound cheerful.

"Okay. Well, tell me about it later." I promised her I would catch up on the situation when I got back, then headed out the door. "I'll send you pictures when it's done. See you later."

The brisk weather outside was a stark contrast to the warmth of our shared apartment. I walked with purpose, trying to avoid making eye contact with the people I passed. The streets were full of people without homes, a group I was all too familiar with from my time at Baby Dolls. Despite the danger, I couldn't help but feel grateful for my job and the relative safety it provided. I knew what life was like for working girls on the streets. Drugs and abuse took a toll on their minds and bodies, and I was grateful to have avoided that fate.

Where would I be if I didn't start working there? Working girls on the streets didn't last long. Shuddering, I picked up the pace.

As I walked, my thoughts turned to my life and all the twists and turns that had led me to this point. Baby Dolls had its problems, but it was still better than the alternatives. The work was unpleasant, but the staff did their best to keep us safe. I never felt completely safe, but when I was asleep, I was able to escape to a world where I was with my friends and my loved ones. This tattoo was my way of bridging the gap between my waking and sleeping worlds. I could look at it and know that a part of Klein would always be with me.

  Lost in thought, I hadn't realized how far I'd walked until I reached the tattoo shop. Larry was in the process of opening for the day, and I watched as he turned on the neon "open" sign. A glimpse of someone sleeping caught my eye, hidden between the buildings. Feeling a pang of empathy, I walked into the shop, wishing I had an extra jacket to offer the homeless person.

  "Hey Larry, are you ready for me?" I asked as I stepped into the compact space of Pins and Needles. The walls were painted in a bold black and red hue, and the room was equipped with two tattoo stations and a small front counter. My eyes were drawn to the numerous plastic frames hanging on the walls, and some of the images made me do a double-take. Did people really get these designs permanently inked onto their bodies? Shaking my head, I turned to Larry, who was preparing his station. There were two doors in the back, one with a gender-neutral bathroom sign and the other marked "employees only." It must be the break room or storage space. Quiet rock music was playing from the speakers on the front desk.

  "Just a minute," Larry replied, "I just have to wrap everything up to keep everything sterile. I already have your design stenciled out." He sprayed disinfectant on a black massage table before covering it with plastic. The thought of the entire process being covered in blood made me shiver. But, I reminded myself, Jess would have warned me if I was going to bleed everywhere. Right?

"All done! Come on back," Larry announced. The sight of all the plastic covering the area made it look like a scene from a TV show about a serial killer. Despite its ominous appearance, I was relieved knowing everything was sanitary. As he prepared, I watched him unwrap sterilized needles and disposable ink containers.

"Stand here so I can get the placement where you want it. Across the collarbones, right?" Larry asked.

"Right," I replied, still feeling nervous despite my long walk. My pulse was pounding in my ears. Larry had me stand in front of a mirror to ensure the stencil was placed exactly where I wanted it. He marked my collarbones to indicate the midline and the ends of the design, taking his time to line everything up perfectly for my body frame. After spraying the stencil onto my skin, I was able to preview what the finished tattoo would look like. It was perfect, and a smile spread across my face.

"Happy with the placement?" Larry asked.

Nodding my head energetically, I exclaimed, "It's fantastic! Exactly what I wanted!" Now, if only getting a tattoo was just that easy. Larry patted the table, indicating for me to lie down as he prepared the ink he would be using.

"Does this color palette look okay to you? I'll be using a mix of blacks, grays, and a small amount of white." He reassured me, with a professional demeanor, "If at any time you become uncomfortable or need a break, just let me know."

I tried to make myself comfortable on the table and prepare for the pain. "The colors look good to me. As long as it comes out like the picture," I responded, trying to mask my nervousness.

"I'm going to do my best." Placing a gloved hand on my chest, he asked, "Ready?"

"As ready as I'll ever be," I mumbled as the first needle touched my skin. The pain was sharp and immediate. I cursed, realizing it was just as bad as I had feared. When I had asked Jess about the pain, she had just laughed at me. *Well, of course, it hurts. Did you think they were licked on by unicorns?*" Very funny, Jess.

Larry continued tattooing, and the pain came in waves. Some areas felt like nothing, while others felt like blades scraping against my bones. I tried not to grit my teeth or pull away, instead clutching the sides of the table.

The intense pain of getting a tattoo was not lost on me, but I was determined to endure it. This was something I had wanted my entire adult life, and I was not going to let a little discomfort get in my way.

Laying on the table, the whirring sound of the tattoo machine was almost deafening. The vibration of the machine seemed to travel through my skull and down my spine. Larry, the tattoo artist, was completely focused on his craft, working with a quiet determination to create a masterpiece on my skin.

With each dip of the needle, I felt a jolt of pain. It seemed like every time I thought the session was over, Larry would dip the needle in again for another round. As the hours passed, I tried my best to distract myself from the pain by thinking of Klein and what he would think of my decision to get a matching tattoo.

My thoughts turned to my silver-eyed friends. What were they up to right now? Would they ever encounter a unicorn? The thought of these magical creatures was a welcome distraction from the discomfort I was feeling. I tried to paint a picture in my mind, but all I could see were the innocent-looking white unicorns that were often depicted in art.

Just as I was lost in thought, I felt a gentle touch on my shoulder. It was Larry checking in on me. "Everything okay? Do you need a break?" he asked.

Shaking my head, I said, "I'm okay, you can continue." Larry nods and goes back to work. I can't wait to see the finished product. I hope it doesn't take longer than he estimated. My mind drifts back to the financial aspect of my decision, and I realized I only brought enough cash for the quote he gave me.

The thought of money brings my mind to Jelaria and the added debt from Lycanthus. My brow furrows as I think about the dangerous jobs he usually gives out, like assassinations and kidnappings. I try to shake off the thought of someone being tortured in the caves of the Abyss for information. These dark fantasies of mine are my least favorite, often filled with blood and violence. They make me squirm and sometimes even force me to leave my dream.

Suddenly, a cool splash hits my collarbones, and I let out a gasp in surprise.

"Just cleaning up! This might sting a little." He warned me too late as he took a damp paper towel to wipe my stinging skin.

"Fuck!" I exclaimed as the antiseptic solution made contact with my skin. The sharp sting felt as though it was intensifying the pain from the tattoo, but before I could voice my discomfort, Larry quickly applied a soothing ointment to my skin, bringing relief and comfort to the area.

"Sorry about that," Larry said, breaking the silence. "Did you want me to take a picture before I wrap it up?" He stood up straight, his back cracking as he did after having been crouched over me for hours without taking a break.

"Yes, please!" I handed him my phone, and he snapped a few pictures before handing it back to me. I took a look and saw that the tattoo was a little puffy, and there was a small amount of blood leaking out, but the placement and shading were fantastic.

Larry cut out a sheet of clear bandaging, which looked like it should be waterproof. "This is a new tattoo wrap," he explained. "It helps the ink heal cleanly. Just don't take it off for 24 hours." He placed a long sheet of clear plastic over my collar bones, pressing down lightly, and it instantly stuck, creating a protective layer over my raw flesh.

Getting up, I looked at the tattoo in the mirror, tilting back and forth to admire the way it looked on me. I felt a little lightheaded, but it went away after standing for a few minutes. My stomach was rumbling, so the lightheadedness was probably from a lack of food. I had only brought enough money for the tattoo, so food would have to wait.

The plastic covered the tattoo, but you could still see it peeking out. And what I could see was amazing. Larry was a great artist. "Thank you, Larry," I said. "I love it. It was worth the painful four hours it took to complete."

"So, is it going to be cash or…" Larry paused, looking me up and down.

There it was. I had thought that he wouldn't reveal that side of him to me. "Just cash, please," I said as I pulled out the money I owed. He took the cash and handed me several papers to review. Despite his slight disappointment, he still accepted my payment. While Jess may be okay with taking clients outside of work, I was not.

"These are all your aftercare instructions. Touch-ups are free, so if there's anything I need to fix, don't hesitate to reach out," he said, pointing to the papers. He also handed me a new sheet of clear bandages. "After you remove it, wash the tattoo with antibacterial soap and reapply the bandage. You can leave the second one on for up to seven days."

I carefully slipped on my jacket, trying not to agitate my freshly tattooed skin, and thanked the artist with a nod of my head.

The journey back to Baby Dolls seemed so much chillier compared to the trip there. I hugged my jacket tighter, shivering slightly as I walked. Upon passing a gas station, I decided to stop and treat myself to a scalding hot cappuccino to warm my hands, using the last few dollars I had left. Ah, much better. I took a sip, immediately burning the roof of my mouth. "Dammit!" I shouted to myself. Despite the pain, I was grateful that the scalding liquid didn't spill onto my tender tattoo, which could have been disastrous.

I took out my phone and sent a picture of my new tattoo to Alex. He didn't respond immediately, and I assumed he was busy serving at the diner. He worked almost every day, with hours that changed depending on who called in. He stayed up late, so we usually talked to each other at night. I also sent the picture to Jess, but she didn't respond either.

Taking another sip of my coffee, I felt like the skin had burned off of my tongue. Even though it hurt, I continued to drink, determined not to waste it.

Upon returning to my room, I heard a heart-wrenching cry and quickly rushed inside.

Jess was lying face down on her bed, which was now separate from Amber's. The bedding was stripped off, and there was a noticeable absence of clothing and makeup in the room. My heart sank as I wondered if they had broken up. Tentatively, I approached her side, watching as her back heaved with sobs.

"Everything okay? Where's Amber?" I asked in a soft voice.

"She's... she's gone," Jess replied, her voice hoarse from crying. Reaching out, I started to rub soothing circles on her shoulder.

"Gone? Did something happen? Is she hurt?" I asked, trying not to panic. Hopefully, she had just moved away or found another job—and not something worse.

Jess turned her head towards me, her skin red and splotchy, tears filling her eyes. "Her family came for her this morning. I didn't even know she was talking to them." She started shouting, her face contorted with grief. "She was supposed to be my best friend. How could she do this?" she cried, tears continuing to fall down her face, ruining her makeup.

"Isn't that a good thing, though?" I sighed in relief and continued rubbing her back. "I know it's hard to see right now, but maybe this is what was best for her."

"Best for her! What about me?" Jess shouted. "She could have at least given me a heads up! Something! Hey girl, I'm leaving. Try not to get too attached!"

With a nod, I sat on my bed, allowing Jess to vent and express her feelings. I could relate to the feeling of betrayal and abandonment, having experienced them myself. I picked up my phone and placed it on the charger, silencing any notifications so I could fully focus on Jess. Right now, she just needed me to listen.

"You're right," I said, "She should have given you a heads up so you wouldn't be caught off guard."

"Exactly! If I were leaving, I would tell you guys," Jess continued. "She told me that she and her family had no contact anymore. I know I should be happy that they came for her, but I just feel so betrayed."

Jess turned her face into her pillow, her sobs intensifying. I nodded, listening attentively as she talked. In the corner of my eye, I saw a notification flash on my phone, but I ignored it. "Yeah, I understand," I said in a soothing tone.

"Here I am, ruining my face over this. I have to work tonight. I shouldn't be crying," Jess said, sitting up and wiping her eyes. "Time to put on my big girl panties and stop being a baby!" She mustered determination in her eyes.

As she looked at me, she noticed the clear bandage covering my new tattoo. "I forgot! How did it go? Did you get the Larry special?" she asked with a wink, causing a fresh tear to roll down her cheek.

I cringed at the memory of getting my tattoo. "No, I paid him cash. He did a pretty good job; really captured all the details I wanted," I said, pointing to my chest.

"Awesome, I can't wait to see it when it's healed. How was the pain level?" Jess asked, her curiosity overcoming her sadness.

"Awful! I don't know how you have so many tattoos. I felt like I wanted to jump out of my skin."

Laughing, she patted the tattoos covering her tanned legs. "Yeah, I know! It's almost like the pain is erased from your memory before it's time for another one. I have a whole gallery of ideas on my phone for my next tattoo." Pulling out her phone, she started flipping through images, showing me a couple of ideas. "Maybe some new ink would cheer me up?"

"Yeah, nothing like the scrape of needles on your skin to make you feel better," I joked. Some people did enjoy the pain, treating it like a form of therapy. The cost was probably similar to therapy if we were being honest. Taking my phone in hand, I checked my messages. Smiling, I saw it was Alex responding to the picture I sent him.

*Alex: *wow emoji* That came out incredible!*

Jess saw my face and smiled. "Ooo, texting your boyfriend?" She went to the vanity and took a makeup wipe to remove what was left on her face.

"He's not my boyfriend, just a good friend. We haven't even gone on a real date yet," I tried to protest. But it was getting harder to deny that I was growing feelings for him.

"*Yet*. Just a matter of time," she said with a frown. Pouting at me, she whined, "Then you'll leave me too, and I'll be all alone here." Tears were starting to build in her eyes again.

"You know I don't plan to be here forever, and you shouldn't either!" I said. I knew this wasn't a life that could go on forever, and deep down, she did too. "I promise I'll tell you before I leave, okay?" Hopefully, that would be sooner rather than later. I didn't want to stay here a moment longer than necessary. I had been here long enough already. My words seemed to placate her, though, and she didn't start sobbing again. She began to paint on her makeup like an artist, blending out the lines. Her eyeliner was sharp, just a quick flick of the wrist, and she had it perfect.

"Hey, I'm starting self-defense classes on Monday. When Alex and I go, would you like to join us?" I watched her as I spoke. I was sure Alex wouldn't mind, and maybe it would cheer Jess up to have something else to focus on.

"You wouldn't mind me crashing your date?" she asked.

"For the last time, Jess, it's not a date! So no, you wouldn't be crashing anything," I argued with her. Sighing, I went to my phone and typed out a response for Alex, asking if it was okay if Jess came with us on Monday.

Me: Thanks! Hey, question about Monday, is it ok if Jess comes with us?

Alex: Yeah it is . She should learn to defend herself too. Will Amber be coming?

Me: No.... She went back home to her family. Jess is really torn up about it.

Alex: Good for her. That place is no good. I hate to sound that way but I hope all of you guys get out of there someday.

Me: Me too....

Thinking about the money I had saved, I felt a sense of pride mixed with uncertainty. The idea of leaving Baby Dolls, where I've been working as a dancer was becoming more appealing by the minute. I've saved enough for several months of rent in a small apartment, and it's time for me to move out. The problem is, I don't have any real work experience or skills except for dancing. I recalled seeing a "now hiring" sign in the window of a bookstore that I visited with Alex and decided to take a chance and visit the store's website to fill out an application. What's the worst that can happen?

They could reject me, and I'll have to continue working at the dance club. But the job at the bookstore offered decent pay and benefits and requires someone who's willing to work full-time and late hours. I thought back to all the late nights I've spent at the club and realize that this could be a good fit. I quickly filled out the application on my phone, taking only ten minutes to complete, and hit the "submit" button. A spark of hope ignited within me as I anticipated their response.

Chapter 10

Jelaria

A grand feast was spread out on the table before Klein, its rich aroma filling the air. In the center of the table was a whole roasted pig with an apple lodged in its mouth—surrounded by smaller dishes of various meats and vegetables. The feast was sumptuous and costly, its cost rivaling that of feeding an entire village for a month.

Once a month, Lycanthus would insist on hosting these extravagant meals. He invited as many of the guild members as possible. The idea was to display his power and dominance over his followers. Tonight, fifteen guild members were gathered at the table, their once lively conversation reduced to a tense silence.

After dinner, Lycanthus would hold meetings with each member or small groups, delegating the tasks he wanted completed. The prospect of the work to be assigned to Klein and Mystic was making it a strained affair. The only ones who seemed to be enjoying themselves were Lycanthus himself—who relished in his own grandeur—and Stella, who sat on his right, fawning over him with adoring looks as she ate.

Klein ate his meal with a neutral expression, savoring the flavors of the baked chicken and herb-crusted fish. The food was expertly prepared, and the wine was served by the household slaves—which were common among the aristocratic Fae. The slaves, purchased from Bastards Bay like Klein and Mystic, were tasked with performing menial tasks and housework. Despite being given more freedom due to their abilities, Klein and Mystic were still slaves—their shackles made of blades and blood.

Lycanthus had plans for Klein and Mystic that night, a task they must complete, regardless of the consequences. If they refused, they would be punished in the rooms of the Abyss, just as they had many times before. Klein had vowed to himself and Mystic that he would find a way to escape, even if it were the last thing he did.

The money that Lycanthus paid to the Guardian only added to the weight of the chains that bound them. Klein knew that he could never leave without Mystic and that Lycanthus would find new ways to add to their debt. Klein had many different bank accounts to make it difficult for Lycanthus to track their gold, and as soon as they had enough, Klein planned to confront Lycanthus—laughing in his face and savoring the moment.

Mystic sat beside Klein, eating her meal and casting guilty glances at him from under her lashes. She took all the guilt for their debt onto herself, despite Klein's repeated assurances that they were in this together. But no matter how many times he told her, she still blamed herself for every last coin. Klein knew that Lycanthus would find some other reason to add to their debt, but he remained determined to escape with Mystic by his side.

"Always good to spend time with my family! Only the best for my children!" Lycanthus's voice rang out as he addressed the table. He wore a fine suit with gray pinstripes tailored to fight his large frame. Golden hoops lined his pointed ears, and the pocket watch chain hung from his breast. He had a large braided beard with golden beads, and his blonde hair was pulled back in a low ponytail, giving him the appearance of a pious leader who was relaxed and carefree.

However, Klein could tell by Lycanthus' tensing neck muscles that he was actually in a foul mood. There was someone who was going to pay with blood tonight, and Klein knew that one of them would deliver the killing blow.

Klein's chicken tasted like ash in his mouth as he ate. Food was merely fuel for his body, giving him the energy to get through his days. There were times when Klein could take pleasure from eating, like on the market day, but the weighted stares he received from the jealous guild members dampened his appetite. Lycanthus had always treated him and his sister with extra care, giving them the best and most lucrative jobs.

The servants cleared the dirty plates and made sure all glasses were full. With the table cleared, they began serving dessert—a frozen berry pudding. The sharp taste made Klein's lips pucker and his mouth salivate, but it wasn't to his liking, so he passed the remainder to Mystic. She always had a liking for sweet things, and he was rewarded with a large smile from her as she took it.

Stella was staring at Klein with a glint in her eye that spelled trouble. "Master Lycanthus?"

"Yes, what is it, pet?" Lycanthus gave her his full attention.

"Klein and Mystic are taking on the Ostara Sapphire job, and I want in on it. Klein told me no, though. Can't you make them change their minds?" She whined, making a fool of herself in front of everyone there.

"Is this true, Klein? Are you taking on that job?" Lycanthus asked with concern. "It's going to be dangerous. I don't want to lose my best children."

"We were thinking about it, oh great and mighty leader," Mystic said mockingly, giving him a salute. "Stella can stay here and water the flowers or whatever you keep her around for."

"Watch your tone, girl. Stella serves me in many ways," Lycanthus warned her.

Mystic leaned back in her chair, not caring about her tone. "Oh, I'm sure she does."

"So, what kind of job will you be giving us tonight?" Klein asked in a low voice, trying to draw attention away from his sister.

"No more business talk until I can give you all your assignments," Lycanthus grunted, keeping his eyes on Klein. "I guess you've decided to take my offer to lessen some of your debts to me."

Klein pushed his glass away, keeping his face calm. "Let's get on with it then. Just tell us who we need to kill, and we'll be on our way."

"If you're in that much of a rush, I'll make sure your meeting is the first one I have," Lycanthus boomed across the table. "I know how much you love the jobs I give you." The smile he gave them was feral. Someone's night was about to get a lot more gruesome.

"Of course, Lycanthus. Anything for our savior," Klein said, giving up on not trying to offend him. It was too late for that after Mystic's antics anyway.

Lycanthus' tone was unaffected, and he chuckled. "That a boy! It looks like everyone has finished. You and Mystic can stay behind. Everyone else, out!" he yelled, his voice full of firm authority, leaving no room for questioning.

Everyone quickly left the dining room, relieved to be free of the forced proximity to each other. The competitive nature of the Thieves Guild didn't allow for lasting friendships, and more than one person here wanted Klein's head for some reason or another. The room was finally empty; not even the servants stayed behind.

"So what's the assignment?" Mystic asked in her melodic way, picking at her nails with a knife she must have stolen from the dinner table.

"There is a rogue member of the guild I need you to hunt down. He fled to Bastards Bay this morning and is probably trying to book a ship off the continent," he growled, baring his teeth. "I want his head. Whether or not it's attached to his body is up to you."

That Fae must have gotten away with quite a bit of gold to merit a sentence like that.

"When do we leave?" Mystic questioned, realizing it might already have been too late to catch him. "If he caught any of the merchant ships out this morning, he would already be long gone."

"Oh, he's still there. Spending my gold in the arms of some whore, to be sure. You'll leave immediately. There is a small boat waiting to take you to the bay." He said, his fist coming to rest under his chin. "Do not fail me on this."

He handed Mystic a folded slip of paper. Unfolding it, she showed it to Klein. They saw a drawing and name, Frances Weatherdeen. Neither of them had done work with him in the past, but they knew him as a seedy fellow. Frances always took jobs under the table to keep the money for himself. Not good for guild business, so it wasn't surprising that he pulled a stunt like this. His greed was finally catching up to him.

"Where was he last seen?" Klein asked.

"I have eyes on him at the Orchid Flower. The fool. Make sure he suffers a little before you kill him." Lycanthus told them, his tone deadly.

"That's easy enough for me to find someone in that brothel..." Klein said, trailing off. Standing up with a bow, he took his leave with Mystic close on his heels.

Assassination was a difficult task for most, but he was Kleptis Klein of the Silver-Eyed Siblings—and he would not fail.

Walking along the rocky coastline, the small boat bobbed in the calm waters, as promised by Lycanthus. The journey to the bay was swift and easy, and the rolling waves provided a soothing rhythm. Mystic harnessed her wind magic, effortlessly guiding the vessel towards its destination with graceful movements. The wind caressed their faces, carrying the salty spray of the ocean, as she navigated the boat over the tranquil waters.

"Hopefully, Frances hasn't moved on by the time we get there. The stupid male, what was he thinking?" She asked while using the wind to keep the small boat steady.

"Probably that Lycanthus wouldn't notice right away. Idiot. He should have known that Janubis keeps tabs on every single gold piece. He should have left while he had the chance. Now, we're left to clean up this mess."

Mystic tilted her head and smirked. "Well, he wasn't always the brightest, was he?"

The pair arrived at the shores of Bastards Bay, tied up the boat, and made their way towards the buildings. Dressed for their mission, Klein was wearing fighting leathers that were concealed under a dark black cloak. Mystic, who had transformed into her serpentine form, stayed coiled around Klein's arm and body, ready to strike at a moment's notice. Her fangs were capable of delivering a deadly dose of venom. This was a common tactic they used when they wanted to make a kill without drawing too much attention. In a place like a brothel, where a single Fae would be less suspicious than two, Mystic's form was invaluable. Despite her distaste for the Orchid

Flower, being the brothel where she used to work as a child, she knew the place and its layout well.

The residents of Bastards Bay gave Klein a wide berth as he strolled through its grimy streets, as his reputation as a member of the Thieves Guild preceded him. No one dared to try to pickpocket him, as they knew the consequences of crossing a member of the Thieves Guild. His name and reputation echoed through the Bay, and Klein was widely recognized and respected.

With a slight drizzle in the air, Klein's boots were quickly coated with mud as he made his way through the tight alleyways of the stacked buildings in Bastards Bay. The stench of decay and rot filled the air, assaulting his nostrils with its intensity. It was a familiar odor in the Bay, where the smell of death was never too far away. The sound of raindrops hitting the cobblestone streets echoed through the alleyways, adding to the dreary atmosphere.

The Orchid Flower was a three-story wooden mansion that had seen better days. Its once-proud facade was now in dire need of repairs, and its neglect was extremely obvious after centuries of abuse. Despite the rain and mud, Klein strode into the building, not bothering to wipe his boots or shake off his cloak. The sound of the rusty hinges screeched as he opened the door, causing Mystic to flinch within his sleeve.

Inside, the brothel was filled with female Fae of all races, all trying to look provocative as they fanned themselves on the carpeted stairs. Nymphs, elves, and even a few selkies were among their ranks, trying to attract the attention of potential customers. Klein ignored the sultry looks thrown his way as he searched for the madam, Belladonna, the owner of this crumbling establishment.

It didn't take long for Klein to find her. She was seated on a large, high-backed chair that was designed to resemble a throne, dressed in her finest attire. Her brown hair was braided around her head, giving it the appearance of a crown. She sipped wine from a silver chalice as she surveyed the room, like a queen observing her court. As the Madam of the Orchid Flower, the largest brothel in Bastards Bay, she was indeed the queen of whores—at least in Klein's mind. She also happened to be his bitch of a mother. Belladonna had never treated him as a son, having thrown him onto the streets as a small child. She only claimed credit for his success after he survived the Pits.

When Klein entered the room, her eyes lit up, and she shrieked, "Klein, my handsome boy, wonderful to see you again." She reached out her arms as if to offer him a hug, but Klein kept his distance, eyeing her with distaste. "Anyone catching your eye tonight?" she asked suggestively, batting her eyelashes at him.

The Orchid Flower was a well-known establishment for scoundrels and criminals and was a great place to find information, as long as one had the gold to pay for it. Despite his mother's repeated requests, Klein had never taken advantage of the other services offered at the brothel.

Klein felt a wave of anger coming from the presence in his mind. It never liked when he had to come here. *That makes two of us.*

"Not today, I'm afraid. Business only."

She pouted her lips, looking put out by the fact that Klein didn't want to be a customer in her establishment, as if Kleptis Klein would ever pay for sex. It was almost insulting. There were plenty of beautiful, high-born Fae who would jump at the chance for a night with him. The fact that most of the Fae working at the brothel were not here by choice didn't sit well with Klein either.

"No Mystic with you today?" Belladonna purred. "I thought she never left your side. I hope you're paying her well."

Klein let out a roar, causing Belladonna to shrink back. "Never say her name again, or I might find that I no longer need your help," he warned her.

Fake tears lined Belladonna's eyes. "So angry, trying to scare your dear mother? I only want to be sure your needs are being met."

Klein pulled the piece of paper from his pocket and showed her the face of the male he was searching for. Frances had long brown hair and green eyes. He was attractive, as all elves are, but there was a look in his eyes that suggested not all of his brain cells were functioning properly.

"Enough games," Klein said. "I'm looking for Frances. I know he's around here somewhere."

"Oh yes, he showed up this morning with gold to burn," Belladonna said, tilting her head. "Did he do something naughty?"

"Just point me to the room, and I'll be on my way," Klein replied.

She waved her hand in a flourish, "Anything for you, my love. Room 13, he's up the stairs and to the right." As Klein walked towards the stairs, he heard her calling from behind, "Oh, and don't be shocked by what you see. The gentlefae has a thing for youth."

Her words filled Klein with rage. Was she implying what he thought she was? His blood grew icy as his anger rose. Mystic tightened around his arm defensively, sensing the shift in his mood. This was a sensitive subject for her, and Klein knew Frances wouldn't be leaving the Orchid Flower alive.

Frost started to coat Klein's hands as his anger was visible on his flesh. He noticed it and pulled back the magic, causing the frost to melt away. His mind went to a dark, cold place as he began to move towards the stairs. Dealing with Fae like Frances made this job almost too easy sometimes. Klein walked up the stairs with controlled movements and reached for one of the hidden blades in his cloak, keeping his hand on it. Mystic slithered down to wind herself around his arm and wrist, ready to strike at a moment's notice.

The rooms passed by in a blur until he reached door number thirteen, the number painted on it in chipped gold paint. Without wasting time, Klein kicked it down with a loud bang. Wooden shards flew inward, Klein knew he should be more subtle, but Frances had really pissed him off. The cost of the door repairs and the blood cleanup would be worth it.

A look of shock crossed Frances's face when he saw Klein. He was lying on the bed naked, surrounded by three very young females. When he realized who had broken into his room, his green eyes widened even further. Death had come for him, and it wouldn't be quick or painless.

"Frances is going to be busy for the rest of the night," Klein said in a low voice. "Please head back down the stairs."

The females gathered their clothes, sensing the danger in the air, and rushed out without getting dressed. Klein promised them that he would make sure they were paid. He would pay them using the stolen gold, claiming it had already been spent by Frances. Anything to help ease the suffering that he knew they had endured.

Frances was shaking on the bed and looked ready to bolt, the smell of fear and urine tanging the air. Giving him no time to run, Klein flung out his arm, sending his sister flying right at Frances's face. Mystic released, transforming midair into her Fae form. She landed right on top of him with her blade pressed to his throat. When she was angry like this, she would stay partially transformed, large fangs filling her mouth and the gold ring in her eyes expanding to swallow the silver.

Panicked, Frances shook beneath her as he wailed, "Mercy, please! I'll give the gold back! I only meant to borrow it for a while!" He looked pathetic laying there, his shriveled length exposed for all to see.

"Not our problem," Klein growled, his voice rough with anger. "You will find no mercy from us, nor do you deserve it."

Mystic lunged forward, sinking her fangs into his neck, releasing a non-lethal dose of venom. He immediately stilled, no longer able to move his body. "Now sit there like a good boy, and let us teach you the meaning of pain." Mystic hissed as she slid off his body to stand with Klein. "I wouldn't bother trying to move. My venom is something you can't fight." Mystic's fangs shrank down to normal size. "You know, I had to practice for years to get the dosage just right. Enough to incapacitate a Fae but keep them awake to feel everything we were doing to them. A neat trick, isn't it?"

Standing in front of the bed, Klein's eyes were hard as he stared down at their victim. If you could really call him that, after all he's done.

"Where to begin?" Klein said, pointing his dagger at Frances

They took their time and dismembered Frances, piece by piece. He didn't scream—or, more accurately, he couldn't scream because of the venom. Klein took one of the pillowcases and placed Frances's bloody head inside, ready to deliver to Lycanthus. The bed was a mess, with blood soaking the once-white fabric. The whole mattress would probably need to be replaced, but Lycanthus was going to generously cover the cost—without knowing it. On the way out, Klein tossed Belladonna a small fortune. The prospect of a ruined room didn't bother her in the slightest.

Chapter 11

Mel

    The air was thick with the sweet and fruity scent of strawberry sparkling wine, casting a celebratory mood over the room. The walls glimmered with the twinkling lights that hung from every corner, creating a warm and cheerful ambiance. I, along with my fellow dancers, were decked out in shimmering dresses and towering high heels, ready to take the stage. New Year's was a big event for the club, and Micheal paid extra attention to the details. He wanted us all to look our best tonight, more so than any other. It was all so fake. I hated it.

    I wish I could stay asleep so I didn't have to do this anymore. I just want to be done with this life.

At least Alex doesn't have to see me like this. I made the decision not to reach out to him until the night was over and I was safely back in my own bed. The past few days of talking to him have given me a new perspective and made me feel like I have other options besides the ones I'd been given. I had to push through this and endure one more night of being a pawn in this place before I could truly start thinking about quitting and building a better life.

Baby Dolls may not be a high-end establishment, but the arrival of New Year's brings out the wealthiest patrons. The club was filled with men dressed in designer suits, who toss back glasses of cheap wine while they watch beautiful women remove their clothes.

We had to put on a façade of elegance and grace, which was easier for some of us than others. In the corner of my vision, I spot Annalise struggling to keep her cocktail dress from revealing her bony legs, a scowl etched across her face. When she catches me gazing her way, she flips me off before storming away. I raise an eyebrow and take another sip of my drink. *Tonight would be a normal night, and my monsters won't find me here.*

I was draped in a gorgeous golden silk dress, the fabric hugging my curves and illuminating my skin with its rich color. The high neckline of the dress concealed my bandaged tattoo, still a little tender from the recent ink. My make-up was carefully done with a smoky eye, a mauve lipstick, and a light blush highlighting my cheeks. My strawberry-blonde hair cascaded down my back in a gorgeous copper waterfall. After a few glasses of the sweet and fruity sparkling wine, I started to feel a bit more relaxed and carefree.

"Let's take these men for all they're worth," Jess said with a forced smile that failed to reach her eyes. She was dressed in a stunning emerald green dress that brought out the vibrant green of her eyes. Her lips were painted a rich shade of red, and her eye makeup was simple yet effective, enhancing the almond shape of her eyes. "Are you dancing tonight?" She asked me.

"No, Harvey is still paying for my time," I shrugged. "I haven't seen him all week. I really hope he treats me ok, and then I can get the hell out of there. Becky is supposed to give me the room key whenever he shows up. Honestly, I hope he doesn't show." I took a deep drink from my glass of sparkling wine, hoping it would help me forget about my situation and make the night a little better.

"I thought you were done with him?" Jess asked with genuine concern in her voice.

"So did I," I replied with a sigh. "I'm still thinking about it. Micheal talked to me earlier about Harvey being here tonight, and it was already a done deal. He wants me to dance, but only for him in the privacy of one of the upstairs rooms, which is fine by me. He also paid in advance." I told Jess, rubbing my fingers together. The envelope stuffed with bills, begrudgingly given to me, was already safely put away in my room

"You could make so much more money dancing for everyone," Jess says, pouting her full lips. She was still upset about Amber's sudden departure. "Why don't you tell Becky to tell Harvey to go away? It's not worth it."

"I know, but maybe he'll give me a big tip," I shrugged. "I know dancing would make me more money, especially on a night like New Year's Eve. I'll consider telling Becky tomorrow. I need to take advantage of the money while I can." I still hadn't made a decision on how to tell Jess that I was thinking of leaving.

Jess shook her head, the disappointment clear on her face. "If you say so, girl. It's your life."

We continued to move through the packed room, mingling with the guests and lending a hand to the bartender, taking drink orders and delivering them to the waiting tables. Loren, the bartender, expressed her gratitude by treating us to a pair of raspberry martinis, which were sweet and tangy, more like a dessert than a drink.

The edges of the club are guarded by tall, imposing, and well-muscled men. Michael has hired extra security for the night, and they stand at attention by the doors, dressed in all black, exuding an air of menace that keeps the patrons and dancers in check. Their eyes constantly scan the room, ignoring the revelers and performers alike. I know that at least two of these guards are stationed on the top floor, just in case any of the clients become unruly. Although it's rare, it has happened before.

Men were constantly approaching me, offering compliments on my outfit and propositioning me for a night of entertainment. Despite their advances, I declined each offer—as the substantial sum Harvey had paid me tonight more than compensated for my rejections. I was also wary of how Harvey might react if he were to find out that I had been with someone else.

This past week, I had made a decent amount of money, all while doing nothing. And tonight, I'd make even more. Did I want to lose out on that? My secret hiding spot was now teaming with cash, tempting me to finally stop working here. How much did I need to start over? Surely, the money I'd saved would be enough. But where would I go? How could I ever make it out in the real world? The words I heard in my childhood echoed in my mind, and I had to take a deep breath to calm my nerves.

My monsters won't find me here.

Movement on the stage caused me to look up, and I saw one of the girls dancing. I am struck by the grace and beauty of one of the dancers. Her sparkling sequined dress reflected the light, and she slowly shed it as she moved. The view from the floor masked any discomfort she may have felt and made it appear as though every move was effortless. Seeing it from down here was so different. You can't see how uncomfortable they feel, can't see the struggle to make every move sexy and beautiful. Even Anna seemed to make every move look effortless, the lights hiding away any imperfections.

Just as I had become engrossed in the performance, I felt a firm grip on my hand, pulling me away from my thoughts. I let out a small gasp of surprise, and upon turning to see who it was, I found Harvey, who was urging me to follow him.

Might as well get this over with.

"Happy New Year. Shall we head upstairs?" I purred.

"What's the rush?" Harvey replied, letting out a low laugh. "Let's have a few drinks and show the other men what they're missing out on tonight. You're all mine. Right, Princess?"

"A drink would be nice, thank you," I responded, trying to keep a pleasant expression on my face despite my growing discomfort. "And yeah, I'm all yours."

"This night and every night," Harvey growled possessively.

I forced a flirty laugh, trying to hide my reluctance. "Sure, Harvey, whatever you say." Harvey led me over to a hidden table at the edge of the club. I was surprised he wanted to stay for drinks, as most men were always in a rush to get upstairs. I sat across from him, trying to hide my disgust at having to spend extra time with him.

"You look ravishing, my princess," Harvey grunted, licking his thin lips as he looked at me. He motioned for me to sit across from him, and I was grateful that he didn't ask me to sit on his lap like some of the other men I saw around. "Did you miss me this week?" he asked, running his stubby hand down my arm.

"Yes, Harvey," I complied, regretting my decision to keep our arrangement going. Something felt very wrong. I shouldn't be here.

"Master Harvey will do just fine," he declared, snapping his fingers to get the attention of one of the other girls. Jess came over to take our drink order, her eyes filled with concern as she took in the situation. I tried to give her a reassuring look, conveying that I would be okay, but inside, I felt a sense of growing dread.

"I'll have a scotch neat, and for the lady, a glass of sparkling white wine," Harvey said, handing Jess a fifty-dollar bill from his golden clip, which was filled with several hundreds. "Keep the change," he added gruffly, leering at her.

Jess thanked him and hurried off to get our drinks. Harvey seemed to be feeling generous with his money tonight, and I hoped his generosity would extend to our room later. Jess quickly returned with our drinks, placing them in front of us, but she seemed hesitant to leave. Harvey narrowed his eyes and spat out, "You can leave now. I won't be requiring any harlots tonight." He looked at Jess with disdain, not mentioning that I, too, was a hired escort. Jess gave me another pitying look before leaving.

Harvey took his drink and sniffed it before taking a long swallow. "What a horrible, unfortunate creature," he muttered, referring to Jess. "Ruining herself with those wretched tattoos. Truly disturbing." I shuddered as I thought about my own tattoo, which he would soon see. I wondered if I could keep my dress on and to avoid him noticing it.

Sipping my drink, I tried to come up with ways to conceal my tattoo from Harvey. There wasn't really a way around it. He was going to see it. Maybe he'd be so disgusted by it that he would leave and never book me again. The thought didn't sadden me, and I was seriously thinking about making tonight my last night. Provided I could find a job that paid well enough.

The coffee shop hadn't gotten back to me yet, as it had only been one day, but I'd been obsessively checking my phone. I didn't have it with me now. It was locked away in the dressing room, along with the phones of all the other girls, to protect the identity of the men who visited Baby Dolls.

My head was feeling light from all the drinks I'd been consuming, and I was caught off guard as Becky approached our table with the room key. She slid it across the table to me in a discreet manner. To my surprise, it was for room eight again, leaving me to ponder if there was any significance to that number for Harvey. Becky was dressed impeccably in a form-fitting black business dress that accentuated her figure, her fake breasts pushed up high in a too-tight bra. Her makeup was flawlessly applied, a testament to her years of experience. Not a trace of cigarette smoke surrounded her as if it had dissipated into the air, and she held no cigarette between her lips.

"Have a good time, you two," Becky said with a flirtatious wink before she left to attend to the other girls.

Harvey and I had another drink, and he kept a possessive hand on me at all times as if I might try to escape. The drinks helped me remain calm and compliant for what was to come.

"Shall we head upstairs and continue the party?" Harvey asked, running his hand over his thinning hair, revealing his shiny scalp. "I have a special surprise waiting for you in our room." He grinned, showing too many teeth, as he offered me his hand to help me out of my chair.

"Of course," I said, forcing a smile. "I can't wait to see what you have in store for me." We walked to the elevator, passing several security guards who nodded at Harvey. It seemed that they were familiar with him, and I couldn't help but wonder how they knew each other.

"What kind of surprise did you prepare for me?" I asked, trying to hide my apprehension. I hoped it wasn't some kind of torture device.

He squeezed my hand tighter, a sense of unease growing within me. "This is a gift for both of us, my dear," he said with a grin. I couldn't help but wonder what kind of gift he was referring to, my mind instantly going to the worst possible scenario. The elevator ride was filled with an awkward silence as Harvey held onto my hand in his sweaty grip.

The sound of the elevator dinging signaled our arrival on the top floor, where two imposing guards stood at attention, clad in all black with earpieces to communicate with the rest of the staff. They looked uninterested and bored, as if they had drawn the short stick and were assigned the tedious task of guarding this floor. Despite their stoic demeanor, they still acknowledged our presence with a nod of their heads as Harvey and I walked by. One of them said, "Have a good night, boss." My eyes widened as I heard the words.

"Oh, I will. Tell Micheal I said you guys can take a fifteen." Harvey answered. A tremor of worry ran through me. Me and Harvey would be well and truly alone for at least that long.

The door to the room closed behind us, and I realized the significance of what the guard had just said. Harvey was one of the owners of the club. Besides Michael, I had never met the other owners, but it was finally starting to make sense as to why Harvey was receiving preferential treatment and why he was so confident in his actions. The realization filled me with a mixture of fear and curiosity as I wondered what other secrets Harvey might be hiding.

Gazing around the room, I was taken aback by the transformation that had taken place. Room eight, which I had visited countless times before, now looked like a luxurious suite in a five-star hotel. The drab bed covers, curtains, and furniture had been replaced with rich, jewel-toned textiles, and new, modern appliances shone in the kitchenette that had been added to the left of the room. The plush grey carpet felt soft and inviting underfoot.

I whispered in shock, "Wow, it's so different. I can't believe Michael would spend so much money to upgrade it like this. How did they even manage to complete the work so quickly? It must have cost a fortune."

"Micheal." He huffed. "No, Princess. I paid for all this, just like I paid for you. This room is going to be all yours from now on. Where we can keep having private time together. Can't have you being tainted by the whores downstairs." Brushing his hands down his suit, removing imaginary lint, he looked at me for approval.

"It's beautiful," I said truthfully, still in shock at the lavish upgrade. "But I don't know if I can accept it. It's much too generous."

Harvey put a finger to my lips, silencing me. "Hush now. This room is for us to have private time together. You don't need to worry about the other girls downstairs ruining our special moments." He walked over to the bed, admiring it before turning to me. "Now, let's get you out of that dress and enjoy our new space."

Hesitating, I was taken aback by Harvey's request and struggled to process what he was saying. Did he really want me to live in this room indefinitely? I took a deep breath and tried to calm my nerves. "Maybe we can have a few more drinks first?" I suggested, hoping the alcohol would help me make it through the night. If Harvey drank enough, perhaps he would pass out, giving me an opportunity to escape from this dangerous situation. I gestured towards the bottle of wine and glasses on the table, hoping to steer the conversation in a different direction. I was disappointed when Harvey didn't take the hint.

"No, that can wait. I want to see my princess kneeling for me, naked, in the next minute—or I will become cross. And I'd hate to leave any more marks on that lovely skin of yours."

"Would you like me to dance first?"

"I suppose a dance might set the mood. Go ahead. Dance for me, Princess." He said, pulling out his phone and connecting it to the new Bluetooth speaker installed above the bed. He took a moment to select a song, then leaned back in a chair and watched with eager eyes as the music began to play.

When the beat hit, I moved my hips in a slow, seductive swing, taking my time removing my clothes. First, I removed my shoes; the golden heel pumps slid off with ease as I kicked them away from me.

I focused on my movements, trying to appear confident and in control despite the fear that was starting to take hold. I knew that I should have listened to Jess and told Becky that I didn't want to take on Harvey as a client anymore. But now it was too late, and I was stuck in this situation.

With slow movements, I go to take off my dress. There is a knot at the top holding it together, and as I undo it, my dress falls like liquid over my body, pooling on the floor. My hair was covering my chest and most of the tattoo. Turning around, I bent over, removing my black lace thong, and as I slid it down my hips, I could hear him groaning. There was the unmistakable sound of a zipper being undone.

As I turned around, I saw him standing in front of the bed, waiting for me to kneel before him. If I could just get through this night, I promised myself that this would be my last time as an escort. I would get through this.

My monsters won't find me here.

Slowly, I walked to him, swinging my hips before getting down on my knees. He was pumping himself with one hand while reaching over to grasp my hair and pulled my head back. That's when he saw it.

He let out an angry roar as he saw my tattoo. His grip on my hair tightened, causing me to wince in pain. "What have you done to yourself!" he shouted, his eyes blazing with anger. With a rough shove, he pushed me away from him. I had never seen Harvey look so furious, his face contorted in rage and spittle flying from his mouth. The expression on his face was like that of a demon, causing me to fear for my life.

A vague memory floated to the surface of my mind, but I quickly pushed it away, focusing on the present moment. The panic was rising within me, my fight-or-flight response going into overdrive.

When he throws me away from him, I hit the ground hard, the rough carpet abrasively rubbing against my sensitive skin. The shock of the situation finally wore off, and I regained control of my movements. Scrambling away from Harvey, I grabbed my dress and pulled it over my body, hoping it might calm his anger.

A scream ripped from my throat, "Help! Anyone!" Hindsight is twenty-twenty, right? Seeing how he reacted to Jess should have given me a clue that he'd react this way, but I didn't listen to my gut.

"You stupid slut! How dare you ruin my things!" He screamed as he rushed towards me. I could see the anger in his eyes as his hands stretched out to grab hold of my throat. My survival instincts kicked in, and I instinctively raised my hands to fend him off, but it was a futile effort. He was larger and stronger than me, overpowering me with his size as he pinned me down to the ground with his weight.

Desperate for air, I let out blood-curdling screams, hoping to draw the attention of the guards who were supposed to be protecting me. But either they don't hear my cries for help, or they choose to ignore them. The darkness crept in, clouding my vision as I fought to take in a breath. The fear of death gripped me tightly, and I feared that this was how my life would end at the hands of this madman.

"We can fix this." He muttered. "Laser removal. Makeup. Anything to remove this stain. I won't let this turn out like the last time. I won't let you turn out like Rosa."

His grip is relentless, and as I lay there, listening to his manic rambling, my mind is filled with regret. I thought of Alex and wished I had taken those self-defense classes sooner. I wondered if a few lessons could have made a difference in this moment, but my body felt weak and powerless under his grasp. My consciousness began to fade, and I couldn't help but question the choices that led me to this moment. The thought of it ending like this was unbearable.

A shimmering female voice sounded in my head.

Almost time ….Almost time.

Almost time? For what? For me to die? It certainly felt like that's where this was heading. My lungs screamed for air, sending a searing pain through my body.

Time seemed to crawl by as my vision gradually darkened. I felt myself losing consciousness, and a sense of dread washed over me. Is this what death feels like? I wondered. Through the haze, I could barely make out the sound of someone rushing towards me, accompanied by a faint curse. However, I was already too far gone, sinking into the depths of unconsciousness.

Chapter 12

Telaria

The moon hovered high above Klein, casting everything in its silvery glow. With his wolf eyes, he could see through even the densest darkness, and with the moon's half-full face shining down tonight, there was more than enough illumination for him to navigate by. To him, it might as well have been broad daylight.

Shining like a guiding light, the moon had always been a constant companion for Klein. When he ran beneath its silver light, he felt a sense of freedom that he couldn't find anywhere else. That freedom was what the tattoo on his back symbolized, a promise to make it a permanent fixture in his life.

The trees whipped by, their branches heavy with the rustling autumn leaves. Each of the Courts had their own quirks and idiosyncrasies, and the Mabon Court was no exception. The Lord of this Court used his magic to keep the leaves in brilliant shades of red and orange, especially in his private orchard—although it was a waste of power, it was also a thing of beauty.

Creeping through the dense foliage, Klein and Mystic carefully navigated the labyrinth of trees, Klein's steps hushed by the blanket of soft leaves underfoot. With bated breath, the two of them ventured deeper into the enchanted orchard, their eyes fixed on the breathtaking beauty that surrounded them.

Klein and Mystic had been on the move for the better part of a week, stealthily making their way into the Mabon Court. The quickest and most discreet way to travel was in their animal forms, which they were currently using. Mystic, in her snake form, remained coiled around Klein, who was in his wolf form, as he ran at a lightning-fast speed.

Something felt amiss to Klein as they traveled. The presence that had always been with him since he was young was suddenly gone, not as though it were sleeping, but simply vanished. This was a deeply unsettling feeling for Klein, who worried that the presence might never return. With the comfort that the presence gave gone, Klein felt distracted from their current mission.

Bringing his nose to the ground, Klein sniffed out the prey they were seeking. If the information Mercia had sold him was correct, they should find the sleeping unicorns somewhere in these woods. The plan was simple: Klein would sniff them out and get Mystic close enough to slither beside their sleeping forms. Then, she would bite one, putting it into a deep sleep, and they could take the hairs—a quick and easy operation, in and out.

Klein followed his nose, carefully navigating the trees and bushes. His paws made no sound as he avoided stepping on any dry leaves. The overpowering sweet and rotting smell of apples filled the air, but underneath that scent, Klein could smell the unicorns. They must be getting close. As he rounded another grove of trees, he finally saw them.

The light of the moon cast a bright glow over their russet brown fur, making it shimmer and glisten. The stallion, who stood guard over his herd, was twice the size of a regular horse and had a regal presence, even in slumber. His head was facing the tree line, and his ears were perked up, ready to defend his herd at a moment's notice. The unicorns' horns, made of pure gold, caught the moonlight and shimmered like diamonds. Klein couldn't help but marvel at their beauty.

One of the smaller unicorns, which Klein assumed was a foal, stood out among the rest. Its fur was painted with white splashes and a blaze on its snout, making it truly unique. The sight of the young unicorn filled Klein with wonder, imagining how magnificent it would be if it grew to the size of its father. With the foal selected as the weakest of the herd, they had found their target, and now it was up to Mystic to do her part.

Silently, Klein approached the herd, tucking himself behind a dense mulberry bush. Mystic followed suit, uncoiling herself from around his wolf form. She glided across the mossy ground, her six-foot-long, slender snake body shimmering in the moonlight, her black scales iridescent with an ethereal glow.

As she inched closer to the young unicorn, she was careful to avoid any actions that might startle the majestic beasts.

With calculated precision, Mystic struck, hooding up and injecting her fangs into the foal's leg. The venom should be painless and have no lasting effects on the unicorn, but as she administered the dose, the foal suddenly kicked out, sensing her presence. This prompted a chain reaction, causing all the unicorns to awaken and rear up, their angry neighs filling the air. Mystic was thrown back, her serpentine form tumbling into the bush where Klein was hiding.

With a concerned whine, Klein approached the thorny bush where Mystic was hissing. He sniffed her carefully, checking for any signs of injury. To his relief, he could see the iridescent shine of her black scales as she slowly slithered out of the thorns.

The herd of unicorns had taken off, galloping away and leaving behind only the fallen leaves they had disturbed. The prospect of having to hunt them down again filled Klein with disappointment. He couldn't help but let out a huff of frustration at the thought.

That's when he noticed the foal, still lying in the glen and convulsing from the toxins in its system. Foam was beginning to form at its mouth, and its eyes were rolled back in its head. Klein's heart sank. The kick from the unicorn must have caused Mystic to release more of her venom than intended. If it died, Klein and Mystic would be in deep shit.

As he cautiously approached the fallen foal, Klein sniffed at it, relieved to find that it had finally stopped convulsing—though its breathing was still labored. He transformed back into his Fae form and swiftly plucked the necessary strands of hair. With a handful of thick, white, and approximately one-foot-long strands, he placed them into a bag before transforming back into his wolf form.

Mystic, now next to Klein, slithered up and coiled around his neck and body, careful not to squeeze too tightly. They were ready to depart, but as they turned to make their escape, the crunching of leaves and heavy breathing filled the air. Glancing behind him, Klein saw the enormous form of the stallion leaning down to check on the foal, its white breath huffing against its face. With a roar of rage, the stallion's eyes met Klein's, and before they knew it, the great beast was upon them.

The stallion charged towards Klein, wielding its golden horn like a lethal weapon. With a powerful stomp, the beast caught Klein's side, piercing his flesh and drawing a scream of agony from him. Blood flowed freely from the deep wound, splattering onto the fallen leaves beneath their feet. They knew they had to act fast and get away before the stallion could cause further harm.

Klein dashed through the forest, his heart pounding as the thundering hooves of the angry stallion followed close behind. He twisted and turned, dodging trees and attempting to gain some ground between himself and the beast. Despite the stallion's speed, its massive size made it difficult for it to maneuver through the dense trees. With a fierce determination, Klein raced towards the thickest part of the orchard, hoping to find refuge in its maze of branches and leaves. Or, if he was lucky, he could reach a tree and climb to safety, away from the wrath of the raging stallion.

As the idea came to him, Klein saw a great oak in the distance. It's close enough that if he pushed himself, they could make it. His breaths came swiftly as he forced his body to the limit. Klein was soon upon the tree, and as he scrambled up, his claws grabbed the bark, leaving deep gouges and chips of wood flying off in every direction.

The unicorn was right under him, and he could feel the air whipping as it brandished its horn, nearly removing Klein's tail. But with a jump forward, Klein made it up higher and higher, finally getting out of its reach.

Klein wondered to himself for an instant, why don't we just kill the beast and make our escape? There were a few reasons. Firstly, killing the stallion was more than illegal, and they might have already killed one unicorn tonight. Secondly, taking down the stallion wouldn't be an easy feat.

The unicorn in question, a formidable creature with a golden horn and hooves, paced restlessly under the great oak. Their only hope was that the stallion would eventually tire of chasing them and return to his mares.

Just as it looked like they had the upper hand, their luck was about to run out. The stallion raised its head, opened its mouth, and emitted a strange noise that Klein had never heard before. It was almost like the sound of a war horn, growing louder and deeper. It was causing Klein's sensitive ears to ache. They needed to get out of earshot—*now!*

Klein transformed into his Fae form to communicate with Mystic, who remained in her snake form coiled around his arm. He climbed up a sturdy branch and crouched, ready to make a move if necessary. Mystic kept her head facing towards Klein, her golden eyes fixed on his face.

"Oh shit," Klein muttered as he became aware of the wound on his side once again. Despite the bleeding, it was not life-threatening. Acting quickly, he utilized his magic to create an ice bandage and stem the flow of blood. The unicorn below them had finally stopped making noise and stood there, gazing into the woods as if waiting for something.

"Should I take it out so we can escape?" Klein whispered, already wielding his magic and creating an ice arrow. He reached for his bow and added, "I'm confident my magic can take care of it."

"You won't be doing any killing," a new voice spoke up.

Peering out, Klein saw a faint glow emerging from the woods. It looked like a sunrise, but it was still the middle of the night, and the sun wouldn't rise for several more hours. As the light grew closer, the figure of a Fae appeared, emitting a powerful red and orange light. Klein realized with humility that he had been foolish to consider his own power to be great. Compared to this Fae, he felt like an ant.

"Why have you trespassed into my Orchard?" the male asked, his voice deep and rich like the earth. As he approached, Klein could see him clearly in the dim light. He was a stunning elf with deep red locks of hair that flowed down his back golden eyes that shone like the sun. His skin was the color of the darkest soil. He was draped in layers of fabric, intricately wrapped and patterned, with a top opened to reveal his well-defined chest. The mention of the "Orchard" meant that they were in the presence of the Lord of Mabon himself—and the situation was fucked.

"We were just leaving," Klein replied nonchalantly, taking a seat on the branch. "If you could kindly ask your beast to let us pass, we'll be on our way."

"No, I don't think I will," the Lord replied, reaching out to caress the unicorn's neck. The animal let out a happy neigh, leaning into his touch. "My stallion has told me of the harm you have inflicted upon his foal. Lucky for you, it takes more than a little venom to kill a unicorn," he added with a smirk. "The foal should be up and running, back with its mother by now."

There was a pause as the Lord considered their fate. "Now, what to do with the two of you?"

"You could let us go," Klein suggested, trying to keep his voice steady and confident. "We didn't cause any permanent damage. Surely, you can spare a couple of foolish Fae." Sometimes, all it took was to ask, and you never knew how many times asking had saved them from situations such as this.

He laughed, his voice rumbling like thunder. "No, Kleptis. I don't think I'll let you go, at least not for tonight." His eyes glimmered as he raised his hand, gesturing for Klein to come down from the tree. "My seers have told me of your arrival on this day, and I couldn't wait to meet you. Get down from the tree, and we can talk. My servants are preparing some mulled cider as we speak." He turned away, expecting Klein to follow. "Oh, and Mystic, you can join us as well. Those are your preferred names, are they not?"

"How do you know us? Why should we go with you anywhere?" Klein asked, his voice wary.

"That's irrelevant, I'm afraid," he waved his hand airily, growing impatient with their unwillingness to go with him so easily. "Hurry up, I don't have all night."

With the Lord's overwhelming power, Klein realized they could be brought down with a single blow. So, he decided they better not anger him, and, without a word, he hopped down from the tree, landing in a crouch. However, as he landed, his face contorted with pain as his wound opened back up, blood leaking out. Mystic tightened around him, turning her scaly face towards his side in concern.

The Lord's eyes narrowed. "I figured your sister would have healed you by now."

"Mystic doesn't have healing magic,"

"Is that so? Well, no matter, let me fix that for you. Can't have you falling behind now, can we?" The Lord reached out to Klein's side and pressed a long-fingered hand on the wound. His nails were long and sharp, almost metallic and shining like gold. The glow of healing magic warmed Klein's side, easing the pain. When the Lord removed his hand, all signs of the wound were gone except for the blood soaking Klein's clothes. With a stiff nod, Klein grunted his appreciation and began to follow the Lord through the woods.

Mystic gracefully unwound herself from Klein's arm, her body transforming back into her Fae form as she stepped forward on her own two feet. Despite her normally energetic and snarky personality, she seemed eerily quiet in the presence of the Lord, as if she were trying to avoid drawing any unwanted attention to herself.

Klein and Mystic, now fully exposed and vulnerable, continued to follow the Lord through the forest. With no other options left, they resigned themselves to their fate, no longer attempting to hide or conceal themselves. They had already been caught, and any further secrecy was now useless.

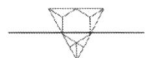

When they reached the village of Mabon, Klein and Mystic were awed by the towering trees that stretch towards the sky, each one intricately carved with houses perched high up in the branches. A network of ladders and bridges connected the various dwellings, creating a seamless blend of modernity and nature. The landscape was dotted with twinning streams, where schools of fish could be seen jumping and splashing in the cool, clear water. The quiet of the night was broken only by the warm, comforting glow of lights shining from within the windows of some homes. The majority of the Fae seemed to be asleep, nestled safely in their beds for the night.

The Lord dramatically raised his hand and greeted them with a grand flourish. "Welcome to Mabon! You wouldn't believe how unbearably boring it's been waiting for you to arrive. You can call me Draken, by the way."

Mystic was cautious and looked at Draken with suspicion. "I'm confused. You were expecting us to come? This all seems too much to be coincidental."

Draken answered with a mad glint in his eyes, "Something like that. I have been waiting a long time for this moment. Now, come along, and let me show you my palace."

What Draken showed them next was not what they had expected. Instead of a grand palace, he led them to the center of the city and stood them in front of the largest tree they had ever seen. It was so large that a whole castle could easily fit inside its wide trunk.

"Magnificent, isn't it?" Draken boasted. "This tree is the heart of Mabon and my palace. You could walk around it for hours and not get all the way to the other side. My ancestors grew it, and we have added our magic to it every generation."

Mystic was in awe, and her mouth gaped open as she stared at the magnificent tree that was carved with large windows and sprouting balconies. Something about this place and this Lord was causing Mystic to act strangely, and Klein couldn't quite put his finger on what was bothering her.

A grand staircase was carved into the wood and led all the way up to a large entrance balcony, where wooden double doors hung with gold hammered into the grains. As Klein looked closer, he saw that gold was woven into all the wood of the trees, as if they had grown that way. Even the leaves had golden veins running through them. This place was so different from Celetrix, and Klein couldn't help but think that it was the power of the Lord of Mabon that made it so.

Walking through the doors, they found the inside to be just as extravagant as the outside. Exotic plants were visible as far as the eye could see, with golden vines hanging from the ceiling and fairy lights woven around them lighting up the hall. Great auburn velvet curtains covered the walls, creating hidden alcoves where shadows could be seen moving within. At certain points in the great hall were large golden statues—seven in total, most depicting Fae with wings and horns. Many were nude or draped with thin fabric.

Klein's eyes widened as he took in the Fae walking around the space. Most were elves, but there were plenty of wood nymphs mixed in as well. They were all scantily clad, drinking wine, and generally at ease. Laughter echoed through the air, and soft music played from a harp.

"Are we interrupting something?" Klein asked.

"Nonsense," Draken replied. "This was a party for you, celebrating the start of the end."

With a shake of her head, Mystic turned a worried eye on their host. "I don't understand. Start of the end?"

A servant in a black robe approached with a tray of drinks, the aroma of spices wafting from the golden goblets. The servant respectfully offered the tray, bowing deeply as they waited for them to take the cups.

"All in good time," Darken said in a deep and soothing voice, grabbing a goblet for himself and taking a long drink. "We have many things to discuss, and the cider will help it go faster." Seeing the Lord drink from the goblet, Klein and Mystic took their cups from the servant and retreated into the fray of the party, staying cautious and taking only small sips, keeping their eyes on the guests.

The Fae in the hall were clearly inebriated and having a good time, with more than one orgy taking place in hidden corners. It didn't seem to phase Draken, so Klein assumed this was a common occurrence. He led them to a room made for hosting meetings, a great round table with seven seats around it, made of black and gold marbled wood with plush red seats. Klein and Mystic knew better than to sit before a Lord, so they stood and waited.

Finally, Draken took his seat facing the door, a wise choice that Klein would have made himself. They took their places across from him, and Klein placed his drink down, not in the mood for silly court games.

"Why did you bring us here?" Klein asked, frustration evident in his voice. "Why haven't you killed us or locked us in the dungeons?"

Mystic chimed in, her voice dripping with sarcasm, "Maybe he just wants to invite us for a threesome."

Draken chuckled in response, "You're more than welcome to join the party if you wish. It is for you, after all." He took another sip of his drink and hummed in satisfaction before speaking again. "When I learned what you two were going to do, I thought about locking you up, but I found this much more exciting. Long life can be incredibly dull, but now that you're here, the fun is about to begin."

His words were cryptic, meant to anger them, and paired with his bored expression—this lord was seriously irritating Klein. He needed to keep his cool while dealing with him or risk incurring his wrath.

"What does that even mean? What fun?" Klein's voice came out harder than he intended, causing the Lord to raise an eyebrow.

"Let's just say the punishment I would have planned for you will pale in comparison," Draken replied, twirling his cider with his finger.

"If you're not going to harm us, may we leave?" Mystic asked, drawing attention to herself.

The lord considered them with narrowed eyes. "Here I am, trying to be accommodating, and all you want to do is leave. How predictable." He sighed. "In any case, I'll be taking back the hair you took from my prized unicorn."

Klein tried to keep the surprise off his face and took a drink to buy time before speaking. "What hair?"

"Let's not play games, boy," the Lord said, his voice hissing through his teeth with anger. "You know what hair I'm referring to."

"We need that hair!" Mystic exclaimed. "We never intended to hurt the unicorn. It just happened."

"Things like this don't just happen," the lord sneered. "In any case, I have something much better for your quest." He pulled out two rings from his clothes and tossed them onto the table. The rings were made of twisted copper, and at their center was a large red ruby, the size of a blueberry in each. "These should get you through any ward. Now, the hair."

Klein wondered why the lord would give them such valuable items. "What is the price?" he asked in a low voice. "Nothing is free. Every Fae knows that."

"The price is a favor in the future," the lord replied, his face once again returning to a bored expression. "Those 'charms' you were planning to make wouldn't have worked anyway. You'll need these rings to get into the Ostara Castle. And you need to go there if we want things to progress."

Klein and Mystic looked to each other, communicating silently. After a moment, Klein turned back to Draken and said, "Agreed, but the favor must be something reasonable and achievable for us. Is that a deal? In exchange for the rings, you'll allow us to depart tonight." He removed the hair from his bag and placed it on the table, pushing it towards the lord. Klein made sure to keep the terms of the agreement clear and concise, avoiding anything that could jeopardize his and Mystic's safety.

"Deal, except for the part about leaving," the lord said with a smile. "You will stay the night and leave at sunrise. That should give you enough time to arrive at your destination on schedule." A hooded servant entered the room, bowing low. "Ethal, here, will take you to your rooms. I must join the revelers in the main hall; can't disappoint the waiting females. Are you sure you don't want to join me?" The lord's voice was a low growl as he gave them a sly wink.

"No, thank you. We'll just wait out the night in the room provided," Klein replied.

The lord got up to leave. "Suit yourself. If you change your mind, you know where to find me."

Ethal gave them a bow and beckoned them to follow her through the doors. The tree was a maze of hallways and passages that they could easily get lost in. Klein wondered if the servant was taking extra turns to confuse them.

"That was strange," Mystic whispered as they were led to their rooms.

Klein nodded in agreement. "Let's just get some rest so we can leave this place as soon as possible."

The hooded servant led Klein and Mystic to a cozy room featuring two plush beds and an adjoined bathroom. The bedspreads were a warm blend of autumnal hues, soft and inviting to the touch. When Klein turned to offer his gratitude to the servant, he noticed she had disappeared—evaporating into nothingness, much like Mystic's ability to disappear at will.

Mystic laid down on her bed, still dressed in her traveling clothes. "Do you think we should go to the party?" she asked, giggling and fanning herself.

"You go ahead," Klein replied. "I'll be here, sleeping."

"You're no fun," Mystic pouted. But she made no move to leave the room. "Fine, we'll just stay here in these boring beds."

The night dragged on. Klein and Mystic tossed and turned in their beds, unable to fully surrender themselves to sleep. Their minds raced with the fear of being suddenly dragged away by the Lord of Mabon and thrown into the dreary dungeons below. The uncertainty and apprehension hung heavy in the air, preventing them from finding solace in rest. The soft and comfortable beds of the room seemed to mock their anxious thoughts as they impatiently counted down the hours until the morning light would finally arrive.

Chapter 13

Mel

    Feeling like I was coming out from deep water, my eyes cracked open. I was filled with confusion and disorientation. The sound of beeping monitors was the first thing I registered, and I struggled to understand where I was and how I got here. My eyes fluttered open, and I was met with the sterile and clinical atmosphere of a hospital room. The overpowering scent of strong chemicals and a faint floral fragrance assaulted my nostrils, making it difficult to breathe.

    My gaze fell upon a small table next to my bed, where several bouquets of roses were arranged. *Where am I? Are those flowers for me?* I couldn't believe there were people in my life who would go out of their way to bring me flowers. A warm feeling of love spread through my chest. But as the memories of the events leading up to my hospitalization came flooding back, the pain in my throat intensified, becoming sharp and abrasive—like swallowing glass.

Guess he didn't manage to kill me after all.

Using the remote, I pushed the button to prop myself up into a more upright position, my surroundings gradually coming into view. The room was filled with the beeping of various machines and monitors, which were all connected to me via a network of cords. A clear plastic bag filled with fluid hung above me, connected to my veins by a tube that ran from my arm to the metal stand beside the bed.

Just as I was inspecting the tape holding the IV in place, the door to my room creaked open, and a nurse in bright pink scrubs stepped inside. Her blue eyes caught mine, and she beamed a smile at me. "You're awake! How wonderful!"

I rubbed my throat, my voice raspy from disuse as I spoke. "How'd I get here?"

The nurse furrowed her brows as if struggling to find the right words. "It sounds like you were involved in some sort of domestic situation." She deftly adjusted the tape on my hand and continued, "I'm not exactly sure what happened."

I remembered bits and pieces of the events that brought me to this place, but the details were still hazy. "I remember that much," I said. "But what I really want to know is...how am I going to pay for all this?" I gestured to the machines and IV, feeling a sense of dread at the thought of the mounting hospital bills. "Even just one night in this place is going to cost a fortune."

The nurse approached my bed, and she took hold of the silver chart hanging from its foot. With a quick flick of her wrist, she scanned through its contents, her blue eyes darting from the page to me and back again. "Not to worry, sweetheart," she said with a warm smile. "It looks like your stay here has been taken care of. A gentleman named Harvey has covered everything. And those roses over there," She gestured to the bouquets, now drooping and beginning to wilt, "those are from him too."

My mind was a jumbled mess, and my voice was rough and scratchy as I tried to speak. "Harvey?" I asked, my hand involuntarily going to my throat.

The nurse gave me a knowing look. "Your father, I'm guessing?"

My chest constricted, and a shiver ran down my spine. Harvey was many things, but he was not my father. In fact, the thought of him being near enough to me to pay for my hospital stay made me feel physically ill. I closed my eyes tight, trying to push the thoughts and memories away.

Before I could dwell on it for too long, the door to my room swung open, and Jess and Alex stepped inside. The nurse gave me a quick wink and turned to leave. "I'll let you catch up with your friends," she said. "I'll be back in a few to help you with your discharge paperwork."

They really waste no time getting you out of here, do they?

As she saw I was awake, Jess rushed forward, her eyes welling with tears as she took my hands in hers—being careful not to pull on my IV. I couldn't help but think how much I hated IV's and the liquid that was slowly dripping into my veins. *What are those weird bubbles in the line? Could they harm me?*

"Mel! I was so worried about you!" Jess's voice shook, and I couldn't help but notice she was close to breaking down.

Patting her hands and letting my voice come out soft, I said, "I'm fine, see?" I gestured to my bruised and battered body. "Or, at least, I will be. What's been happening at the club? How long have I been here? With the way I still feel, it couldn't have been too long."

Alex walked forward to stand next to her, looking angry. He had dark shadows under his eyes as if he hadn't slept in days. "The club will survive without you. You've been here for nearly a week, so just worry about yourself!" His hand reached out to mine, and his eyes softened a little. "I'm sorry, I'm just so mad at the man who did this to you. I'm mad at myself for not being able to stop it."

"There was nothing you could have done," I said, unable to hide the fear from my voice. "I made my choices, and now I have to live with them. Did anything happen to him? Did Michael call the police?"

"Well..." Jess started, looking sheepish.

"No, of course he didn't," Alex growled. "Men like him can do whatever they want and never have to face the consequences." Angry tears filled his eyes. "Please, I'm begging you, Mel. Don't go back to that place."

With tears in my eyes, I replied, "I'm never going back there again." I made a promise to myself, and now to him—hoping it would be true. Turning to Jess, I asked, "Can you do me a favor? Can you get my stuff from our room? There's a hidden place under the floorboards where I keep my stash of cash. It's not much, but it should get me out of here."

"Already done," she replied with a frown on her face, tinged with sadness. This was definitely not a good sign.

"What? Is something missing?" Fear stabbed at my heart. "Did something happen to all the money I had saved?" I knew it wasn't the most secure hiding spot, but banks had a problem letting dirty money be deposited.

She burst into tears. "I'm so sorry, Mel. Micheal got to it before me, and I couldn't get everything. He tore our room apart in a rampage after the ambulance came."

My fears come true as she tells me the worst. "What was I going to do now? I have to get out of here, change my hair, my name. What if Harvey comes back to finish the job he started?" All the possibilities flash through my mind. "Is all the money gone?" I ask, voice shaking.

Jess pulled out a bag hidden behind my bed and rummaged through it, revealing a roll of cash. "I was able to save some of it," she said, handing me the money.

"There's only about three hundred dollars here." I stared blankly at the cash, wondering how I could possibly survive with such a small amount.

"And he didn't take your phone," Jess added, handing it to me. "I think he knew you were leaving and wanted to take everything he could." The phone screen showed several missed calls and thirty unread texts, but I decided to check them later when I was in a better state of mind. I was relieved to see that some of my pajamas had survived in the bag.

"Thanks, Jess," I said with a defeated sigh. "I have no family and no money. I don't know where I'm going to go from here." The thought of selling myself on the street was not an option, and I knew it could be even worse than my previous situation.

Just as I was starting to spiral into my thoughts, Alex's strong voice pulled me out. "Don't worry about that. I talked to my aunt, who runs an apartment building downtown. She's willing to give you the first month free."

"Nothing is free, Alex," I whispered.

"Trust me, she's cool. I told her your situation, and because you're my friend, she's willing to help. All she asks is that you find a job as soon as possible," Alex said, rubbing the back of his neck. "Nothing sketchy, of course."

The tears I had been holding back started to flow down my face. "I don't know how to thank you," I whispered.

"Thank me by getting better." He said firmly. "The room is only a studio, but it's clean, and she even put in a bed for you."

The offer of a bed and a place of my own was too generous. She didn't even know me, but with all my money gone and no job, I had no other options. A small, stubborn part of me wanted to do it on my own, but the bigger part of me knew this opportunity wouldn't come again. With the start of a plan to move into an apartment, find a job, and hide for the rest of my life, I wiped my eyes with my hands and looked at Jess. "What about you?"

"Don't worry about me, Mel," Jess replied. "I'm a big girl. I can handle myself." Despite her words, she didn't look very confident in them.

"That apartment is going to be awfully lonely without you. Maybe you could stay there with me?" I breathed out the words, filled with hope that maybe, just maybe, my best friend would consider giving up her job at the club and start a new life with me.

"I'll visit you all the time, girl. Don't worry, you'll be sick of my company by the end of it!" She laughed, her face still puffy from the tears, but her beauty shone through. My stubborn, beautiful friend, who I wished would never have to endure the dangers of working at the club again.

I sat up straighter, pressing the button to call the nurse. "Let's get the hell out of here. I need this fucking IV out of my veins before I rip it out myself." I laughed, trying to lighten the mood—but in all seriousness, I couldn't wait to be free of this hospital room. "Alex, would you mind driving me to the store? There are some things I need to pick up before I go to your aunt's apartment. The stuff in that bag won't be enough to get by." Plus, there was something else I needed to grab at the store.

"Sure thing, Bella Durmiente." He gave me a warm smile,

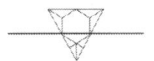

---

helping me get up and supporting me as we made our way out of the hospital room and towards my new life.

We reached the apartment building before the sunset. Alex already dropped off Jess at the club, despite my objections. She was determined to keep working there, and I could only hope that she would eventually find a way out. If she had to do it on her own, I completely understood her situation.

I was about to step out of the car when my phone started buzzing relentlessly. Someone was trying to reach me urgently. I took out my phone, only to almost drop it from my hand when I saw the unfamiliar number on the caller ID. The caller was apologizing profusely, and I immediately realized it had to be one person. I hung up the phone and read the text messages from the same number.

Unknown: Please Princess. You have to forgive me. I didn't mean it! We can fix this. I already made you some appointments to get it removed.
Answer me!
Why did you leave your hospital room? I was on my way to get you. Where are you?

A shiver ran through me as I scrolled through the texts. My lip was sore from where I had been biting it in anxiety. As I looked up, I saw that Alex was watching me with a worried expression. "I'm sorry, Alex," I said, my voice barely above a whisper. "I shouldn't have involved you in this."

"Is that the man who did this to you?" Alex asked, his tone unwavering.

"Yes, I think so," I answered, feeling ashamed. I couldn't even remember giving Harvey my number.

Without hesitation, Alex took my phone and blocked the number, then handed it back to me. "Now he won't be able to bother you anymore," he said confidently.

"I really hope that's true," I replied, filled with a mixture of hope and fear.

The four-story building stood before me, full of new possibilities. It was made of red and brown bricks and seemed newer than some of the surrounding structures. There were bikes chained to a fence that likely belonged to the residents, some of which looked like kid's bikes, and I couldn't help but wonder how many children lived in the building.

Alex walked me to the management office to meet with his aunt. The cold air nipped at our faces as we moved, our jackets and scarves doing little to keep the chill away. As the sun set and the darkness set in, we quickened our pace towards the door. I found myself fidgeting, my hands adjusting my jacket and scarf repeatedly.

"Don't be nervous, Mel. She's going to love you." Alex said, giving my hand a reassuring squeeze. The metal door of the apartment manager's office loomed before us. Alex wrapped his gloved fist against the door, causing the metal to clang and the door to shake. Although I noticed a doorbell on the side, it was covered in tape, indicating it was out of order.

The sound of opening locks and squeaking hinges filled the air. As the door opened, it revealed the petite woman in charge of the building. She looked younger than I expected, with dark brown hair tied up in a neat bun, showing only a hint of gray at the temples. She greeted us with a warm smile, her honey-brown eyes crinkling at the corners.

"Well, don't just stand there, mi jito. Come in! Come it!" She exclaimed, waving her hands for us to enter. As we stepped into the warm apartment, a small dog sniffed at my heels, letting out a growl that made me nervous. "Oh, don't mind Pako, he's all bark and no bite!" The woman chuckled, leading us further inside.

Sure he is. Small dogs like him were always the ones you had to watch out for.

The quilts and hand-sewn pillows decorated the room, each one adorned with Spanish sayings that I couldn't understand. The homey atmosphere was complemented by the cleanliness of the space, which was spotless. Not a single speck of dust could be found on the shelves—filled with religious statues, crosses, and cherubs. Alex's aunt led us to a floral print couch, old but well-maintained.

"Have a seat. Can I get you anything? I was just about to start a pot of coffee," she offered in a motherly and soft voice. *Coffee at this hour*, a woman after my own heart.

"And you, mi jito?" she turned to Alex.

"Yeah, I'll take one too. Gracias, Tía," he replied, wiping his hands on his pants after removing his gloves and taking a seat next to me. The soft cushions sunk in as he sat down.

With his aunt now out of the room, Alex and I were left to sit in an uneasy silence. The atmosphere was palpable with tension, and it was clear that this meeting with his aunt was a significant occasion for the both of us, causing our nerves to be on edge.

As Paco continued to sniff at my shoes and pants, I eyed him warily. The room was very warm, so I took off my jacket, keeping it bundled in my hands. There was a small electric heater keeping the room a toasty eighty degrees—too hot, even in this weather. Paco, done with inspecting me, laid down in a small dog bed, promptly falling asleep and letting out a loud fart. His tongue rolled out of his toothless mouth. He appeared to be some kind of cross between a chihuahua and a rat—and about one hundred years old by the looks of him.

"Your aunt seems lovely," I whispered to Alex, trying to keep my voice low so as not to disturb the peaceful environment. Surrounded by all of the knickknacks, I found myself resisting the urge to touch anything.

"She is. After my mother passed, she became a major part of my life. I don't know what I would've done without her," Alex said with a hint of sadness in his voice, but it was quickly replaced by pride. I could tell he loved his aunt deeply, and it was easy to see why—she was kind, caring, and all the things you could want in a mother figure. I couldn't help but think that having someone like her in my life would've made a big difference when I was growing up.

Asking about his mother's passing was a delicate topic, but I couldn't help but wonder. I hesitated for a moment, searching for the right words, before finally asking. "What happened to your mom?"

Alex took a long time to answer, and I immediately felt guilty for putting him in this situation. Just as I was about to apologize, he spoke. "She died of cancer. After my sister's death, she really started to decline. The doctors couldn't stop the spread, and she refused to go through chemotherapy again after everything she'd been through with Rosa."

"I'm sorry," I said, feeling a pang of sadness for Alex's loss and a twinge of regret for imposing on his family. They had already been through so much, and here I was, adding to their troubles. With tears threatening to spill over, I asked, "Are you sure this is okay?"

"Stop those thoughts right now!" Alex's aunt said as she entered the room carrying a tray with three coffee cups and a plate of sugar cookies shaped like flowers. She placed the tray on the coffee table in front of us. "Alex has told me about your situation, and it's no trouble at all for me to help you out."

"I just don't want to be a burden," I said, my face flushed with embarrassment. "I'm sorry, Alex didn't give me your name, and I should have asked on the way here. I can be such an idiot sometimes."

She gave Alex a stern look and then turned her eyes to me, her face losing its edge. Somehow, her gaze didn't feel like pity; it felt like someone who understood. "You can just call me Tía Lucia," she said, "since my rude nephew probably hasn't told you anything about me. Let me tell you a little about my own situation and why it doesn't pain me at all to help you." She took a seat on a plush chair across from us and prepared her cup of coffee. She liked a lot of creamer in hers, turning it practically all white. "You see, I was once in a similar situation to the one you're in, and I often wished someone had reached out a hand to help me." A depressed look fell over her face as she spoke, lost in her memories.

    I gave Tía Lucia a moment to gather her thoughts and then reached for my coffee. I stirred in the desired amount of cream and sugar, then took a bite of one of the cookies on the plate. The cookie had a satisfying crunch and was overwhelmingly sweet.

    She continued with her story. "My husband was beating me and kept me from my family for years before I finally gathered the courage to leave him. I won't go into details, but let's just say he's no longer in my life." She let out a strained laugh before continuing. "I started working here and managed to support myself. It takes hard work to get back on your feet after an experience like that, but I want to help you if you'll let me." Her voice was encouraging, and I couldn't help but believe in her.

    Taking a sip of my coffee, I considered her words. "I appreciate your help. I had saved up some money, but it's gone now. I'll get a job as soon as I can," I promised.

    "Good! I know you will," she laughed. "Alex has been talking about you nonstop for months."

"Tía!" Alex hissed.

"Well, I won't embarrass him too much, but from what he tells me, you're good people." She placed her coffee on the tray and started searching in her pockets. "Here is your key. It's the room next to mine, so you won't have to worry about loud neighbors, except for Paco. With his bad eyesight, sometimes he barks at ghosts. Do you need any food? I can make something quickly," she asked, her eyes scanning my skinny waist.

"No, thank you. I just bought some food at the store, so I'll manage," I replied, not wanting to take any more advantage of her kindness.

"Alright, if you change your mind, I'll be here. Alex, why don't you help Mel settle in? I've made the bed for her. The bedding is all hand-me-downs, but it's clean," she said, getting up and taking the tray with her. "It's good to finally meet you, Mel. I wish it was under better circumstances, but don't worry, we're going to get along just fine," she continued, giving me a smile full of love, which made me want to cry, but I managed to hold back. I got up, and Alex led me to my new apartment. My heart was pounding with excitement in my chest.

Before setting off to my room, we needed to retrieve the bags from the trunk of the car. At the store, I had used some of my remaining cash to purchase the essentials: shampoo, conditioner, tattoo ointment, some food, and cooking supplies. Alex informed me that the room was equipped with a small kitchenette, complete with a refrigerator and stove, allowing me to cook my meals at home. One grocery bag in particular filled me with excitement as it represented a fresh start and a departure from my past self. Alex helped me carry the bags and showed me around the room, demonstrating how everything worked. It was evident that he had spent a lot of time in the apartment during his upbringing.

"I'll leave you to get some rest," said Alex, as he reached out for an awkward side hug—which was the first we had ever shared. The embrace was sweet, and I leaned into his warmth, turning into a full hug. I could feel his firm muscles through his clothes, and as I looked up, I saw a light stubble on his jaw. Alex was really handsome. How had I not noticed it before?

"Thanks again, Alex. I'll text you in the morning," I replied.

"Looking forward to it!" he waved with a goofy grin on his face before heading out the door, leaving me alone—*in my very own apartment.* I was so excited to have a bathroom all to myself.

As I started putting away my groceries, I placed all the food in the cabinets and put the milk and eggs in the refrigerator. Taking the last bag, I went to the small bathroom. It was just a six by six square space with a toilet, a standing sink, and a small shower. Everything was white and shining, and Lucia really meant it when she said things were clean in here.

I gazed at my reflection in the mirror, and I couldn't help but notice the dark circles around my eyes, making me look haunted. The bruises on both sides of my neck—even a week after my hospital stay—looked horrifying. My skin was paler than usual, making my veins stand out prominently, giving me a sickly undertone, and making my freckles appear darker. Thank goodness Jess had packed a cosmetic bag for me, as I was going to need a lot of concealer to appear human again. The thought of meeting my new landlord with this appearance made me grimace. No wonder Alex's aunt had been so kind to me. I must have looked like something the cat had dragged in—or, in my case, *Paco had dragged in.*

With determination, I opened my bag and pulled out my prize—the hair scissors, gleaming, and a box of hair dye, ready for use. It was time to change my appearance, and maybe, if Harvey saw me again, he wouldn't recognize me, or he would be so disgusted that he wouldn't want to. I had even gone as far as buying brown contacts to hide my mismatched eyes.

Grabbing the scissors first, I started chopping away at my hair, first giving myself a bob, but then I decided that wasn't enough, so I went even shorter, giving myself a punky pixie cut. *Perfect!* Even I didn't recognize the girl in the mirror. Opening the box, I saw that there were two steps—first, I had to bleach my hair, and then I could put on the color.

The process took much longer than I had anticipated, but as I wiped the condensation from the bathroom mirror, I saw that my efforts had not been in vain. The bright pink pixie on my head had transformed everything about the way I looked. It made my heart-shaped face more defined and drew attention to my cheekbones. I felt like I could take on the world with hair this colorful.

With a mix of excitement and nervousness, I sat on the edge of the bed as I checked my phone. An email from the coffee shop had arrived, and my heart skipped a beat as I clicked on the link to read it. The smile on my face grew wider with every word as I realized they wanted to schedule an interview with me. The earliest slot available was tomorrow at noon, and without hesitation, I took it.

As I thought about what to wear for the interview, I glanced at my single bag of clothes. My options were limited, but I remembered that Jess had saved a few of my turtle necks, which I was grateful for. They would help conceal the bruises from my near-death experience and give me the confidence I needed for the interview.

Closing my eyes for the night, I felt a glimmer of hope for the first time in a long time. Maybe this wasn't the end, but it was the start of something amazing. And I was ready for it. I drifted off to sleep with a smile on my face, feeling grateful for this new beginning and excited for what the future held.

Chapter 14

Mel

I sat at the kitchen table, surrounded by the comforting scents of freshly brewed coffee and melted cheese. I struggled to shake off the feeling of emptiness that had plagued me since I woke up from my medicine-induced coma. My fantasy world, a place where I could escape to and lose myself in, had been absent for the past week. I was used to being able to recall every detail of my dreams, but now all I was met with was a dark void. It was a disorienting sensation, almost as if I had lost a part of myself.

Despite my concerns, I knew I needed to be on top of my game for my interview at the coffee shop. I had remembered that the baristas there were a creative bunch, so I wasn't too worried about my new hair color—the pink was a stark contrast to my natural hue.

I paired my new hair with a light pink turtle neck and high-waisted wide-leg black pants, a comfortable yet professional outfit that would make a great impression. According to the coffee shop's website, there was a uniform policy, so I was hoping that I wouldn't have to buy a whole new wardrobe.

To ensure that the bruises from my recent hospital stay wouldn't be a topic of concern, I utilized the power of makeup to cover them up, grateful for its ability to transform my appearance. The final touch was putting in my new brown contacts, which gave me a soft, doe-like appearance, a welcome change from my previous eye color. With a newfound sense of confidence, I was ready to face the interview—and whatever the future had in store for me.

After I finished getting ready, I took out my phone to send Alex a good morning message. I also wanted to let him know that I scored an interview at that coffee shop.

Me: Good Morning! I have some exciting news!
Alex: *Sun emoji* Morning, I can't wait to hear it!
Me: Remember that coffee shop we went to?
Well, I remembered they were hiring and applied.
And I got an interview! It's at 12.
Alex: Congrats! That's great news! I'm sure you're going to kill it!
Let me know how it goes.

The coffee shop was situated in the heart of downtown, just a stone's throw away from my new apartment. Despite living in the city for a while, I was still unfamiliar with the surroundings, so I relied on my GPS to guide me to my destination. I made sure to dress warmly for the cold weather, wrapping myself up in my favorite black jacket, scarf, and my trusty pink beanie hat that I had worn almost every day since the winter season started. My beanie almost matched my hair, which was sticking out of it haphazardly in every direction. I'd never had hair this short before, and I was still figuring out how to style it. *Should I let it be free and wild, or should I use some product to make it lay flat?* I guess I'd find out eventually.

As I walked down the street, I was surrounded by a few new buildings interspersed between the older ones. The sky was clear, and the sounds of the bustling city filled my ears. Every available parking spot was taken, and I couldn't help but wonder how the city planners could have forgotten to include enough parking in this area. The neighborhood was just as run down as the area where the club was located, but there were many more restaurants and small shops, which I was eager to explore once I had more time—and money.

I noticed a large building with dark-tinted windows. When I looked up to see the sign, it read, "All Woman's Gym. Start learning to protect yourself now! First class free!" It was like a sign from the gods, or at least that's what it felt like to me. Although I couldn't see what was happening inside, the dark tinted windows must have provided a sense of comfort to the women working out. I made a mental note to visit the gym on my way back.

Finally, I arrived at The Book Keepers Coffee Shop, my potential new place of employment. As I pushed open the door, a small bell jingled, announcing my presence. I was greeted by an employee whose vibrant hair stood in stark contrast to the all-black uniform they were wearing. The uniform consisted of a simple yet stylish ensemble of a black shirt and pants paired with a navy apron bearing the shop's name in crisp, white letters. The employee's dark makeup and piercing, a double nose ring in one nostril, added to their unique style.

"Thanks! Actually, is the manager around? I'm here for an interview," I said, removing my hat and attempting to flatten my hair. I apparently had gone for the messy, I-don't-care look that day.

The employee's smile widened as she took me in. "Melancholy, right? That's actually me. My name is Avery. It's a pleasure to meet you! Come on back, we can talk in the break room."

"Colly, actually. I don't use my full name," I corrected her. I had made the decision last night to go by a different name—just to be safe. The name Mel was gone and lost forever, along with the memories of the jewel-colored room that I hoped I could eventually erase from my mind.

"Okay, Colly," Avery agreed, her hazel eyes sparkling as she led me to the break room.

The room was smaller than I expected, with a few brown tables surrounded by white plastic chairs. There was a fridge, sink, and microwave in the room, and short cabinets hung on the walls. The brown cabinets were covered in signs about clocking in and taking breaks, and various posters displaying the company policies adorned the walls. All the information was written in business jargon, making me question how a normal person was supposed to interpret it. Perhaps that was the intention.

Avery led us to a table with a tablet and a pile of paperwork on it, which I assumed was for the interview. We sat down, the chairs squeaking across the floor, and Avery took the papers in her hands, quickly reading through them as her eyes moved back and forth, focused on the task at hand.

"Sorry for the informalities," said Avery, the manager of The Book Keepers Coffee Shop. "I haven't been in this position for very long, and all these interview questions seem pointless to me." She furrowed her brows as she tried to think of the right questions to ask. "I mean, who works here for any reason other than money? It's a no-brainer!" she chuckled at her own joke.

"Money is definitely a big factor for me," I replied, smirking. I was already starting to like Avery's straightforward attitude.

"That's what I like to hear," Avery said, tapping her pen against her lips. "What's your favorite book genre?"

Hesitating, I tried to figure out the best way to answer this question without revealing my love for steamy romance novels. "I'd say fantasy romance," I finally answered.

Avery's eyes lit up. "Spicy romance?" she asked with a conspiratorial grin.

I couldn't help but smile back. "Yeah, something like that."

She leaned back in her chair, causing it to squeak, and continued the interview. "What I really need to know, now, is your availability and whether you have transportation. Can you start tomorrow?"

"I'm available anytime, and I just moved close by, so I can walk to work without any problem," I replied, trying to sound professional.

"Brave girl," Avery commented. "I don't even want to walk to my car in this weather. But you know what, I wanted to hire you as soon as I saw your hair."

I ran my hand through the short pink strands, feeling self-conscious. "I wasn't sure about the haircut at first, but thank you," I mumbled.

"It looks adorable," Avery gushed. "You look like a cute little pixie girl straight out of a book!"

"So, do I have the job?" I asked nervously.

"You do! The hours are long, and the customers can be entitled and rude, but as long as you can handle that, the job is yours. Willow, one of the employees you'll meet soon, called in sick, and we could really use the help," Avery confirmed.

"What time?"

"Well, like I said, the hours are long. Do you mind coming in six to four?"

Surely she can't mean six in the morning? I'm going to have to retrain my body to wake up early. "Didn't the ad say late hours? Sorry, I'm not much of a morning person." I mumbled. Was I seriously going to turn down a job just so I could have my beauty sleep?

She looked at her tablet. "Yeah, that's right. Your regular schedule will be two to eleven pm. This would just be temporary while we get you all trained up. I'm sure you have made coffee before, but some of the drinks can be complicated. Two weeks tops." She gave me a hopeful stare.

"Well, okay. I can manage to drag myself up for that. I really need the job, and a few hours of sleep is nothing! I might look like the undead, but I will be here!" I said resolutely. *I could do this. I needed to do this.*

"Perfect! Then, I'll see you tomorrow bright and early! I'll send some more paperwork to your email." She started furiously typing on her tablet. "You'll need to fill it out tonight. It's just payroll information, insurance, and all that jazz. Oh, and uniforms come out of your first check. I should have some in your size in the back. Wait here." She set her paperwork and tablet down to get it.

When she came back, the uniforms were in a brown shopping bag. "There are two sets in there. If you need more, you can order them from the employee website."

She waved goodbye to me as I walked out the door, the proud new owner of a real job. Taking out my phone, I promptly set my alarm for the next two weeks. I'd have to wake up at least at five to get here on time. *Ugh, it's totally fine—totally fine.* It's not like I was dreaming of Jelaria anyway.

As I walked down the busy street, I saw the gym again. Since I was trying new things today, I might as well check this place out. The inside was painted in all grays and blues. There was a large wooden front desk where a girl sat, talking on the phone. She was blonde and pretty, with her hair in a tight ponytail. "Yeah, Jim, I'm going to have to call you back. Someone just walked in." She looked me up and down as she hung up. "How can I help you today?"

"Hi, I was looking to sign up for the free class?"

She rolled her eyes. "Obviously. Well, classes are every two hours, from eight am to eight pm. We have beginners classes and advanced." There was bubble gum in her mouth that she chewed loudly, blowing bubbles and then popping them.

She seemed *real* nice. Trying to not sound like a bitch I answered her. "Beginner, please." Hopefully the teacher would be nicer than this chick.

"'Kay, well, there is one tonight at six if you want to sign up." She pulled out a clipboard from somewhere behind the desk. "Just fill out this waiver. You only get the one free, and if you don't show up, you don't get another one," she snipped at me.

Seriously, rethinking my decision to go to this gym, I took the clipboard. This place was close to my apartment, and I did need to learn to defend myself. With gritted teeth, I filled out all the necessary information and handed it back to her.

"See you later, then." She looked at me up and down again, "or not."

After that *lovely* experience, I walked the rest of the way home. Home. I liked the sound of that. My phone started buzzing in my pocket, so I took it out to see who was texting me.

*Alex: So, did you nail the interview? *Smile emoji**
Me: I got the job. I start tomorrow at six.
I might have to electrocute myself in the morning, but I'll be there, lol
Alex: Nice. I knew you'd get it!
Maybe I'll stop by when you get a break, and we can grab a coffee.
*Me: Sure, I would like that *smile emoji***

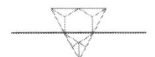

The All Woman Gym beginners class was small, with only about ten students plus the instructor. Her name was Jill, and she was a mature forty, very muscled, with dark brown hair—that had blonde highlights throughout, pulled into a ponytail. She was tan, with long bronze legs, which she showed off in her gym shorts and workout tank. Clearly, she knew her way around a dumbbell.

As she waited for us to settle in, she was checking off a list of everyone here—I guess they took attendance seriously around here. I had told Alex that I had decided to try this gym, and he was very encouraging, probably just happy I was finally taking his advice.

"Welcome to beginner's kickboxing. My name is Jill, and I'll be your instructor today!" Her voice was deep and calming as she started leading the workout. "Now, I like to start these classes by getting to know my new students." Her eyes found mine. "Why don't you tell us a little bit about what you want to gain out of this class today."

Way to put me on the spot. "Umm me?" I asked, hoping she was looking through me to the girl behind. She nodded, though, so I guess she wanted me to answer. "Hi, I'm Colly. And well, I signed up because..." *because I almost died, and I don't want to be weak again.* "Because I want to learn to defend myself."

"That's a great reason to take this class and a really common one. Lots of women want to learn to defend themselves and don't know where to start. Thanks for sharing, Colly!" She smiled and moved on to the next woman in the class. Some had similar answers, but most were here wanted to lose weight. No weight loss needed for me, thanks. If anything, I was hoping that taking some classes might thicken me up a little—add some muscle to my slim frame. Afterward, she took us through a simple warmup, stretching our muscles and getting them ready to work.

She addressed the class with a serious expression, "Okay, class, I want to talk a little bit about defense. These moves I'm going to teach you will help you get out of holds and give you time to run away. I know it's tempting to try and put your attacker in their place, but it's unrealistic. Most men are going to be bigger than you. Most men are going to be stronger than you."

That's a bleak thought but true, and as I look around, I can see the rest of the class agreed. She continued, "The best thing you can do is make as much noise as you can and find help. Never let them take you somewhere else. That's how you disappear. If you can't escape and no help comes, you make your stand there!" She clapped her hands. "Alright, let's demonstrate some holds!"

We spent the next half hour in pairs, grabbing each other and trying to break the grips our partners had on us. It was surprisingly fun, and by the end, I felt like I could get away from someone if I had to. After that, we went through a set of basic jabs and kicks. She had us do sets of them over and over until the sweat was dripping down my back and face. I don't think I've ever worked that hard in my life! When I went to the fountain to grab a drink, the instructor followed me.

"Good work out there, Colly. Can I expect to see you again tomorrow?" She asked, wiping the sweat from her brow.

"Maybe I really did enjoy it! Do you guys have any membership discounts or anything going on right now?"

She looked thoughtful as she said, "Let me talk to Tammy; she's the front desk girl. I'm pretty sure we were running a New Year special that should still be going on. I'll be right back." half-walking, half-jogging, she left the class. Hopefully, the membership would be affordable, and I would be able to come here again.

Not long later, she came back with a huge grin. "Great news! I got her to extend the sale for you. It's only thirty a month for your first six months! You just have to fill out some forms, and you'll be all set!"

That wasn't a bad deal at all. I could afford to spend thirty a month on self-improvement. After signing up for the gym and getting a new job, I was feeling really accomplished. Sure, I was sweaty and completely broke after paying for one month of classes, but I was more free than I had been in a long time. I hoped tonight, my dreams would come back to me, and then everything would be complete.

Chapter 15

Jelaria

    Klein and Mystic arrived back in Celetrix within a week, running the whole way as if being chased by an angry dragon—to be fair, they might have been. There were still a few loose ends to tie up before they could attempt the job in Ostara that would make or break their lives.

    The rings the Lord of Mabon gave them would be a big help, but what they really needed was an amulet of invisibility. If they had one, Klein just knew there would be no way they could get caught. Such amulets were few and far between, made from old magic that was no longer available to the Fae. The gods had long ago abandoned this world, and the power they once held was gone with them. Not that Klein could remember the gods—they had been gone long before he was born before any of the Fae currently living were born. All they had were old stories and objects of power left behind.

    The only place to find an object like that was the Dark Market in Bastards Bay. The seedy market only catered to those who knew how to reach it. They planned to make a visit to the Dark Market before continuing on to Litha.

Mystic was already packing her bags for the trip in her room across from his. The desert lands were so different from any they had been to before, so they needed to pack specific clothing for the harsh sandstorms and blinding heat.

The plan was to leave as soon as they were finished with any outstanding business with the guild. Klein still had to report to Lycanthus before they could go. The Guild Master needed to be informed of all plans, or the consequences would be brutal. According to the terrified guild member he had asked, Lycanthus could be found in his office. The Guild Master was likely in a bad mood today, but when wasn't he?

As Klein walked through the hall, he was practicing what to say—he had to prepare his words carefully. Lycanthus would want his cut of the Ostara Jewel job, that was certain. But perhaps, if Klein got him to weigh the risks they were taking to get it done, the percentage would be more in their favor.

"Come on, Kleptis. Don't linger outside my door like a harlot!" Lycanthus's voice rang out from behind the great white oak door, the skull knocker glinting in the hallway light.

Klein entered the room, taking long, confident strides. He saw Lycanthus sitting at his desk, pouring over paperwork and ledgers. His button-down shirt is open, showing off the strong planes of his green chest. Focused on his work, he couldn't be bothered to look Klein in the eye as he said, "What is it now, boy? Sister in trouble again?" His voice was gruff and impatient. It was not a good time to push him, but Klein needed to talk to him before they left. Lycanthus tapped his fingers on the desk, the sound like war drums to Klein's ears.

"Guild Master, as you know me, and Mystic are taking on the Ostara Sapphire job."

"Yes." He said, still not looking up—too absorbed in whatever report had his attention. "Well, spit it out. I don't have all day."

Trying to keep his tone respectful, Klein continued, "The job comes with great risks. Seeing that we may end up imprisoned, or worse, our commission should be higher. If we pull this off, the Thieves Guild will go down in history as the most notorious in the world. Surely that would be worth eighty percent instead of the usual sixty."

Lycanthus looked up from his paperwork, his eyes narrowing as he took in Klein's words. "Eighty percent? You must think I'm a fool, boy. The risks are always high in our line of work, and you knew that when you joined this guild. If you don't want to take the job, then don't. But don't come to me asking for more money because you're scared of getting caught." He leaned back in his chair, his arms crossing over his chest. "And don't forget who holds the power here, Kleptis. I could easily find someone else to take on this job and give them the usual commission without a second thought." Bringing a hand up to twist on the braids in beard, he added. "It costs a lot to run this place. Do you think the servants are free?"

Klein swallowed hard, his heart racing with fear and frustration. He had hoped that he could convince Lycanthus to see reason, but it seemed like he was fighting a losing battle. "I understand, Guild Master. It's just that—"

Lycanthus interrupted him, his voice stern. "No buts, Kleptis. You know the rules of this guild. If you want to take on this job, then you do it at the usual commission." He leaned forward, his gaze intense. "And don't you ever question my authority again. Understood?"

"I know what the cost of a Fae life is, Lycanthus. I just don't want to risk my or my sister's life for anything less than eighty. You could always find someone else willing to risk it—if you can." Klein shrugged, pretending it didn't matter either way. *So much for keeping his tone light.*

"You've got balls, boy, I'll give you that!" He laughed. "Tell you what—if you both survive this, you can have seventy." Lycanthus leaned back in his chair once more, his attention already returning to his paperwork. "Just don't go saying I never did anything nice for you. Now, get out of here. I have a meeting to prepare for." Lycanthus waved Klein off with a ring-clad hand.

No, Lycanthus definitely wasn't hurting for gold. The emerald pinky ring on his finger was worth more than most Fae made in a year. Klein wouldn't be surprised if his jewelry were spelled to bring fortune and good luck, making it priceless.

Klein nodded, his jaw clenched in frustration. He knew that arguing with Lycanthus would only make things worse, so he forced himself to remain calm. "Thank you. And not to worry, we always survive."

"Yes, I suppose you do," Lycanthus said in dismissal.

Klein nodded, his anger simmering beneath the surface as he turned to leave. He knew that Lycanthus had the power in this situation, but that didn't mean he had to like it. As he walked back down the hallway, he couldn't help but feel like he was walking into a trap. But he didn't have a choice. If he wanted to complete the Ostara Sapphire job and finally free himself from the Thieves Guild, he had to do it on Lycanthus's terms.

With that out of the way, it was time to find Mystic. She should be in her room packing bags and preparing for the big job at hand. As Klein walked into her room, he saw clothing thrown everywhere—bags lying empty on her unmade bed. "Mystic, where are you?" Klein shouted, not seeing her in the mess. Books were piled on every surface, along with dirty cups and plates. "Don't you ever let the servants in here? It's a fucking mess." Klein muttered under his breath.

She stepped out of her bathroom, hair soaking and wrapped in a towel, "Is it time already?"

"Yes. Is there a reason you're still not ready?" Klein questioned her, feeling exasperated.

Placing a hand on her hip, she said plainly, "Do you think I've just been sitting here all day? No, I was out doing something useful. Why don't you take a look in the pouch on my nightstand before you give me looks like that."

Walking through the mess, Klein found the nightstand she was talking about. It took him a minute—since it was covered in dirty dishes. But on top was the pouch, as she said it would be. He took it in his hands, dumping out the contents on the only available surface. A necklace fell out of the small bag. The pendant was made out of bone and shaped like a rough triangle. Around the edges were runes carved into the surface; it's an amulet of invisibility. "How did you get this?" He gasped out.

"Remember that bottle of whiskey I stole the other day?" Mystic said as she started getting dressed behind a brass partition. It was solid with a floral design pounded into the metal—a gift from Klein on her birthday last year.

"Yes, I recall. What does you drinking all morning have to do with this?"

"You *seriously* think I spend all my time drinking? Don't answer that. Anyway, the owner of the Dark Market has a weakness for fine liquor," she tossed her hair using wind magic to dry it, keeping the black half visible, "and beautiful females. It didn't take much convincing to get him to give it to me." Once done getting dressed, she sauntered out from behind the partition, coming to pick up the amulet.

"You stole it, didn't you?"

She batted her eyes as if to say *who, me?* "Gave it, stole it, same thing. He won't remember much, so it doesn't matter." Smirking, she started sorting through her clothes, packing what she was going to need in a small cloth bag. "Now, do you mind? Some of us have packing to do if we're going to leave on time."

That explained why Klein didn't see her last night or this morning. At least her disappearance led to something useful this time and saved them a trip to the Bay—and the cost of the gold. Klein realized that he didn't always give Mystic the credit she deserved. She had as much, if not more, skill at thieving than him. And if he was being honest, it was her laid-back attitude that led people to believe she was harmless. Klein had forgotten it was just for show—a mask to hide the killer lurking underneath.

Letting Mystic get ready, he returned to his room, making sure he had everything in order. The clothing they were going to need was the light, airy fabric of Litha. The wind and sand were ruthless, so everything needed to be covered. He wrapped the long white fabric around himself in a way that only his silver eyes would be on show.

They would walk for the first half of the journey. Once they crossed the border, there were riding drakes they could rent—great lizards made for the heat and sand. The drakes were fast and knew how to navigate the desert without guidance. Trying to walk would be a fool's errand, and you were likely to end up lost. The bodies of such travelers were often found years later, with nothing but bones left—picked clean by the birds, or worse.

Once they were ready, they left through the southern gate. Getting past these guards was no trouble. Like all the guards of Celetrix, they could be bought with a few coins. However, getting through to the border of Litha would be a different story. They would have to wait until nightfall to sneak around the wards separating the courts. Luckily, the rings they were gifted were genuine, and they could get past any ward undetected. They had tested them at the Mabon border, and they worked flawlessly. That, paired with the amulet, should get them through easily. If only they had two of the amulets, then they would be unstoppable. Hell, they could walk right through the gates, and no one would notice—not that Klein would be willing to test that theory.

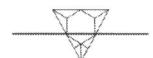

It was nightfall as they moved into Litha territory. Already, the weather was sweltering. Klein could only imagine what it was going to be like during the day. The sand shifted beneath Klein's feet, slowing his speed considerably. They had avoided the guards and just made it through the wards. *Piece of cake*. Things were really starting to look up about this job, and they had a strong feeling that this was going to be the end of their time with the Thieves Guild. The moon was shining bright as it guided their way, and the stars urging them south. All the signs pointed to success.

The first outpost of Litha wasn't far, but it would still take a few hours of running to get there. Klein took on his wolf form and ran across the ground that, slowly transformed into lifeless sand. Dunes lay in every direction. Staying near the main roads—but not on them—they were still able to follow the signs leading to Litha.

The road was marked by glowing towers of rocks, set at intervals so travelers wouldn't get lost. It was still dark, but after a few hours, Klein started to see the outline of the small outpost coming into view—the flat roofs creating a silhouette against the night sky.

Before they entered, they transformed back into their Fae forms. Klein was lean and tall. And Mystic, shorter and more slender. Klein attempted to dust off his clothing, his hands still covered in red sand. Next to him, Mystic stood smugly clean, protected by the layers of his fur as they traveled through the desert.

They put on blank faces and walked with confidence as they strode into the outpost—perfectly normal travelers, definitely *not* thieves trying to get to Ostara.

The fabric of their clothing billowed around them in a light breeze, keeping them covered head to toe. It was made to be comfortable and light while also holding all of their hidden weapons beneath the folds. There were few Fae walking the street this late at night, but the ones they did see paid them no mind. After all, those living here would have expected guards to have given them a rigorous search and had them turn in all the proper paperwork. *Don't these fools know how easy it is for thieves to get in? It's like they want to be robbed.*

Looking for an inn was easy, as the outpost was small, and there was only one—a sandstone building with a flat wooden beam roof. The inn was aptly named Outskirts Inn, and inside, there was a female sand nymph working as the hostess for the night. She had golden skin and golden hair, almost like sand in the sunlight. With the ability to swim through sand like water, this was the perfect place for one of her kind.

"Traveled far, have you?" She asked them, taking in Klein's dirty clothing.

Mystic gave the hostess a dazzling smile. "No, not too far. We'd like a room for the night. With two beds preferably, and if it's not too late dinner."

"Of course, I can do that. Especially for a beautiful female like you. Will you be staying long?"

Klein gave his sister a stern look. "Just for the night."

The hostess fetched them the food quickly and directed them to their room. It was an easy transaction, as Outskirts Inn was used to travelers just passing through.

The food was a simple fare, hard bread rolls and steaming bowls of stew in covered dishes to keep them warm. Nothing fancy, but with so few resources in the deserts of Litha, Klein wondered how they survived at all—being combined with Ostara and the Kingdom of the Seelie Fae must have its perks.

As soon as they were alone in the small square room with nothing more than two beds and sandstone walls, Klein couldn't help but confront Mystic. "Do you have to flirt with someone everywhere we go?" he asked, his tone tinged with annoyance.

Mystic sat on her bed with her tray of food on her lap, her demeanor casual. "I wasn't flirting. I was just being friendly. You should try it sometime," she replied, a mischievous glint in her eye. "Besides, I even got us dinner after hours."

Klein grunted in agreement and began to eat his food, his expression solemn. The stew was warm but mostly water, and the bread was so hard he suspected it had been baked days ago and left out in the summer sun to dry.

After they finished their meager meal, they took turns keeping watch while the other slept. They split the hours into four, alternating who got to sleep first. Tonight, it was Mystic's turn. As she drifted off to sleep, Klein could hear her steady breathing. It was a skill they were both trained in. Sleep quickly and lightly—always ready at a moment's notice.

Hours passed, and just as Klein was beginning to think the night would be uneventful, a sound caught his attention. The slow scraping of boots echoed through the room, signaling someone's approach. Whoever they were, they were failing miserably at being stealthy. Klein stayed on his bed, keeping a hand on his blade, ready for whatever might happen next.

Quiet words were whispered just beyond the door, sending a chill down Klein's spine. He strained his ears, his instincts honed by years of danger, and heard every word. "I'm telling you, they are loaded. The gold that they were carrying will be worth it," one voice said. "And the sister, a fine little thing like her. I bet he'd pay us handsomely for her, even after we've had our fun." Vulgar laughter followed their crude remarks about Mystic and their plans for her.

Fools, Klein thought. They had clearly never robbed someone before. He gripped his blade tightly, his muscles tensing with anticipation. He could feel his magic humming with excitement, eager for a taste of these unworthy males—or maybe it was just his own thoughts. Either way, they had no idea what they were in for.

Keeping his blade at the ready, he relaxed his body, waiting for his chance to strike. Let the fools get close, then strike. He closed his eyes, deciding he didn't need to see them for this. That would be too easy.

He heard a slight shifting sound from Mystic's bed, alerting him that she was awake and aware of their attackers. The doorknob turned as they creaked the door open, trying to be quiet but failing miserably. Amateurs. It was laughable that they thought they were going to rob Klein and Mystic. The clothing they wore had disguised them not nearly well enough, Woven capes covering their bodies, faces still on display. No thief in their right mind would dare it, knowing who they were.

Klein waited, ready to strike, as the floorboards creaked under their movements. They moved to surround Klein's bed, seeing him as the greater threat. Every wrong move they made seemed to emphasize their inexperience.

But then there was a slight whisper of fabric moving, and Klein realized his mistake too late. As he went to quickly strike out and kill them both in one blow, he was surprised to find his body immobilized. He opened his eyes in shock and looked up at his attackers, his heart pounding in his chest.

Both of the males had fair hair that shone like gold in the dim light, and their eyes were the color of watery blue, looking smug as they stood over their helpless victims. Klein knew that they were probably Fae from Ostara because they had used their plant magic to summon vines of rope to wrap around his body, rendering him immobile. As he looked over to his sister, he saw that she was in the same predicament, and panic surged through him. Had someone found out about their plans? Was it possible that someone from the guild had betrayed them? Stella?

The vines were wrapped tight, and Klein bared his teeth, a growl escaping him as he tried to free himself. The vines were strong, though, and he couldn't seem to manage it. He realized that at least one of his attackers was well-trained in incapacitating victims, and a feeling of dread washed over him.

"Look at what we have here. A couple of Yule Fae far from home," one of the males laughed. "Take care of the sister while I get rid of the extra baggage," he directed the other one, indicating he would take on Klein. The first attacker drew a blade, bringing it close enough to touch Klein's neck, the sharp edge cutting into it slightly. They hadn't known their names, so they couldn't have been sent from the guild—just some unlucky fools looking to make some quick gold.

With little time to think and his body bound, Klein focused on making some magic of his own. Staring to build it up, he began coating his skin in ice, creating a thick suit of armor and making sure the point of contact with the blade was well-covered. His attacker gasped out in surprise as Klein became a demon of ice, spikes protruding from his body sharp and deadly, cutting into the vines. Klein's face broke out into a feral smile.

It wasn't often that he got to take this form. He didn't like to use this trick very often, as using it cost him, draining all his magic stores. It would take days to replenish it fully. They still had at least a week of travel ahead of them, so he wasn't too worried about it. Standing up, Klein shook the broken vines from his body, the attackers backing up towards the door as if they could escape his wrath after the things they were planning. Klein didn't take rapists lightly, and he didn't plan on them making it out of this room alive.

The smell of fear emanated from the trembling thief's body as he dropped the knife, still dripping with Klein's blood. "Please, I have a family," he cried, his pants stained with urine.

"So do I," Klein growled. A roar of rage erupted from deep in his chest as he sent spikes of ice aimed at the thief's fast-beating heart. The thief collapsed to the ground with a wet thump, his blonde head of hair rolling away from him. Klein's aim had been off due to the excitement of taking on his ice armor form. He let out a mad laugh as he turned to his next victim, but to Klein's disappointment, that thief had already been taken care of.

Mystic was lounging on her bed, looking as though she hadn't just killed someone. At her feet was the body of the Ostara male, still twitching in the throes of death. His eyes were rolling to the back of his head, and foam poured out of his dying mouth, gargled screams faintly leaving his lips. Using the attacker's blade, Mystic was casually cleaning her nails. "Did you have to make so much noise, brother? You probably woke up the whole inn," she purred.

Dispelling the magic from his skin, Klein sent glittering ice to linger in the air. "Yeah, yeah. Let's just get out of here."

Mystic jumped up and began gathering her things, keeping the blade from the male she killed. "I always did enjoy sleeping under the moon," she said, giving Klein a sly smile.

Blood dripped from the ceiling onto the rug in front of the door, staining it a deep shade of crimson. Despite the gore, he couldn't help but feel a sense of satisfaction at the sight of the male who lay in pieces before him. They deserved what they got and much worse. Klein and Mystic hastily packed their belongings and made their escape through the window, leaving the bodies to rot where they fell. At least they had managed to scavenge a meal from this outpost, Klein mused, even if it tasted terrible.

Before venturing back out into the unforgiving desert, they stole a couple of sand drakes from a nearby barn. Chances were good that the drakes belonged to the men they had killed, but it didn't matter now. The drakes were large creatures, about the size of a horse, with scaly skin that came in varying shades of muddy brown. Their sharp teeth and barbed tails hung low to the ground, giving them a deadly appearance. As Klein and Mystic approached them cautiously, the drakes watched them with interest, their intelligent eyes narrowing slightly.

In the hay on the ground lay the guard who had been watching over the drakes. Mystic had put him to sleep with her venom before he knew what was happening. It took only an instant, and he didn't make a sound. They should have invested in better guards if they didn't want someone stealing their mounts. But it was their fault, not Klein and Mystic's.

Mounted on the drakes, Klein and Mystic let the creatures use their instincts to guide them through the sandy terrain. The drakes knew this land far better than they ever could. After traveling a safe distance from the outpost, they found a rocky area free from the wind to rest for the night. Klein and Mystic commanded the drakes to settle down, and the creatures obediently tucked their long-necked heads close to their bodies.

Under the starry sky, Klein and Mystic slept curled up together like it was the most natural thing in the world. And for them, it was. They might not have been siblings by blood, but they were siblings of fate. The presence that had been watching over them both as they slept finally returned to Klein after many nights, bringing with it a wave of warmth and longing.

Chapter 16

Mel

    It was my first day working at the coffee shop, and everything felt overwhelming. Learning all there was to know about this place was a lot to take in. From using the register to handling the machines, there were several videos I had to watch on the company tablet to learn everything. While the videos were simple and easy to follow, I still felt underprepared when it came time to actually do the work.

    This job was so different in some ways from working at the club, but customer service was still at the forefront. At least I didn't have to sleep with the customers like I did before. The machines made coffee and steamed milk on their own, and my job was to prepare and serve the drinks. It sounded easy enough, but I couldn't quite get the hang of the proportions yet, and some of my drinks tasted foul. We had to dump them down the sink rather than serve them to anyone.

While I struggled, the milk steamer glinted at me, the sounds of bubbling inside as it worked perfectly. The metal machines seemed to mock me with their ability to do their job so effortlessly. I couldn't help but think they were stupid robots out to get me.

Avery assured me that I would learn it all in no time, but after I got my first customer complaint, I was feeling a little out of sorts. Who knew people could get so worked up over coffee? Seriously, it was just one extra sugar. The lady didn't need to bite my head off about it.

As my break time approached, I let out a sigh of relief, grateful for the chance to catch my breath. I couldn't wait to see Alex and enjoy my free meal, especially since I was broke and this was my only meal of the day. The coffee shop's menu mainly consisted of ready-made sandwiches and baked goods, but hey, it was free. I decided to indulge myself and selected a giant cinnamon roll, its buttery and sugary filling oozing from its swirly depths. Taking a bite, a contented hum escaped my lips, savoring the divine taste of the icing on my tongue. Despite my temptation to finish it all before Alex arrived, I moved to an empty table and waited for him.

A few moments later, the doorbell jingled, and I looked up to see Alex entering the coffee shop. His face was pink from the cold outside, and it took him a moment to recognize me with my new hair. But as I waved him over, a smile slowly spread across his face, and he walked towards me. The table and chairs we sat in were made of dark wood, creating a cozy and comfortable atmosphere. I had picked the same table as last time, hoping to recreate the same enjoyable experience.

"Hey, sorry I'm late! Parking was awful out there!" Alex said, sounding apologetic. "Loving the new hair, by the way. And whoa, are those contacts?"

I smiled in response. "Yeah, I thought it would be better to change my look... just in case. It's fine, you're not even late! I still have twenty-five minutes left on my break." It was reassuring to see him again, and his flustered demeanor only made him more endearing.

"I get that. If that creep ever comes around, you know you can always call me, right?" Alex said. "I'm going to order a sandwich. Do you want anything?" Alex's concern for me was touching, and I appreciated his offer to help if needed.

Pointing to my monster cinnamon roll, I laughed. "No, I think this is more than enough." Honestly, I should have bought him something, but I didn't have a single dollar left to my name. My first check couldn't come fast enough. I was used to fending for myself, even if it meant surviving on one free meal a day. It was a big change from my previous job, where I was paid daily in cash. Now, I had to wait for my bi-weekly paycheck like everyone else. It made me wonder how people managed to make ends meet when they lived paycheck to paycheck. It was nice of him to offer to come to my rescue, but I wasn't a princess locked in a tower. I could take care of myself—just like I had been for the last twenty years. While he was waiting for his food, I received a text from Jess that caused my eyes to widen with worry.

> Jess: Hey girl, be careful out there. Harvey came into the club looking for you.
> Me: Fuck, I wish he would just forget about me. Stay safe and avoid him if you can!
> Jess: Oh, I will girl.
> That is one man I don't want to mess with.

I heard Alex's footsteps approaching. I forced a smile on my face and took in a deep breath, trying to push away the anxious thoughts that had crept up on me. Harvey couldn't hurt me here, I reminded myself. I was safe. *My monsters won't find me here.* I watched as Alex sat down across from me, his hands full with an avocado sandwich and a cup of coffee.

"So, read any good mangas lately?" I asked, trying to sound casual and carefree. I wanted to take my mind off the text message that had just made me worry.

He took a massive bite of his sandwich and tried to chew it quickly as if he was afraid I would change the subject before he could answer. "I haven't really had the time lately," he admitted. "I've been working a lot and helping my aunt with the apartments. Plus, with you being in the hospital, I was just too worried about you." His cheeks and ears turned pink, and I felt a surge of affection for him.

"Sorry, I don't know if you want to talk about it," he continued. "Jess gave me the basic details. But we don't ever have to talk about that place again if you don't want to." He sounded nervous, and I could tell he was trying to be careful not to say anything that might upset me.

"Relax, Alex," I said, putting a hand on his arm. "It's okay. I'm comfortable with my past, and I just want to move on. Thanks for caring about me, though."

He nodded, looking relieved. "Right, okay. Well, if you ever want to talk, I'm here for you." He took a sip of his coffee and winced.

"Is it bad?" I asked, concerned. "I'm the one who made the last batch of coffee, and I really wanted to get it right."

"No, it's fine, just hot," he replied, his eyes watering a little. "Pretty sure I burned off what little taste buds I had left." He laughed and proceeded to wipe his tongue with a napkin. The coffee was definitely bad, and I cursed silently to myself.

"How's the first day going?" he asked, changing the subject.

"It's going," I replied with a sigh. "There's a lot to learn. Who knew making coffee was so complicated?" I picked up my cutlery and cut into my cinnamon roll, taking two large bites. The soft dough melted in my mouth, and I let out a happy moan. Sometimes, I seriously considered a sugary snack to be more satisfying than sex, but maybe that was because all the men I'd been with had been selfish pricks.

"You've got this!" Alex said, trying to cheer me up. "I was thinking if you have time later, we could watch some episodes of Ramen at your place. I'll bring pizza." His cheeks turned crimson as he asked to hang out. I honestly thought we were moving past the point of embarrassment. After all, he'd seen me at my worst.

"I don't have a TV in there yet," I replied, my mouth feeling dry as I talked. Maybe I wasn't over my embarrassment yet.

"I can bring my laptop. It's nothing fancy, but it's better than watching on a phone. Not that I think watching on the phone is bad or something," he said, looking down at his food. The sandwich looked toasted to perfection, and it came with a side of chips. It was all pre-made, so it was pretty hard to mess that up.

"Well, when you put it that way," I laughed, giving him a winning smile. Spending time watching anime with Alex seemed like the perfect way to spend my evening. "Okay, let's do it. I really need to get some furniture when I get paid. Do you know of any good thrift stores around here?"

He took a drink of his coffee, looking up in thought. "If you wait until the end of the month, people leave a lot of stuff when they move out. I bet we could find you a decent couch and coffee table."

"Really? That sounds awesome. What time should we get together?" I pulled out my phone to look at my schedule. "Oh, crap! I forgot about my gym class! Is it ok if you come over at like 7:30? That way, I can go to class?"

"Colly! Breaks over!" Avery called out to me, interrupting our conversation.

"Colly?" Alex gave me a questioning look. Smiling, I put a finger to my lips and gave him a little wink. He took the hint and didn't correct her. "See you later, Colly. And have fun at your class!"

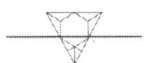

Walking back to my apartment, I could feel the chill in the air seeping through my jacket and nipping at my cheeks. My tired legs ached with each step, and I could feel the sweat trickling down my spine from my workout, making my shirt stick uncomfortably to my skin. Despite the discomfort, my top priority was getting to my apartment for a hot shower. As I approached the building, I noticed Alex's car parked outside. He must be visiting his aunt. I fished my phone out of my pocket and quickly sent him a text to let him know I had arrived home.

Me: Hey, I just got back. I'm going to shower real quick, then you can come over.

Tell your aunt I say hi!

I scoured my closet and drawers, desperately searching for something decent to wear. With each passing second, my hopes sank lower and lower. Most of my clothes were either crumpled on the floor or stuffed in the laundry basket, waiting to be cleaned. With a heavy heart, I settled on a pair of my favorite pajamas, feeling disappointed that I couldn't find anything better. Glancing at the pile of dirty clothes in the corner, I knew I had to do laundry soon. But with my jam-packed schedule, finding the time to wash my clothes felt impossible. For now, I had to make do with what I had, even if it meant wearing my worn-out clothes for the next few days.

While my frustration mounted, I knew I had to wash my clothes soon, or I would be left with nothing to wear. However, the situation seemed hopeless. I checked my pockets, but I had no change for the laundry machines, and I didn't want to bother Lucia, even though I knew she would let me use hers. Left with limited options, I had to resort to the bathroom. Standing in front of the shower, I mentally prepared myself for the unpleasant task ahead. It wasn't the most convenient option, but it was the only one I had.

Still not receiving a response from Alex, I locked the door and darted to the shower, snatching some of the clothes from the pile of dirty laundry. As I scrubbed myself and my clothes, the familiar scent of my body wash surrounded me. Its clean, comforting scent of rosebud honey filled the room as I rinsed and wrung out each piece of clothing. After I hung everything up, I kept my underwear inside the shower, just in case Alex needed to use the bathroom.

After I finished my shower, I slipped into my fluffy bunny pajamas, briefly considering whether it would be embarrassing to wear them around Alex. But ultimately, I shrugged it off, reminding myself that comfort was key. While I dried my hair with a towel, I noticed a chill in the air. When I looked around, I noticed the window was slightly open, with the curtains fluttering in the breeze.

Puzzled, I couldn't remember opening it. I quickly closed and locked it before hearing a knock at the door.

With a towel wrapped around my head, I answered it to find Alex standing there with a box of pizza in hand. "Hey Mel, ready for some action-packed Ramen episodes?" he asked, looking at my towel. His cheeks turned pink as he said, "Sorry, do you want me to come back later?" I grabbed his arm and half-pulled him through the door.

"It's fine. Now that my hair is short, it dries really fast. Mmm, pizza! What kind did you order?" I opened the door wide for him, and he walked the rest of the way, placing the pizza on the counter. "I don't have plates, but you don't need plates for pizza, right?" I pulled out a roll of paper towels and handed one to him.

Opening the brown box, the smell of cheese wafted through the air. He grinned as he revealed the delicious pizza. "I wasn't sure what you liked, so I just got pepperoni. Hope that's okay."

"Pepperoni is great. I'm not picky," I replied, taking in the sight of the steaming hot pizza.

He wore a backpack adorned with interesting patches, probably containing his computer equipment. As he scanned the room, I noticed a hint of concern on his face. "Where should I put my laptop?" he asked.

"We could sit on the floor?" I suggested. The only piece of furniture I had was the bed, and that would be weird. Like, do we lay down together? Plus, it would be a bitch to wash pizza out of my only bed set.

"Sure. Sorry, I didn't even think about it," he said, chuckling as he began setting up his laptop on top of a sturdy cardboard box. It was just high enough for us to sit with our backs pressed against the foot of the bed and still be comfortable.

Grabbing a slice of pizza, I sat down cross-legged and took a bite. The cheese stretched tantalizingly as I took a bite, then snapped, hitting me on the forehead. I let out a small yelp and quickly grabbed the towel off my head, using it to wipe my face. I tossed it haphazardly onto the bed, not caring about the mess. At least it would be better than having tomato sauce on my face for the rest of the night.

After Alex got it all set up, he grabbed himself a slice and sat down next to me, his legs brushing against mine. He didn't notice my pizza incident; too busy doing stuff on his laptop. The screen had the episode ready to play, and he hit the space bar to start the show. His body was warm next to me, and every time his knee brushed against mine, little tingles jumped up my spine. I was tempted to move closer, but I didn't want to give him the wrong idea. It was too soon for me to want to have someone physically like that. If I was honest with myself, I could still feel Harvey's hands on my throat, the weight of his body over mine.

I tried to be brave and say I didn't care—I was comfortable with my life before. But deep down, I didn't know what a normal relationship was like. What if all Alex wanted from me was my body? What if this was all a lie?

Lost in my thoughts, pizza forgotten, I didn't notice that Alex had moved in front of me. He grabbed my chin, bringing my eyes to his. "I've got you, Hermosa. Don't let your thoughts win. We're in this together, okay?" His voice was soft and soothing like he was comforting a wounded animal.

My lips curled up as a flash of anger rushed through me, and I slapped his hand away. "I don't need your pity."

The color drained from his face as his mouth fell open. He looked like he was hunting for the words that would fix this situation, and I immediately regretted my moment of rage. "I wasn't pitying you."

"Sorry," I whispered, "I don't think I'm ready to be touched yet."

"No, I'm sorry. I shouldn't have grabbed your chin like that. I'm such an idiot." He stood up, starting to collect his things.

I shook my head, not wanting Alex to leave just yet. I couldn't explain it, but I just needed him to stay a little longer. So, I reached up from the floor and grabbed his hand, making him turn to look at me. "Stay," I whispered, my voice barely above a breath. My fingers intertwined with his, hoping he would understand that I wasn't ready to be alone yet.

He didn't ask any questions; he just nodded and settled back down next to me. We continued to watch a few more episodes, but there was an awkwardness between us now. He was more careful about leaning too close to me, and I found myself missing the warmth of his skin against mine.

As the night grew late, Alex got up to leave, giving me a warm goodbye. I knew he was going to leave without a hug. And even though I wanted him to hold me, I couldn't bring myself to ask. Maybe it was too soon, and maybe I wasn't ready yet. All I knew was that I was grateful for his company, and I hoped that he would stay in my life a little while longer.

Chapter 17

Mel

    The following two weeks went by quickly. I worked most days and went to the gym when I got out. Ever since I started my new routine, I've been feeling so much better. It's amazing how much a change of scenery can do for your mood. With my work training finally complete, my new schedule was about to start. *Thank god!* I didn't think I could wake up that early one more day.

    Today was January 20th, my twenty-fourth birthday. In light of that, I decided to skip the gym today and go straight home. There was a comfy bed waiting for me, just begging me to rest in her comfy arms. *Is my bed a girl? Is it weird if it's a boy? Maybe I should get one of those anime body pillows. Then things could really get weird.* I started laughing at my own jokes as I headed home from work.

Walking back to my apartment, I passed the gym with its blacked-out windows. I felt a little guilty for missing my self-defense class. My head hung in shame, and my steps slowed down. Making the final turn toward my apartment, my thoughts drifted toward my dreams and Jelaria. When I was working out at the gym, I felt like Klein was training for a heist. I felt stronger—like the next time someone tried to hurt me, I would be able to stand on my own.

Alex had met me for lunch every day without fail, and it was nice to have someone reliable in my life. My first check had already come and gone, spent on necessities. My apartment now had plates and dishes—like I was a normal person or something. There was a small round table and two chairs, making my apartment much more homey. I was able to buy them from a thrift store that Alex had helped me find. He had even taken care of setting them up for me. *I really don't deserve his kindness.*

Ever since the night he came over, Alex had been more cautious with his touches—always asking for my consent before leaning in for hugs. It was sweet and made me feel comfortable, but I found myself ready for a little more. Had anyone ever asked for my consent before? As an escort, I suppose it was just implied that I was consenting, for a price, of course.

My thoughts took a dark turn towards Harvey. Since Alex had blocked his number, I hadn't received any more texts or calls from him. Jess would let me know when Harvey came to the club looking for me, but it seemed like he finally got the hint that I was gone.

Poor Jess needed to get out of there, too, but I wasn't going to fight her on it. She was a big girl and could make her own life choices.

It was my birthday, but I didn't have any plans to go out. Jess had sent me a text this morning letting me know she wouldn't be able to see me because of work, which was a bummer. But it's not like I ever did anything special for my birthday anyway. The only thing I wanted for my birthday was to get my dream world back. The last few weeks, it felt like Jelaria was being wiped from my memory. When I woke up, I would only remember bits and pieces—a scrap of white cloth blowing in the breeze, hills of rolling sand. It was frustrating, to say the least. Just sand, sand, and more sand. It almost felt like, now that my life was coming together, I didn't need the dreams as much. Some days, I couldn't even remember half of what happened in them. At least I had Alex to distract me.

With a heavy sigh, I opened my apartment door and flicked on the lights.

"Surprise!" The sound of my friends' voices was all around me. As I looked around, blinking back my tears, I saw Jess, Amber, and Alex. My small room was decorated with purple and green streamers. There was a small cake and presents on my little table.

"You guys! You didn't have to do this!" I gushed, rushing to give Amber a tight hug. "I thought I'd never see you again!"

"Yeah. Well, a certain red-haired someone wouldn't leave my thoughts, so I had to come back. Besides, why would I miss you getting older? What are you now, like thirty?" She said with a laugh.

Jess's cheeks were pink as she gave me a hug after Amber. "Amber has been texting me all week, helping me plan this." Jess said.

"I'm glad you're back. But what about your family?"

"Oh, I'm just here for a couple of days," Amber told me, glancing over at Jess. They were so in love, it was adorable. Hopefully, they would find a way to make it work somehow.

"Well, I'm so glad you made it!" I said, with a huge smile on my face.

Next, I went to greet Alex. He was wearing a silly party hat, messing up his curly black hair. Deciding *what the hell,* I gave him a huge hug, too. His strong arms wrapped around me, and a feeling of contentment came over me. His warm breath brushed my ear as he said, "Happy birthday, Hermosa." Butterflies were doing a happy dance in my stomach at his words. I looked up what it meant the other day, and it basically means beautiful. And I was okay with being called that.

"Who wants cake!" I exclaimed as I pulled away. "Please don't sing! I've heard it before, and I really can't afford new windows if you break them!"

"Ouch! My singing isn't that bad!" Jess laughed, wincing a little. Amber pat her on the shoulder with a grin. We had all gone out to karaoke in the past, and Jess was more than a little tone-deaf.

The cake sat on the table like a work of art—a masterpiece crafted with a buttery yellow sponge dotted with juicy raspberries and creamy white chocolate swirls. The aroma of baked goodness wafted through the air, teasing my taste buds with its tempting scent. I served myself a large portion. As I took a bite, the flavors exploded in my mouth, a perfect balance of sweetness and tanginess that sent shivers down my spine. It was so good that I almost regretted having to share it with my friends. With only two chairs, we all sat on the floor to eat our cake slices, not wanting to be rude, and take the only seats.

Alex had set up a little speaker to play music, and we took turns picking songs. Jess and Amber had brought a couple of bottles of wine and plastic cups, which they passed around. "We weren't sure what kind of cups you had," Jess explained with a laugh. "And this way, you won't have to do any dishes!" She had been teasing me about my sparse collection of kitchenware since she came over last week, and I couldn't help but grin at her mischievousness.

"Hey, I said I bought dishes; that didn't mean wine glasses. Those are for rich people!" I joked back, taking one of the cups and pouring myself some moscato. "At least I have a wine bottle opener, okay? That has to count for something."

Jess's head fell back as she laughed, her red locks tumbling down her back. Amber came over to check on us. "What's going on over here?" she asked with a smile.

Giving her a withering look, I turned to Amber. "Nothing, just Jess is teasing me like usual."

After a few glasses, we were all singing loudly and having a great time. We even convinced Jess to belt out a song for us. It wasn't as bad as I remembered, but maybe that was all the wine talking. I knew I'd have to apologize to Lucia later for all the noise we were making—but hey, you only turn twenty-four once.

Jess and Amber were dancing together and whispering under their breath. Things were getting hot and heavy between them, and I was beginning to wonder if I was going to have to kick them out soon. Before things could go any further, Jess abruptly turned to me with excitement in her eyes. "Presents!" she exclaimed, breaking away from Amber, who shot her a longing glance. They needed to sort out their feelings for each other.

"Open this one first!" Jess handed me a large, heavy box. "Me and Amber pitched in to get you this. It's like a birthday-housewarming present."

I eagerly tore off the pink wrapping paper to reveal a 24-inch TV. "This is too much!" I protested, feeling overwhelmed by their generosity. It was the most expensive gift I had ever received.

Jess stumbled over her words as she waved a dismissive hand at my protest, her speech slurred from the wine. "Oh, just shut up and say thank you!"

"How can she shut up and also say thank you?" Amber chuckled, patting Jess on the thigh.

Jess scowled, flipping her the finger. The gesture might have been more effective if she hadn't lost her balance and fallen forward, pressing her hand to Amber's lips. Amber immediately leaned in, taking the offending finger in her mouth and giving Jess a heated look that caused a blush to rise on her cheeks.

Ignoring them, I turned to Alex, who was holding a gift bag and looking shy. "It's not a TV or anything, but I hope you like it."

"You didn't have to get me anything," I protested again, feeling a bit embarrassed at how much they had all spent on me.

But Alex just smiled and said, "I wanted to." I pulled out a t-shirt with all the main characters from my favorite Ramen anime on it. It was the perfect size, and I held it up to my body, grinning. "Thanks, Alex, I love it!"

"There's one more thing in there." He reached into the bag and pulled out a couple of manga novels with a girl in a sailor costume on the cover. "I thought you might like these. They're some of my favorites."

I flipped through the pages, intrigued by the storyline. "I've never seen these before, but they look really cool. Thanks, Alex!" The cover had a girl with two buns in her hair and a fierce look on her face. Above her was a little text bubble that read, 'In the name of the celestial body in the sky, I will punish you!'.

"It was my sister's favorite too. It's a little cheesy, but it's good. I read the whole thing after she... you know."

Bringing them to my chest, I told him, "Then, I'll be sure to read every single one." He gave me a warm smile, and as I turned to see what the girls were up to, I found them making out on my bed. *Oh no! Not my bed.*

"Amber! Jess!" I shouted at them. "I think it's time for this party to end!"

They laughed as they got up—their lipstick smeared and hair disheveled. "We were just about to call for a car! Don't worry, girl. I'm sure you want some alone time with your boyfriend!" Jess winked at me as she pulled her phone out to order a car from the app.

"I'm not... we're not..." I stuttered. She ignored me, still looking at her phone.

Alex looked just as embarrassed as me, waiting in awkward silence for the car to come to pick them up. Luckily, it came quickly. Jess and Amber departed, arms interlocked and supporting each other as they made their way to the car. Amber promised she would text me when they made it to the hotel where she was staying for the weekend.

I looked at Alex, hoping the boyfriend comment didn't scare him off. "Want another drink?" I asked, but before he could answer, there was a knock at the door. "Maybe they forgot something," I said, heading to answer the door. Looking through the peephole, I didn't see anyone. "Maybe it was just the wind or a stray cat?" I opened the door to check, but again, nothing.

As I went to close the door, I noticed a box on the ground. Picking it up cautiously, I brought it inside and placed it on the table. The wrapping paper covering the small box looked expensive, and I had no idea who would send me a gift like this in the middle of the night.

"Someone bring you a gift?" Alex asked from over my shoulder.

My hands trembled as I read the gift tag. It said, 'For my princess' in fancy cursive. It didn't say who it was from, but I knew. Opening the box, I found a golden collar and immediately threw the whole thing away from me. Suddenly, I was on the ground, hyperventilating and unable to catch my breath. Bile coated my mouth as I brought a hand up to my neck. I was back in that room, fighting for my life. My heart pounded, and my muscles went rigid as I prepared to die.

A hand touched my shoulder, and I let out a primal scream. But when I looked up, instead of seeing Harvey, I saw Alex. As I realized I wasn't actually in danger, my body curled in on itself, and tears broke through my eyelids. So many apologies were stuck inside.

"What do you need me to do? Should I call someone?" Alex asked softly, his eyebrows drawn together. He was being careful not to touch me, and I hated that. I hated being seen like this—like a weak little girl. I hadn't been her in a long time.

He leaned down close to me, bringing his face to mine. "Look at me, Mel. Tell me what to do."

My emotions were all over the place. I was angry at myself for letting Harvey have any power over me, but I also couldn't seem to stop my body from reacting. Being alone right now wasn't an option, so I said the only thing I could. "Can you please stay tonight?" My voice shook, and I pressed my lips together to try and steady them. Wiping my face with my hands, I was determined not to let another tear fall.

He extended his hand towards me, and my entire body flinched involuntarily. He noticed my reaction and withdrew it immediately, and his lips pursed with concern. "Can I help you up?" he asked in a soft voice. I nodded, lifting my hand, and he reached out to help me stand up. He led me to the bed and gently helped me sit down before turning around to go to the kitchenette. I watched as he got a glass of water from the sink and handed it to me when he was done. Taking a sip, I tried to gather my thoughts, unsure of what to say or do next.

I looked up at Alex, who was still standing in front of me, looking like he wanted to say something but didn't know how. I tried to crack a smile. "Some party, huh?" I attempted to sound casual, but the rasp in my voice gave away my true feelings. I patted the bed beside me and offered him a seat, but he sat down hesitantly, not moving too close. "I'm not a china doll, so please stop treating me like I'm about to break," I growled.

"I'm sorry," he breathed as he scooted closer, bringing his hand to my back and rubbing slow, soothing circles. "I just want to make sure you're comfortable." I leaned into his touch, feeling his warmth and the safety of his presence. I dragged my eyes up his body, and I could see his pulse racing fast at his throat as he swallowed. How could this man care so much about me? How can he treat me like...like I'm not just a body he can use however he pleases.

Bringing my hand to his face, I smoothed out the line of concern marking his forehead. "Let's just go to bed," I whispered, wanting this nightmare to be over. "I don't want to talk about it." My body was exhausted, and my mind was spinning with the memories of what had just happened. I didn't know how to process it all, and I didn't want to burden Alex with my problems. All I wanted was to forget and find some solace in sleep.

He nodded and took the cup from my hand, setting it down in the sink before turning off the lights. As I moved to the top of the bed, I snuggled under the covers, leaving room for him on my left. I couldn't help but feel apprehensive—I had never just slept next to someone like this before. Usually, they just left after they were done with me. Alex seemed hesitant at first before moving to his side of the bed and sliding under the covers.

We both kept our clothes on from the party—my clothes were soft, but he was in jeans. That couldn't have been comfortable to sleep in, but he didn't complain, keeping everything in place. Needing the comfort of his arms, I glided my body closer to his, moving my head to his broad chest and wrapping my arms around him. His arms came down to pull me closer, and he began to touch my hair, fingers combing through the short pink strands. It felt so nice that I could have purred like a cat.

A content sigh left me, and I snuggled closer, wrapping my legs around his. Warm breath tickled my skin, and the sound of his heartbeat filled my ears. We stayed like this until sleep found us. Not once did he make a move to make this into something sexual—all he offered me was the comfort I needed. And as all the tension left my body, my mind drifted off to sleep, more relaxed than I had been in a long time.

At that moment, I couldn't help but feel grateful for Alex's presence. It was the first time I had ever been held without expectations, without the fear of being used for someone else's pleasure. I felt safe and loved, and I never wanted this feeling to end. It was the first time in a long time that I had felt hope that maybe things could get better, that maybe I deserved better. And as I drifted off to sleep, I knew that I wanted to hold on to that hope, to hold on to Alex and the peace that being in his arms had brought me.

Chapter 18

Jelaria

Klein and Mystic had been riding through the unforgiving desert for over a week—their once confident stride now replaced by weary trudging. The sun beat down relentlessly, leaving their skin parched and cracked. Klein's throat was so dry that even swallowing hurt. He couldn't remember the last time they had a decent meal or even a drop of water. They were running on fumes, and it seemed like the endless expanse of sand would be their final resting place.

Mystic broke the oppressive silence with a bitter curse, "These damn lizards were supposed to know how to navigate this shit storm. Maybe the ones we stole are duds."

Klein scowled, his eyes flickering over the bleak landscape as he tried to think of a plan. They had long ago depleted their supplies, and if it weren't for his ice magic, they would have surely perished by now. The magic took a toll on him, sapping his strength with every use, but it was their only lifeline in this burning wasteland—the only thing keeping them from succumbing to the intense heat. Klein had to be careful not to use too much, or they'd run out of water even faster. Klein had been filling their canteens repeatedly, but with no food, it was hard to summon the energy for anything else.

A frustrated groan escaped him as sweat poured down his face. He wiped his forehead, leaving a trail of sand and grime on his skin. The city of Litha was their only hope, but it seemed to be nothing more than a mirage. Klein wondered if they were better off giving up, succumbing to the desert's merciless embrace.

"We need to keep going straight," Mystic said, pointing to the horizon. The endless expanse of sand stretched before them, red grains glistening in the harsh sun. "It's our best shot at finding the city."

"And how do you know that," Klein grunted in response, his patience long gone. He was itching for a fight, a release for his pent-up frustration. His stomach growled, reminding him of their desperate situation. If they didn't find something to sustain them soon, he knew he would snap.

Mystic's voice was laced with confidence as she spoke, "I just do. Let me take the lead. You can trust me!" Her drake, a sleek and nimble creature, let out a huff of protest at the sudden change of direction. Its eyes flickered with uncertainty, but it eventually complied with her orders. Klein scowled, still feeling doubtful, but he had no better plan to offer. He moved his own drake, a larger and more menacing beast, to follow slightly behind Mystic's. Despite its imposing appearance, it seemed to be no match for the speed and agility of Mystic's drake.

The red sands stretched out endlessly before them, the only relief from the scorching heat being occasional outcroppings of jagged rock. The blazing sun beat down on Klein's skin, causing sweat to ooze down his back in sticky rivulets.

If someone caught them now, they'd be well and truly screwed. The thought gnawed at Klein, filling him with a sense of dread that he couldn't shake off. He glanced at Mystic, who was leading them through the desert with confidence. Despite her words of assurance, Klein couldn't help but wonder if they were following the right path. The red sands seemed to stretch on forever, and Klein couldn't shake the feeling that they were going around in circles.

If only they had someone else with them—someone with fire magic who could burn the lifeless bodies of the Ostara thieves they'd stolen the drakes from and left to rot. If the bodies were turned to ash, he wouldn't have to worry about being caught. But Klein was a greedy male, and he couldn't stand the thought of sharing the bounty with anyone else—especially someone like Stella. As the days passed, Klein's resolve began to waver, and he started to wonder if his greed had led them down the path of no return.

Mystic kept her eyes on some distant point, keeping the drake steady following a straight line—at least, Klein hoped it was a straight line. There was nothing out here as far as he could see, and his vision was pretty damn good. But maybe Mystic could see something he couldn't. With neither of them having true sight, it was anyone's guess how she knew her way. However, she did always have an instinct for finding her way out of trouble. Klein hoped this was one of those times and the city would appear on the horizon. Once they got close enough to set their eyes on it, they could release these great beasts of burden and continue on foot to get past the guards.

They passed red sand dunes and sand holes. And that sand pile over there looked like a building at first, but no only sand. Klein was on edge, and he kept his eyes peeled for any threats that may come their way. As the sun began to set, casting the sky in ruby red and purple hues, they saw not a single cloud in the sky. It was beautiful if he had been in a good enough mood to enjoy it—which he wasn't.

Klein's throat was parched, and he took a long drink of water to cool his dry throat. But as he tipped his canteen, only the last drops rolled out. He swallowed them down with a sigh when he heard a deep rumble coming from the sand behind him. Something was wrong. Turning to Mystic, he could see that she had noticed as well, her eyes widening in panic as she looked back. Even the drakes could sense something was amiss and had started to pick up the pace, kicking sand out from under their feet. Their low growls sounded panicked, and their breaths came fast.

The rumble grew louder now. "We need to move faster," Klein said in a rough whisper, kicking his heels into the drake's leathery hide.

There were dangers in the desert that lurked in the sand, and if they had stayed close to the common trails, they would have been protected by the underground wards. However, they had strayed too far and were now vulnerable to the creatures that roamed free. They urged their drakes to pick up the pace, but it was no use—as they heard the sound of sand breaking behind them. A blood-curdling roar echoed through the desert, and Klein felt his heart drop as he recognized the sound. It was a creature from his worst nightmares, a predator that haunted these lands.

Klein slapped himself hard to stop the panic from rising. He could taste the blood in his mouth where he had cut his lip on his canine. "Don't look back!" he rasped, urging his drake to go faster.

Mystic nodded her head, her breathing coming out in quick gasps. "What is that thing?" she asked, her eyes filled with terror. She kept her focus on her drake, which was bucking and foaming at the mouth in panic. She could barely hold on.

Klein felt the pressure in the air increasing, and he knew they were in grave danger. He concentrated all his energy on building up his magic, focusing on creating a shield over their skin. He had a plan forming in his mind, but it was a last resort. The last time he had used it on Mystic, she had ended up with frostbite and had to pay a healer to recover. It was an extremely painful spell, but it was better than being dead. He hoped he had enough magic left to pull it off.

Mystic's drake suddenly moved, causing her head covering to come off, flying behind her like a cloud of white smoke. She turned to look back, her eyes widening as she took in the creature that was now hot on their heels. "Is that a lightning wyrm?" she cried, her voice trembling with fear.

Klein's breath turned icy as he focused on the shield, feeling the magic building up within him. He heard Mystic gasp as the sudden drop in temperature spread through their bodies. The ice began to form, crystal clear and hard as steel, covering their skin in a protective layer. It was a difficult spell to cast on two people at once, but it was their only chance. Klein grunted with the strain of using so much magic; his mind focused on finishing the shield just in time.

A deafening roar shattered the stillness behind them, signaling the approach of their doom. Lightning flashed across the sky, illuminating the terrified drakes as they reared up and hissed in panic. A dome of blue light encased Klein and Mystic, and he could feel his hair trying to stand on end, the static energy building up around them. But the ice shield was holding it down—for now.

With a tremendous boom, Klein was thrown from his drake. Blinded by the attack, he hit the ground hard, his body aching but still alive. The shield had cracked and wouldn't withstand another blast like that. His heart pounded in his chest as he shouted out for his sister, desperation filling his voice. He feared he had failed her and that they would both die in this wasteland.

A voice whispered back to him, "Here!" He turned towards the sound, relief flooding through him as he saw Mystic still alive. As his vision cleared, he took in the carnage around him. The drakes were in ruins, their bodies torn apart and smoldering. The lightning wyrm, its attention fixed on its latest meal, gleamed with an ethereal blue light. Its scales shimmered in the lightning flashes, iridescent and mesmerizing. Its eyes emitted a radiant yellow glow, and its wings crackled with the power of electricity. Its long, slender body, coiled and uncoiled, ready to unleash bolts of lightning upon its next victim.

When Klein got close enough to Mystic to see her, aside from the redness on her flesh from the ice shield, she was unharmed. "Shift!" Klein demanded of her, and she immediately complied. They both transformed into their animal forms, with Mystic clinging to Klein's body in despair. They hoped to outrun the creature while it was distracted. She wrapped her body around his, and Klein took off in a sprint. He felt the wind pushing them from behind, with Mystic's power working to make them move as fast as possible.

Klein's paws moved at blinding speeds, taking them as far away as they could get. Their only hope was to cross the wards, where they knew it couldn't follow. The pressure lessened around them the further away they got, and just when Klein thought they were in the clear, the sound of breaking sand startled him. Mystic's grip on his neck tightened a little as they heard an angry roar from the creature. But Klein didn't stop; he forced his feet to keep moving even as they felt like they wanted to fall off. He just kept breathing in and out, trying to bring as much oxygen to his muscles as possible. Mystic's magic was helping to keep them moving. They had to keep moving. In the distance, Klein could see one of the glowing stones marking the path.

His fur stood on end from the electricity in the air, and he just knew that the wyrm was about to fry them. They were closing in on the marker for the wards, so Klein started to believe they might make it. With one final dash, Klein's paws moved them past the glowing stones. The wyrm let out a blast of lightning, but it was too late to reach them. Sparks hit the wards, and an invisible wall now sent the lightning into the sky to dissipate. The wyrm paced back and forth along the wards, looking for an entrance. Unable to find one, it finally left with a frustrated huff, sending one last spark at them before it went.

Collapsing onto the ground, Klein's breath came in ragged gasps as he struggled to catch his breath. With great effort, he shifted back into his Fae form and looked up at Mystic, who appeared much more composed in her snake form. "So sure that was the right direction, were you?" he grumbled, still winded from their mad dash through the desert.

Mystic transformed back, looking fresh and vibrant compared to Klein's worn-out appearance. "It was the right way, I'll have you know," she said, pointing behind Klein.

He turned his head, his eyes shifting to the color of white silver to see better. In the distance, the lights of the town of Litha shimmered in the dark. "Lucky guess," he muttered.

"Nope, call it serpent's intuition," Mystic replied, tapping her temple.

"Sure, sure, let's just get to the town. I need a meal and a hot shower, or I'm going to kill everyone in a ten-mile radius," Klein said, only half-joking. He knew he was in no condition to cause harm to anyone, even if he had the magical ability to do so.

Mystic let out a teasing laugh. "Always so dramatic! Fine. Let's go, but I get the shower first."

As they entered the town of Litha, they were immediately struck by the striking red sandstone buildings that loomed over them. The city was laced with waterways and canals, adding to its serene, oasis-like atmosphere. Overhead, date trees and towering palms provided ample shade, offering a welcome respite from the unforgiving desert.

Finding an inn with a large bathhouse was no problem, and they decided to stay for the night. After purchasing provisions and taking some much-needed rest, they had no real reason to stay in Litha and hoped to be gone by the next evening.

Mystic headed to the bathhouse first, eager to wash off the sweat and dirt that had accumulated during their journey. The bathhouse was a sight to behold, with intricate carvings and mosaics covering the walls and ceilings. The air was thick with the scent of exotic oils and perfumes, and the sound of running water was a constant background hum.

Meanwhile, Klein stayed behind to order food for them. The inn's menu was a feast for the senses, with the aroma of spices and the sight of colorful fruits and vegetables making his mouth water.

He decided on a hearty curry dish with plenty of rice and a selection of fruits for dessert. The innkeeper promised to have it delivered to their room promptly.

While Klein waited for the food, he took the opportunity to explore their new lodging. The room was well-appointed, providing a clear improvement over the previous inn. The beds were large, and the walls and floors were constructed of red sandstone, creating a warm and inviting atmosphere. The blue and green hand-woven rug added a touch of color and texture to the floor. The table and chairs offer a practical space for dining or completing tasks. At the same time, the curtains on the large window are sturdy and lined, effectively blocking out the intense heat of the surrounding desert and creating a serene and comfortable refuge from the scorching outside conditions.

There was the quiet sound of rushing water coming from the walls, and as Klein leaned in to check them more closely, he found them cool to the touch. The plumbing in this town was second to none—using modern systems to keep the building cool while also allowing for extravagant bath houses. With the sand getting everywhere, it was more of a necessity here than anywhere else. There was a white bathing robe waiting for Klein on his bed.

Just as Klein was settling in, Mystic returned to the room, looking refreshed and revitalized. Her hair was blowing around her face as she used her air magic to dry it. Klein couldn't help but feel a little envious of her powers at that movement. "That was wonderful!

You need to try it," she said, perching on the bedside table. The brass legs scraped against the hard stone floor.

The food still hadn't arrived, so Klein decided to take his turn at the bathhouse, leaving Mystic to wait in the room. The building had both outdoor and indoor baths, as well as private bathing pools for an extra charge. If this were a vacation, Klein might have considered spending the gold, but not today. "I'll be back soon," he said as he walked out the door.

There were free showers near the entrance to the outdoor baths, separate for males and females. Walking in, Klein found a small changing room with sandstone shelves carved right into the red walls. Each shelf had woven wicker baskets to store clothing. Being leery about leaving his weapons, Klein took one of the baskets and put all his things into it. He took it with him around the corner to the next chamber.

Inside this room was a line of brass shower heads and drains on the floor. There was no real separation between the shower stalls besides small half-walls between each one. The Fae weren't shy about nudity, and open-air bathhouses were normal around Litha. But being naked left you vulnerable, and Klein despised feeling that way. Luckily, it was late at night, and there was no one else in there with him.

Taking his time, Klein washed off all the dirt and grime he had collected while traveling through the unforgiving desert. The water stung his skin as he scrubbed. He used the provided soaps they had on the half-walls, small square bars that suds up easily. The scents were mild and made for a Fae's sensitive nose, only smelling clean. It was a nice touch for the guests that Klein was thankful for. Being able to shift into a wolf had left him with senses stronger than most, and strong scents were almost painful for him to be around.

After getting clean and dressing back in his traveling clothes, Klein returned to the room where the food had finally arrived. A variety of dishes, each one aromatic and inviting, were arranged on platters of gleaming brass. As he took a seat, the smell of exotic spices and sweet fruits filled the room, and his stomach gave a loud rumble of appreciation. Mystic had the food set out on the round wooden table and had already demolished her portion and was eyeing Klein's as well.

"Don't even think about it," he scolded her as she pouted. She had a bad habit of eating his food if he wasn't around.

She tilted her head innocently. "I wasn't going to eat it. I just wanted to check it for poison."

"Mmmhmm, sure," Klein said with a contented sigh as he savored the taste of the rabbit curry. The dish was a mild blend of spices and vegetables, including potatoes and carrots, served over a bed of fluffy brown rice. Despite his aversion to spicy foods, Klein found the flavor to be just right and ate with gusto, fueling his body after long days of harsh travel. He was careful to pace himself, not wanting to eat too much too quickly. As he ate, he passed the fruit on to Mystic, who was more than happy to oblige. The fruit was a little too sweet for Klein's taste, but he was grateful for the nourishment all the same.

Clean and well-fed, they went to lie down on their beds for the night. The mattress was on the firm side, and the blankets were rough and scratchy. He couldn't help but feel slightly disappointed after the delicious meal and the luxurious shower, but he knew it was still a better option than sleeping on the ground outside. His eyes started to feel heavy with exhaustion, and he reached over to turn off the standing lamp. Mystic, who had taken the first watch, settled into a comfortable position, ready to keep watch throughout the night. Despite the discomfort, Klein felt grateful to have a roof over his head and a safe place to rest for the night. He closed his eyes and let himself drift off into a deep slumber.

As Klein began to drift off, he could feel a presence in the back of his mind watching him. *Back at last,* he thought. But as always, there was no response.

The next morning, Klein and Mystic navigated through the bustling streets of Litha and were struck by the energy of the town during the day. The streets were lined with vendors selling an array of goods, ranging from spices and fabrics to jewelry and trinkets. They recognized some of the vendors from the markets in Celetrix and were pleasantly surprised to see the familiar faces in this desert oasis. The heat was bearable, thanks to the numerous fountains that provided refreshing mist throughout the city. With all the water features, one might think the people of Litha would be gifted with the power of water. Klein was sure there were some water elementals living here. However, Litha predominantly had the power of fire. Water belonged to winter, along with the ice that Klein was blessed with.

As that thought came to him, Klein saw a group of fire dancers performing in the square. They used their power to send colorful flames to circle their bodies as they danced. They wore airy clothes that displayed their exposed skin at the navel, and as they moved, the fabric's hidden slits showed off flashes of dark skin. One of the dancers, who seemed particularly skilled, caught Klein's attention. She weaved her flame through her fingers and hair, unafraid of burning herself.

Klein watched as the fire dancer effortlessly manipulated the flames, creating patterns and shapes that seemed almost alive. Her movements were graceful and fluid as if she was dancing with the fire instead of controlling it. The heat from the flames was intense, but she seemed completely unaffected. Her exposed skin glistened with sweat, but it was the fire that stole the show. The onlookers were mesmerized, watching in awe as she danced to the rhythm of an unseen beat. He couldn't help but feel a sense of respect for her mastery of her magic. It took a lot of discipline and practice to control one's power, especially fire. It was a dangerous element, but in the hands of someone like the fire dancer, it was a beautiful thing.

The female dancer wore a band of lilac fabric around her chest, and her pants were made of the same color, folded back to allow for ease of movement. Her dark hair was styled in two long braids, adorned with silver ribbons and bells that jingled with her movement. Her outfit allowed glimpses of her alluring brown skin to show through as she danced. The flames she wielded were blue and gave off intense heat, which Klein could feel even from where he was standing.

Noticing his attention, her eyes lifted to meet his. They were a deep blue, almost purple in color. Licking her lips, she lifted a hand to beckon him closer, tempting him into a dance with fire. He almost went with her when he felt the presence in the back of his mind let out a burst of anger. Was it jealous of the female he was looking at, he wondered. Thus far, he had rarely felt such a strong emotion come from it.

"Should we stay an extra day in the city?" Mystic purred from Klein's side. "She looks willing enough; just don't make her mad, or she might burn off your balls!"

Giving her a dry look, Klein deadpanned, "My balls and I would be just fine, but thanks for your concern. Let's just get what we need and get out of here."

She rolled her eyes. "Well, maybe spending a night with her would lighten up your bad attitude. We're on an adventure! Shouldn't you be excited or at least not look so solemn? I swear, you'd think we were marching to our deaths!"

"You do realize we're probably going to be killed for this?" he replied with deadly seriousness.

"Only if we get caught!" she retorted, smiling with all the confidence in the world as if they hadn't been almost eaten by a wyrm the night before. They continued through the town, looking for the supplies they needed before moving on.

The buildings were all made of the same red stone but were decorated with pops of color everywhere—flat roofs with building after building stacked high, though not as high as the castle of Litha in the middle of it all. They avoided it like the plague, not wanting to be noticed by anyone important, as had happened in Mabon.

Deep purple and yellow flags hung across the walls, fluttering above the walkways. The Fae here were cloaked in bright fabrics in jewel tones that brought the city to life. Their white and tan clothes, perfect for traveling in the heat, made them stand out as not belonging here, as if their coloring didn't do that enough. The people of Litha had rich, dark brown skin in varying shades from pitch black to honey. Their hair and eyes were the same, making the people from other parts of the continent obvious. They weren't the only ones who looked out of place, as Klein saw several Ostara Fae shopping in the market.

They bought all the supplies they needed, ready to brave the sandy desert once more. If they stayed on the correct track this time, they should arrive at the edges of Spring in a few days. Besides the two thugs they encountered at the border town, the Fae here seemed pleasant and happy. The kingdom of the Seelie tended to be the light to Unseelie's dark, although with the more modern times, they were living in, that divide wasn't as great as it once was. They were no longer at war with each other and were living in relative harmony.

Klein and Mystic had both purchased new outfits made from the same cotton fabric that was popular in these parts. Their old clothes had been torn and dirty from their first trip through the sands. The cost of the job had slowly risen, and Klein had kept a tally in his mind to keep track of it all. Mystic had found a new pair of jeweled slippers in jade green that she had wanted to buy, but Klein had turned her down with a stern look. He had told her that if they were successful in completing their job, they could get them on the way back. Hopefully, she would forget about them by then—but that was very unlikely.

As they walked around Litha, Klein had seen signs of the Church there. He didn't know their reach had stretched this far. A small temple of red sand inlaid with crystals—a place of worship that, while beautiful, had left him feeling disturbed at some of their practices. Ignoring the priestess in her long flowing robes handing out pamphlets, they had made their way out of the oasis town. They had walked the rest of the way on foot, not wanting to push their luck like they had at the last place.

The guard had let them pass without any issues, more concerned about those coming in than those leaving—more fools to them. The sun had still been high overhead, and Klein had kept his face cloth wrapped up tight to protect his skin from the rays. They had traveled in their fae forms until nightfall when they had been free to run in animal form. The transformation had been rare enough that they hadn't wanted anyone to recognize them. Klein hadn't wasted any magic keeping themselves cool, not wanting to run out if they had run into any other nasty surprises.

Noticing the frown on Klein's face, Mystic had turned to him. "Are you ever going to let me live it down? How was I supposed to know there was a lightning wyrm out there in the sand!"

"Not let it go? Mystic that lightning wyrm could have killed us," Klein replied with a deep sigh, still clearly annoyed by the close call.

"I know, I know," Mystic said, her voice slightly apologetic. "But you have to admit, it was pretty exciting, right?"

Klein just gave her a look and continued to move forward through the sand, not wanting to entertain her antics any further. Mystic could be impulsive and reckless at times, but Klein knew it was because of her that they ended up in the right place.

As they traveled in silence, Klein kept a mental tally of their progress and expenses while Mystic occasionally pointed out interesting sights and sounds along the way.

Finally, nightfall came, and Klein was able to transform into a wolf under the cover of darkness. They moved quickly and quietly through the sand, Kleins senses heightened in his animal form.

After a few hours of travel, they stopped to rest, and Mystic burrowed herself into Klein's fur for comfort. As they slept, the stars and the presence like a butterfly watched over them. Klein couldn't help but wonder what other dangers lay ahead on their journey.

Chapter 19

Mel

The next day, I slowly opened my eyes, feeling the warmth of a body next to me. For a split second, I panicked, but then the memories flooded back. Alex had stayed with me last night. As I tried to shake off the sleep, my dreams from the previous night came back to me, still a little blurry—but one moment stood out more than the others: the flame dancer. A groan escaped my lips as I thought about how jealous I had gotten in the dream of the Fae who had been looking at Klein with heated desire.

I must have made an audible noise because Alex rolled over to look at me. His brown eyes met mine, and a sleepy smile spread across his lips. "Good morning, Hermosa. Did you sleep okay?" he asked.

"Yeah, I did. Thanks for staying with me. That was one of the best nights of sleep I've had in a long time," I replied, stretching my body and making a happy noise. "I wish you could hold me to sleep every night," I blurted out before I could think, immediately feeling embarrassed. "Sorry, I didn't mean to imply that you should stay here from now on."

Alex's expression softened. "I've been trying to figure out what to do myself," he said, his voice tinged with sadness. "I don't want you staying by yourself now that he knows where you live. And, well, I like holding you too."

I smiled at him, feeling a little less embarrassed. "Thanks, Alex. I appreciate it. Maybe Jess could stay with me. Or you could take turns?" I asked, not wanting to impose on him any more than I already had. Jess worked late on the weekends, though, so it was slim that she was going to be able to stay here.

"We can talk about it tonight." He said, getting up from the bed and doing some stretches of his own. "For now, let me make you some breakfast, and maybe we could do a quick workout?" He asked, giving me a hopeful look.

Laughing, I told him, "Yeah, I'd like that."

The morning was shaping up to be a good one. Alex had made a breakfast of eggs and potatoes. I made a mental note to stock up on breakfast meats if he was going to cook for me regularly. After eating, we did a bodyweight workout where he taught me how to throw a punch with my whole body and the best places to kick a man, including the solar plexus and the insole of his foot—of course, the balls, too. Alex then had to leave for work, leaving me alone to get ready.

I refused to give in to fear and instead put on dark makeup like war paint, smoky black eyes, and red lips to give me the strength to face the day. I knew my stalker now knew where I lived, but I wouldn't let some sad man scare me again. Putting on my uniform under my warm coat with a huff of determination, I left for work. It was my first late shift, and I wondered what the crowd would be like. Did people come to coffee shops that late, I wondered?

Walking in the brisk weather, I passed the gym I had been taking classes at. With my new work schedule, I was trying to figure out when to come to the classes. They weren't open twenty-four hours, so my only real option was before work in the mornings. They had a 10 a.m. class that would probably work for me. I hoped it would be the same instructor and not Tammy, as she seemed to have a problem with me, even though I hardly spoke to her.

Making it to work a little early, I spotted Avery working the cash register. She gave me a wave and continued to help the line of customers. It looked like another busy day. Heading to the break room, I used the tablet to clock in and hung my jacket on the silver coat rack. Tonight, Willow would be teaching me how to close out everything and lock up. Avery said that as long as I was good at counting, it should be easy since the register did most of the work. I was feeling confident after weeks of practicing with the coffee machines, and I was no longer spilling drinks all over myself.

The book section of the store was managed by someone else, so I wouldn't have to worry about that. It was a little sad, as some of the books looked interesting. I made a mental note to buy a few for myself, perhaps with my next paycheck after paying rent. I still had to read the books Alex gave me for my birthday, but I had forgotten to bring one with me today.

When I was ready to work, I went behind the counter and started helping Avery fill orders. Looking around, I didn't see any sign of Willow. Avery saw me looking and said, "He's running late... again. Don't worry. He should be here before I have to leave at three!"

"Oh, okay." We continued to work like this until three thirty, with Avery staying late with me so I wouldn't be alone. She didn't complain, but I could see the frustration on her face. Willow was often late, and I knew she was close to firing him if he didn't start showing up on time.

Finally, the man arrived. Willow was recognizable by his short brown hair and bright green eyes. The stubble on his chin indicated a rushed morning or a disregard for personal grooming, likely the latter. With a playful smile, he apologized for his tardiness. "I'm sorry, guys. My dog was feeling under the weather, and then my landlord stopped me on the way," he explained.

"Don't care, Willow! Go clock in. I want to go home," Avery scolded him, used to his excuses by now.

Willow and I worked through the night shift, which seemed very similar to the day shift. As a late-night coffee drinker myself, I shouldn't be surprised. Alex couldn't meet me for my lunch break tonight, saying he had to talk to his dad about something but not elaborating. But he did say he would pick me up when I got out of work, not wanting me to walk in the dark.

After closing out the registers and cleaning up, it was already time to go. Willow asked me to take out the trash bags on my way out. Dragging the heavy black bags out into the alley where the dumpster was, I heaved them into the big green cans, almost dumping one of the bags on myself. *Thanks, Willow.*

As I was turning to leave, a very soft sound caught my attention. It sounded like meowing. I searched around for a bit but didn't find the source. With my curiosity piqued, I shone my phone's light towards the source of the sound and found a tiny kitten. Glowing eyes shone back at me, and a weak meow came from it.

"Come here, kitty," I called, making little clicking sounds with my tongue. Cautiously, the small kitten emerged, looking scared and wet. It was a black and white tuxedo kitten, shivering in the cold. Reaching out my hand, I let the kitten sniff my fingers. It tentatively approached and gave me a lick. With the kitten's acceptance, I gave it a little scratch behind the ears, causing it to purr loudly. "That's a good kitty. Where is your mommy?" I asked.

The kitten just tilted its head and let out a sad meow. "Oh, she's gone, huh?" I said sympathetically. "Okay, let's get you warmed up." Picking up the kitten, I tucked it into my coat. Maybe I could take it to a shelter or something in the morning.

The kitten burrowed into my jacket and purred, sending vibrations through my chest. When I returned to the front of the store, Alex was waiting for me in his car. My phone started vibrating in my pocket, and when I took it out, I saw that he was calling me—probably not realizing that I had gone out through the alleyway. Sneaking up to his window, I let out a "boo!" and opened the door. He didn't jump at all, the brat.

Smiling, he asked, "How was work?" As I was about to answer, the little kitten poked its head out of the collar of my jacket. "Made a new friend, I see," Alex said, letting out a low laugh. "Where did you get that little guy?"

"Yeah, I found him out by the dumpsters. Poor thing must have lost his mother," I replied, giving the kitten some chin scratches. "I couldn't just leave him there. But don't worry, I plan on taking him to the shelter in the morning."

"Okay. Well, I don't think Tía would mind if you kept him. She's pretty lenient when it comes to animals," he said, pulling away from the coffee shop.

"I don't know. I've never had a pet before, and I don't even know how to take care of him," I said uncertainly.

"Cats are easy," Alex scoffed as we drove to my apartment. "Give them food, water, and a litter box, and they're all good!"

His words echoed in my head as I tried to decide what to do. By the time we arrived at my apartment, I had made up my mind. "A trial run!" I declared.

"Trial run?" Alex looked confused.

"Yeah, I'll keep him for now, and if it doesn't work out, I can find him another home." I nodded enthusiastically, hoping that everything would work out.

We entered the apartment, and everything seemed normal. But as Alex hesitated at the threshold, a furrow formed on his brow. "Come in!" I encouraged him.

"Are you sure you wouldn't be happier having Jess stay with you?" he asked, looking unsure.

"She has to work late, and this place is kind of far to try and get here at night. You don't have to stay. I don't think Harvey is going to sneak in through the window while I'm sleeping or something." As I said the words, I shuddered at the thought. *Thanks for that, brain.*

I placed the kitten on the bed, and he started walking in little circles and kneading the blanket, making himself at home. I'd have to take a closer look at him later, but he seemed like a boy to me.

Alex took off his jacket and backpack, leaning them on the chair. "I talked to my dad to let him know I would be staying here for a while. I brought some clothes and stuff. I hope you don't mind."

"Of course, me casa is su casa," I laughed, trying out my rusty Spanish.

"Close enough!" Alex laughed. "I'm just going to get changed, and then maybe we could watch some TV or something."

As he disappeared into the bathroom, I looked down at the kitten. He was already curled up in a little ball, fast asleep. I couldn't help but smile at the sight of him. Maybe taking care of a cat wouldn't be so hard after all.

While Alex was in the bathroom, I quickly changed into my pajamas and set up the TV on the table, positioning it so that it faced the bed. I couldn't wait until the end of the month when one of the other tenants would leave some more furniture behind. I wanted to make the apartment feel more like home and not just a place to crash.

I watched the kitten sleeping on my bed. He needed a name besides "kitten" if he was going to stay with me. While I was pondering on what to call him, Alex burst out of the bathroom, his cheeks red and his mouth opening and closing like a drowning fish. In his hand were my soaking panties. "I'm so sorry," he stuttered. "I was changing, and I hit the shower and, and..."

"Oh my god! Just put them down!" I shrieked, rushing to take the wet panties from him. Grabbing them, I tossed them back into the shower, where they made a wet plop. *How embarrassing!* Clearing my throat, I turned to Alex, who was fidgeting with his T-shirt.

"Let's just pretend that never happened," I said, trying to forget the embarrassing incident. Why was I so weird about him seeing my underwear? Other men had seen me in much, much less. "So, what should we watch? Want to continue Ramen?" I asked, quickly changing the subject. The TV was internet-compatible, and although I didn't have Wi-Fi, I could connect to my phone as a hotspot. Sitting on the bed, I started flipping to the correct show, trying to be careful not to wake Charlie. *Hey, the cat has a name now! Yay!*

We watched several episodes cuddled together, and being with Alex like this was something I could definitely get used to. As I stole glances of his warm brown eyes, I couldn't help the butterflies dancing around in my belly. He hadn't made a move to kiss me yet in all the times we've been together. But I really wanted to know what it would be like with him. Would his kisses be sweet and soft, or would they burn me with their intensity?

Leaning up, I decided that I wanted to find out what it would be like to kiss him. My lips brushed against his, and his eyes widened in surprise as he realized what I was attempting. He lowered his head at the same time, causing our heads to crash together, and my lips landed on his cheek instead. Laughing, I wiped his cheek and grabbed his face with both hands. "Let's try this again," I said in a seductive whisper.

He pulled back, causing my heart to drop. Was I reading the signs wrong? Didn't he like me? "Are you sure?" he asked, his voice low, his eyebrows drawn together with concern. "You've been through a lot, and I don't ever want to pressure you."

"Yes, I want this," I said firmly, drawing him close to me again. Closing my eyes, I brought my lips to his. His kiss was soft and exploring, so gentle. He kept his hands at his sides, but I wanted more from him. I moved his hands to my hips, then brought one of mine up to grip the back of his neck, pressing myself against him and inhaling deeply. He smelled like hot coffee and crisp summer morning air; I could drown in his scent.

Pressing my tongue against the seam of his lips, I asked him to open for me. His tongue met mine in a slow, sensual dance, and I could feel my core heating with the idea of taking this farther. Letting out a soft moan, his hands started exploring above my clothes, brushing up against my breasts, and my nipples hardened under his touch. I wanted to feel him, too. Taking my free hand, I dragged it down his chest, feeling his well-defined muscles. Kickboxing was really paying off for him, and as I found the valley of his abs, he let out a hissed breath.

I could feel his hard length through his sweatpants, but as I reached for it, he stopped me. Placing my hand back on his chest, he drew my eyes to his. "Let's just take things slow, okay, beautiful?" His voice was rough with desire. I could tell he wanted me, but I nodded shyly, my face warm.

Giving me a heated look, he kissed me. I felt my heart skip a beat, and my body ignited with a fiery passion. It was as if he had unlocked a hidden desire within me, urging me to give myself up to him completely. I couldn't resist his touch, and I didn't want to. I wanted to be consumed by him, to feel his every breath on my skin, to be lost in the depths of his love.

As he pulled away, I looked at him, my eyes full of longing and confusion. This was more than just physical attraction. This was a feeling that I had never experienced before, a feeling of being truly loved. He reached out his hand and gently stroked my hair, planting a kiss on my forehead.

At that moment, my heart swelled with emotion. I wanted to give him everything, to be with him forever, to never let this feeling fade away. "But... Don't you want to?" I asked, my voice filled with uncertainty.

He pulled me closer to him, his embrace strong and comforting. "I absolutely want to," he whispered, his voice filled with tenderness. "But you're worth the wait, and I don't want to jeopardize this."

Tears welled up in my eyes as I realized just how much he cared for me. He wasn't just after a physical connection; he wanted something more, something real. I snuggled closer to him, resting my head on his chest as he gently stroked my hair and hummed softly.

At that moment, I knew that I was safe with him. I knew that he would protect me, that he would cherish me, that he would love me with all his heart. And for the first time, I drifted off to sleep, thinking of a future filled with the warmth of his love.

Chapter 20

Telaria

Finally, it was time to leave the unforgiving desert behind. Despite his best efforts, Klein could still feel the sand lodged in every crevice and crack of his body, a constant reminder of his displeasure with this arid environment. Being a winter Fae, he was not suited for the heat of the desert, and he vowed never to return if he could help it. The thought of leaving the endless sea of sand behind and reaching the tropical paradise of Ostara filled him with anticipation. Even though the humidity of Ostara would be overwhelming, it was a welcome change from the unforgiving desert.

As they made their way through the lush greenery of Ostara, Klein couldn't help but revel in the abundance of life around them. Vibrant flora and fauna—it was a stark contrast to the barrenness of the desert. Already dreading the return journey, Klein turned to Mystic and declared, "Let's never do this again."

"Agreed," Mystic replied, wiping sweat from her brow.

Walking together, they planned what they wanted to do when they were free of debt. So far, they had discussed staying in Celetrix or moving to Mabon or Yule. The experience of traveling through the South had made it clear that they didn't want to live there. The heat was too much, and the lack of water and resources made it a challenging place to survive. They yearned for the familiarity of the cooler climates and rich landscapes of their home.

The trees grew denser as Klein and Mystic moved along, and they noticed an abundance of fruit hanging from almost every branch. Klein recognized a few types of fruit easily enough and decided to make a meal out of them. Mystic, always cautious, took a bite of each fruit before Klein consumed them, thanks to her immunity to most poisons. This precaution had saved them in the past when they had encountered indistinguishable but toxic berries.

The humidity crept up on them like a layer of grime on their skin that wouldn't leave, and the relief Klein felt when they first arrived in Ostara quickly wore off. Removing all the top layers of their outfits, Klein and Mystic stowed the excess fabric in their packs. The trees provided plenty of shade from the scorching sun overhead.

Animals scurried underfoot—rabbits, squirrels, and other small animals of the underbrush—but the creatures seemed to have no fear of them. Klein had to wonder why. He and Mystic were predators in their own right, and usually, that alone would cause creatures like these to flee. Perhaps something about the magic of Ostara kept them calm and easy to hunt. Klein took out a few rabbits that crossed his path, planning to make a meal out of them the next time they stopped to rest.

As they wandered through the lush greenery, they stumbled upon a shimmering pool of water. Klein and Mystic were immediately drawn to its inviting coolness, but they inspected the pool for any potential danger before deciding to take a break and bathe. The water was crystal clear and a vibrant shade of blue, filled with a variety of colorful fish swimming in lazy circles. Large lily pads surrounded the pool, each one decorated with delicate white and pink flowers. A few plump frogs were soundly sleeping on the leaves; their eyes flicked open briefly as the duo approached, but they quickly settled back into slumber as they realized Klein and Mystic posed no threat. With the all-clear, Klein and Mystic were eager to take advantage of the serene waters and use it as their mid-day rest spot.

Birds sang in the canopy above, communicating with each other and flying from branch to branch. They came in a myriad of colors, more than Klein had thought possible. A rainbow of feathers flapped overhead as the birds continued their chatter, seemingly oblivious to their presence. The town of Ostara was nearby, but they had to wait until darkness to sneak their way into the city. Just because the wards wouldn't sense them didn't mean they should be careless.

Mystic took a dip in the pool first while Klein kept a watchful eye on their surroundings. Out of respect, he avoided looking in her direction, instead focusing on the jungle. After all, they had lived so close and gone through so much on their journey that nudity had become a non-issue. But privacy was still valued, and Klein tried to provide it whenever possible.

While Mystic bathed, Klein focused on cooking the rabbits over a small fire. He discarded the fur and innards a reasonable distance away from the pond, hoping that some creatures would find them and have a quick meal. The fur wasn't valuable, and while it could be useful, they didn't need it. They should have picked up some spices from Litha, but unfortunately, the rabbit would have to be eaten plain. He was sure Mystic would complain about the lack of flavor as soon as she took a bite of the tasteless meat.

Mystic swam in the tranquil, blue waters of the pool, her form exuding a sense of serenity that Klein could see from where he was cooking. Despite her beauty, there had never been any romantic feelings between them. Klein was aware of the scars from her past that still haunted her, memories that she refused to share with anyone. He assumed they were tied to her mother and the life she had attempted to force upon her. Klein never pushed the matter, but he hoped that with time, she would heal and find happiness. He would always be there for her, offering a room in his home should she need it. All he wanted was for her to find peace and move past her pain. He just hoped they would survive this journey and make it to a safe place where she could do that.

Looking up into the trees, Klein's attention was drawn to a mother bird feeding her chicks high up in the leaves. He could make out the nest and the little naked birds inside. The mother bird's feathers were bright red, blue, and green. She fed only the strongest chick, ignoring the others unless they could shove their way to the front. It seemed harsh, but that was the way of nature. As he watched them—contemplating the fairness of nature as a whole, he was startled by a scream coming from behind him.

Turning around to see if Mystic was okay, Klein saw splashes of water as she went under, followed by a spray of bubbles. Acting quickly, he made to jump into the pond, worried there might be a kelpie hiding in the depths trying to drag Mystic to an early grave. The aquatic horses loved places like this, luring unsuspecting travelers into clean, cool water. Klein thought they had checked the pond pretty carefully before she went in, but maybe it had a magic spell to keep it hidden from view.

Just as he was about to jump in after her, Mystic's face broke the surface of the water. In her hands was something slimy and wet, which she promptly threw at him. Too stunned to dodge, the object hit Klein in the face with a splat and began to crawl up his face to sit on his head. Streaks of slime covered his face, and he had to wipe his eyes to see. As he opened them again, he watched as Mystic laughed a twinkling belly laugh at his expense. Reaching up, Klein removed the creature, most definitely still alive, from his hair. It grabbed onto the strands of white hair, causing them to stick up with the gooey substance coming from its skin.

Pulling it from his hair, Klein saw that it was a giant fire newt staring at him with round, solid black eyes. Its eyes narrowed as if it was Klein's fault it was thrown at him. The belly of the creature was a bright red, which would be frightening even if you didn't know that some of them excreted toxins from their skin. If the belly were yellow, Klein would be dead by now, which he was sure Mystic knew when she threw it at him—at least, he hoped she did. He tossed the creature back at her with a grunt, but it missed hitting her as she dove back under the water.

"You'd better come out here this instant!" he shouted at her. The slime was going to be awful to get out of his hair, especially if he allowed it to dry. Deciding to pay her back, Klein dipped his hand in the water and started to drop the temperature of the pond. He didn't want to freeze the water or harm the creatures living there, but he wanted to make it extra uncomfortable for his sister.

Feeling the water change, she let out a loud shriek. "No fair!" she said as she reluctantly got out of the water, drying herself off and getting dressed. As she looked at Klein, she still laughed at the state of his hair. "Wow, that's a really good look for you! Maybe there's a market for newt hair slime!"

Someday, somehow, Klein would pay her back for this. He just didn't know how yet. Revenge was best served cold, or at least lukewarm, and as soon as possible.

"You're lucky I don't find my own newt to throw at you," he grunted, exasperated with his sister's antics.

"Good luck. He was the only one in the whole pond," she said with a smug look on her face.

"We'll see about that," he replied.

After removing his clothes and folding them neatly on a large gray rock, Klein stepped into the cool water himself. The water was just short of freezing, but thanks to his magic, the cold never bothered him anyway.

Dunking his head under the water, Klein began scrubbing his hair vigorously. The slime was thick and already starting to harden, even after only a few moments. Wishing he had some soap or anything to get the substance out, he was getting frustrated. It just wouldn't come out. His hair was sticking straight up in hard spikes. The slime had come off his skin at least, but at this rate, he was going to have to take one of his daggers and shave his head bald to get the rest off.

Feeling her eyes on him, Klein spotted Mystic watching him struggle, a gleeful look on her face. She handed him some cleansing leaves she must have found nearby. The plant had big velvet leaves that foamed up when crushed with water. They were commonly used for making soaps and body washes. Her finding these, however, did not ease his anger towards her. When she saw the rage on his face, the smirk she had been wearing finally dropped. "It was just a joke," she whined.

"Just a joke! I'm about ready to rip my hair out!" Klein growled back at her.

Rubbing the leaves in the water, a light foam started to build in his hands, and as he worked it into his hair, he could feel the slime starting to break down—luckily for Mystic. If he had to shave his head, she might find herself bald as well. After ten more minutes of scrubbing, Klein was finally free and clean, physically at any rate.

Getting out and dressing back in his clothes, Klein started planning their next move. They still had a few hours before nightfall.

They decided to gather some more fruit and get as close as possible to Ostara's walls without passing any guards' wards they might encounter. Distracted by the upcoming heist, Klein reached up to grab a mango from a high branch. Suddenly, he was pulled down to the ground when his shoe got caught on a lifted root. A curse left his lips as his shoe flew into the trees. It caused Klein to stumble and twist his ankle.

Looking down at his foot to check the damage, Klein removed his sock and assessed the bones of his ankle. It seemed to be sprained, and it was already starting to swell and turn red. Yes, it was official: Klein hated Ostara just as much as he hated Litha. He used some of his ice magic to help bring down the swelling.

"You okay, Klein?" Mystic asked from where she was gathering her own fruit.

"Yes, I think so."

Seeing him sitting down under the mango tree, Mystic came over to check his ankle as well. "Looks like a sprain," she said, placing her warm hands over the joint.

"It's not broken," Klein confirmed for her.

As she rubbed at his ankle, the pain began to lessen considerably. It might not be a true sprain after all if it was already healing this quickly. She took some of the extra cloth they had in their bag to help Klein wrap it, but by the time she was done, he felt like the pain was almost completely gone.

She offered a hand to help him up. "There, good as new!" she smiled, and as Klein moved to dust his hands off, Mystic let out a loud laugh, pointing at the back of his pants. "Wow, I didn't know you fell that hard!"

"What are you laughing at?" Klein asked, turning to see what was amusing Mystic. He glanced down at the seat of his pants and realized he had sat on a ripe mango, which was now splattered all over the back of his clothes, looking like vomit—or something worse. Maybe this place was worse than Litha, he thought to himself.

"Let's burn this horrible place to the ground," Klein said, his tone serious. But Mystic just continued to laugh as he tried to remove the fruit from his clothes.

Despite wiping off as much as he could with his magic, a large orange stain remained, mocking him with its brightness. They should have brought more clothing, but they wanted to keep their load as light as possible, planning to buy or steal what they needed along the way. When they transformed into their animal forms, their clothes moved to a pocket realm that Klein didn't fully understand. He knew it was limited in size and that a too big bag would be left behind.

Hopefully, all his bad luck was running out, and the rest of this job would go on without a hitch. They continued on to the City of Litha until they could see the walls on the horizon. They found a tree to climb and spent the rest of the daylight hours scouting the city from their vantage point. Every once in a while, Klein caught Mystic snickering at the state of his pants, and he warned her not to share their story with anyone at the guild, or there would be consequences.

Chapter 21

Mel

My dreams had returned. As I lay in bed, my mind wandered to the adventures of my fantasy friends that I had been dreaming about. They were so close to reaching the Ostara Court, where they could finally find freedom. I couldn't help but wonder what would happen to them once they reached their destination. Would they finally find the peace they had been seeking? Would any of my loyal companions find love? The thought brought a warm feeling to my chest and a hint of jealousy—which was strange considering I would never really be a part of their world—just an audience of their story.

In the midst of my thoughts, Alex came to mind. He had made quite an impression on me, and I hoped he planned on staying around. Perhaps if he did, I could even share my dreams with him.

Suddenly, little Charlie, my new cat, jumped onto my chest, purring contentedly.

I spent an embarrassing amount of time browsing cat butt pictures on the internet and eventually determined that Charlie was a female cat. With good food and a comfortable bed, she was starting to look much better. I knew that low-cost vaccination and spay clinics were available in the spring, and I had already made plans to get her the necessary treatments and care. It was safe to say that Charlie wasn't going anywhere.

As Alex predicted, Lucia was smitten with her big kitty eyes. She even went out of her way to buy me cat food and a litter box, which, as long as I cleaned it daily, didn't emit too strong of an odor.

It was Tuesday, my day off. I had plans for a date with Alex once he finished at the diner. He promised a big surprise, and my heart fluttered with anticipation. He told me to dress nicely, but as I looked at my options in the closet, I frowned. There was nothing there that I considered "nice." Sighing, I decided to visit a boutique after my gym class. I had been attending the late morning class, and it seemed to be working well. Sadly, the instructor was Tammy, but she seemed to take on a different persona when she taught, and I could not tolerate being around her in that state.

Jess had been busy working lately, and I really missed her smiling face. She and Amber have been texting each other since my birthday, and I can't help but wonder how long Jess would stay here. I knew Amber's family had offered to take her in, but Jess was being stubborn. Thinking of her, I grabbed my phone to text her and see if she wanted to join me for a girls' day before my date.

Me: Hey Jess, want to help me find an outfit for my date with Alex?
Jess: oh baby, I thought you'd never ask!
Me: I have my class first, but could we meet at my apartment at 12, maybe grab some lunch?
Jess: *thumbs up emoji*

    I'd been trying to get Jess to go to self-defense classes with me, but by now, I knew it was a lost cause. Slipping on my shoes, I headed out the door, feeling self-assured in my matching mint green workout gear consisting of leggings and a sports bra. I'd ordered a couple of sets online, and they were working out well—considering how cheap they were. The walk to the gym was short, but the whole time I was walking, I felt like I was being watched. The flash of a golden collar ran through my mind and the feeling that accompanied it. A shiver ran up my spine as I quickened my pace, finally feeling relieved as I stepped inside the gym.

    "Better hurry If you want to make it to class. I don't wait for anyone." Tammy said by way of greeting, her ponytail flipping behind her as she headed to the room where the class was being held. *Well, hello to you, too.*

    Hanging my coat and hat inside the changing room lockers, I went to class to see Tammy had already started, of course. Luckily for me, I knew the stretches well enough by now, so I jumped in with the other girls. After a few weeks of class, I was getting a lot more confident in my movements. I'd always been flexible, and years of dancing had given me some muscle tone. And it turned out that dancing and fighting had some similarities. It was all about combining movements and keeping the flow going. Tammy gave me an appraising eye as I went through the movements.

"Good work, Colly! Keep it up," she said in a cheerful voice, almost as if we were best friends. I snorted a laugh and continued moving, sweat beading on my brow. The class ended before I knew it, leaving me longing for more advanced courses, but they simply didn't fit into my schedule. I waved goodbye and headed to the locker room to retrieve my things. My phone buzzed with a notification from Jess.

Jess: Hey, headed your way. See you soon *kiss emoji*

When I got back to my apartment, I tossed my stuff on the bed, looking around for Charlie. Giving a little *psp... psp... psp*. She didn't come out like she usually did, and I started to panic. "Charlie, where are you, kitty?" A chill ran through the room. Why was it so cold in here, I wondered. As I looked up, I saw my window was open. I rushed to close it, looking out to make sure I didn't see Charlie outside. As I snapped it shut, I heard a meow from behind me.

Charlie came out from under my bed, tilting her fuzzy head. "There you are!" I said as I scooped her up into my arms. She started purring as I patted her soft fur. "I was so worried about you! Don't scare me like that." I scolded. Charlie just kept purring, doing the happy cat chirp. The window being open worried me; I know I didn't open it. It was windy outside, but could that be enough to open a sliding window? I didn't think so. *Maybe I should nail it closed.*

A little shaken up, I took my kitty with me to the bathroom while I showered and started to get ready for the day. The towel was wrapped around me as I walked back to my room when there was a sharp knock at the door. Momentarily, I froze, scared of who could be at the door.

"Open up, bitch! It's freezing out here!" Jess said through the door.

Letting out a relieved laugh, I unlocked the door and let her in. "I thought you were going to leave me to die out there!" She complained. "Oh, a kitty!" She cooed, picking up Charlie and giving her some chin scratches.

"Sorry, I was in the shower and didn't hear the door," I replied, rummaging through my clothes to find something suitable for a girls' day. I settled on a warm sweater dress and leggings and left my face bare for now. "So, what should we eat for lunch?" I asked Jess, who was now lounging on my bed with Charlie purring in her arms.

"Hmm, what's close by?"

"There is a little cafe around the block? They mostly have little sandwiches, but it's not bad." I suggested.

"Meh... let's just get some cheap burgers. I want the greasy goodness!" Jess groaned, rubbing her belly.

Laughing, I agreed with her. We headed to the local Wacky D's and got some food off the value menu, which isn't really that great of a value anymore. A few years ago, you could get four burgers for five dollars, and now you're lucky to get one. With artificial food filling our stomachs, we left for the next destination—a dress boutique. Alex said to dress up, but I'd never been on an actual date before. *Maybe the cocktail dresses we wore at the club sometimes would work?*

The boutique was small on the outside, but as we walked in, I saw rows and rows of clothing—a sea of fabrics and shoes in front of me. I didn't know where to begin. As I stood there looking stupid, a small figure floated through the stacks, popping out in front of me. "Hello Girls, how can I help you?" the voice said. It was coming from a petite, elderly woman who was dressed impeccably with horned rim glasses. Her white hair was coiled on her head in a neat braid.

"Hi, I actually need help finding something nice to wear for a dinner date," I told her and then turned to Jess. "Did you need help with anything?" I asked her.

She shook her head. "Nope, today was all about you and getting you ready for the ball, Cinderella."

"Ball? Dude, it is just a date with Alex! He has mostly seen me in my pajamas. I don't think it is that big of a deal," I shrugged, trying to make light of my date. Although, it was going to be pretty special—and if I had my way, Alex and I would be spending a lot of time together. We had been spending time cuddling and kissing, but I was ready to move on in a physical sense. I felt like his hands and kisses were slowly washing away all the touches of those other men, and I wanted to feel whole again.

"Right this way, girls. I have the perfect selection of date dresses in the back," she led us to the dressing rooms with red velvet curtains. It was a little dusty, and I couldn't imagine how she kept the whole place running by herself. Perhaps she had a grandchild or someone to help her, but as I looked around, all I saw was her. "Just wait right here. I'll bring you some stuff to try on!"

Jess was looking through the racks closest to us, fingering the silken fabric of a navy floor-length gown. "This would look great on you," she said, looking up and down. "But I feel like it might clash with your new hair."

Unconsciously, I reached for my pink locks. They were spiky and hard to style, but I was getting used to it. There were times that I missed my long hair, though. The way it gleamed in the light when I curled it, the feeling of it hanging down my back. Letting out a sigh of longing, I said, "Maybe something black? Black goes with everything?"

Just then, the lady came back, arms full of dresses. You could hardly see her under all the clothing she was carrying. Rushing to help her, me and Jess took the dresses from her and hung them up on the hooks on the wall. Patting her hands on her pants, she looked at me. "There should be something you'll like in there. Forgive me, I'm a little tired. I'm going to sit in my chair, but if you need me, just holler." She walked away with a slight limp, poor thing. It must be hard getting old.

The dresses she had picked out for me all seemed to be the correct size, but the styles were a little outdated. As I looked at some of them, I couldn't help but giggle. When I looked at Jess, she had a smirk on her face while holding one of the dresses up to her body. It was polka-dotted with buttons all the way down, resembling an old pinup dress. "You should try that on," I snickered.

"Maybe I will," she replied, moving to go into the changing room first.

I continued looking through the dresses, hoping to find one that would suit me. As I found a pale lavender maxi dress that I thought might work, I heard Jess cough to get my attention. My eyes turned to her. "Oh My God," I breathed as I took her in. The figure-hugging dress accentuated her curves, making her look classy and sexy at the same time.

"I know, right!" she twirled around for me to admire the back. "Quick, take a picture so I can send it to Amber," she handed me her phone.

"Are you still texting Amber?" I asked, not wanting to pry, but I hoped she would take her up on the offer to move in with her. I would miss her greatly, but she would be much better off. As I handed her back her phone, a little crease formed between her eyebrows.

"Yeah," she didn't offer any more on the subject, turning back to the mirror. "I think I'm going to buy it," she announced, returning to the changing room to put her clothes back on. Still looking at the lavender dress, I decided to try it on. When I looked at myself in it, I wasn't sure what to think. It was cute, sure, but the way it hung on me made it look awkward. My figure wasn't as hourglass-shaped as Jess's, and although I had been eating better, I was still too skinny. Sighing, I walked out to ask Jess what she thought.

She stopped me. "Try the navy one. I'm still not sure if it's classy, but this color always looked great on you." I took it from her and went to change out of the other dress. The navy dress was silky and backless, with a long slit on one side and thin, gem-encrusted straps. When I put it on, I couldn't help but smile. It flattered my figure, and I felt hot. But I couldn't shake the feeling that it was too much for a dinner date.

As I emerged, Jess started whistling and clapping. "This is it!" she said, having me turn around to show her the back. "Alex, eat your heart out!"

"Don't you think it's too much?" I asked, worried.

"Nah, girl. It's perfect. Besides, you can never be over-dressed," she winked. We made our purchases and thanked the lady for her help.

We walked back to my apartment, where Jess helped me with my makeup. With my hair and dress being so bold, we decided that my makeup should be softer. Jess worked her magic, powdering my face and placing a blush on my cheeks. When I asked if we should use concealer on my freckles, she scoffed at the idea. "They're part of what makes you so cute. Don't ever cover them!" she said, brushing my face with a thick layer of powder. For my eyes, she chose a light gold and a brown winged eyeliner. With a swoop of her hand, the line was perfect in one go.

"There, you look perfect!" she said, a tear coming to her eye.

"Don't be so dramatic!" I laughed, but as I looked in the mirror, I stopped. As I saw myself, I saw another me smiling back. I blinked, and she was gone. I shook my head, reasoning that it must have been a trick of the light. "Thank you, Jess. I look wonderful."

"Of course you do!" she purred. "Everyone looks good once I'm done with them." Jess was often the one to help all the girls at the club get ready, and her makeup talent was truly impressive. In another life, she would have made a great makeup artist. Maybe Amber would convince her to move, and she could do makeup there.

"Now, I'm going before he gets here. Don't do anything I would do!" Jess shouted, pushing herself up from the chair, leaving me confused. *What would Jess do?*

We said our goodbyes, and Alex arrived to pick me up shortly after. I was excited and nervous. Alex and I had been hanging out for a while, and he had been staying with me lately. We still hadn't crossed the sexual barrier, and I wondered if tonight would be the night. I had no idea how long normal girls waited. Three dates? Ten? I consulted the internet, but the articles only made me more confused as each one had a different answer. I sighed and put my phone away.

There was a knock on the door, and I jumped up to answer it, smoothing my dress. Alex was standing there with a rose in his hand, which he offered to me. He was wearing a smart suit jacket that was open at the front, showing a white button-up shirt but keeping it more casual with no tie. I took the rose from him and invited him in.

"You look stunning," he said, giving me a heated look that set my heart on fire.

"Thanks," I mumbled, finding a glass to put the rose in. "So, where are you taking me tonight, my most mysterious one?"

"I thought we could try a place I've never been before. Do you like sushi?" Alex asked, looking anxious as he shifted from one foot to the other.

I wrinkled my nose. "I don't know, I've never tried it before. Raw fish kind of freaks me out."

"They have other things there too. Not all sushi is made of raw fish," he explained.

"Well, I'm willing to try anything once. Let's go!" I offered him my most winning smile. I was sure the restaurant would have something I would like. Maybe they had orange chicken.

We drove to the restaurant, talking about nothing and everything. By the time we arrived, I was feeling much more relaxed and couldn't figure out why I was so worried. This was Alex, my Alex, and everything with him was easy and nice. The sushi place was made of dark wood with large tables. The hostess led us to the back of the restaurant, where there were smaller tables made for couples. It was quiet back here, and the noise of the rest of the restaurant seemed far away. She took our drink order and handed us leather-bound menus. My eyes bulged when I saw the prices.

"Order whatever you want, Hermosa," Alex encouraged me.

I was trying my best to ignore the prices on the menu at the sushi restaurant, but there were so many different rolls to choose from that I found myself struggling to decide. Seeing my dilemma, Alex started pointing things out. "The California roll is pretty simple, and most people like it! No raw fish at all. Or if you're not filling that, you could try the tempura plate. It's mostly fried vegetables and some shrimp with rice."

"Fried? Yeah, I'll try that." I said, closing my menu.

"Okay, I'm going to order a couple of different rolls that we can both try. California, crunchy, and Philadelphia rolls." He said, pointing them out to me. "They are all really good!"

"Sure, I'll try some," I said, trusting him. He obviously knew more about sushi than I did.

The waitress returned, took our order, and brought us some miso soup. It had a light and salty flavor, which was pretty good. When I asked Alex if it had raw fish in it, he just laughed. "No, no fish at all! That's tofu."

As our food was being served, my stomach rumbled hungrily, and the miso soup we had been served did little to quell my appetite. The waitress placed a plate of fried vegetables and rice in front of me, which was heaped high and smelled irresistible. In front of Alex, she arranged a plate with the three different rolls he had ordered—the California, crunchy, and Philadelphia rolls. To my relief, they appeared much less daunting in person than I had imagined. Upon unwrapping my utensils, I was pleased to discover a fork in addition to the chopsticks.

Alex expertly used chopsticks, and I felt a tinge of envy that I had never learned to use them. "Can you teach me how to do that?" I asked as I watched him.

"Sure!" He leaned over to show me how to hold my hands, pinching the chopsticks together. I tried the skill, trying to pick up the fried broccoli, but it kept slipping from my grip. After it fell for the fifth time, I became frustrated and just speared the broccoli with one of the chopsticks.

"Got it!" I announced, bringing the food to my mouth. The breading had a light flavor, and for my next bite, I dipped it in the provided sauce. "Mmm," I moaned as the sauce hit my tongue and enhanced the taste. Deciding chopsticks weren't for me, I ate the rest of my food using the fork.

Alex offered me a piece of sushi, holding it out to me with his chopsticks. "All in one bite," he explained.

Leaning forward, I tried the unfamiliar fish wrapped in rice. The taste surprised me, and it didn't taste like I expected. It wasn't fishy, and the flavors all blended together in my mouth. Maybe I did like sushi after all. He smiled at me, offering me another piece. We continued sharing food until everything was gone. When the waitress came to ask if we wanted to order dessert, I shook my head. My stomach was too full of rice and fried goodness. Alex paid the bill, much to my protest, and I offered to pay the tip. He agreed, so I placed a twenty on the table, and we returned to his car.

Turning to him after buckling my seat belt, I said, "Thanks for making me try it. It was tasty."

"I'm glad you liked it," he replied. "Now, are you ready for the next part of our date?"

"Yes..." I said hesitantly. "There's another part?"

He pulled out of the parking lot and drove us to the next location, the aquarium. I was surprised to see a couple of cars parked there. "What are we doing here?" I asked, confused. "Wasn't the aquarium closed by five?"

"During the winter, they have nighttime hours. It's really cool. Come on!" he encouraged.

The aquarium, although not overflowing with people, had a handful of visitors walking around. The night brought a unique enchantment to the tanks as the fish appeared to shine and glitter as they gracefully swam by. The idea of visiting the aquarium at night was an unexpected surprise for me, as I had only been a few times before in my life, including a class field trip. As we strolled through the tanks, linked by the hands, there was a peaceful and tranquil stillness that enveloped us.

The next room was illuminated in a more captivating manner than the others. It was the jellyfish exhibit, and it was surrounded by towering cylindrical tanks in every direction. The translucent creatures seemed to sway in an imaginary current, their graceful movements appearing as if they were performing a dance. It's wild to think these brainless creatures can survive. Not only that, but I think I read somewhere that jellyfish were practically immortal. Alex led me to a bench, where we continued to watch the ethereal dance of the jellies.

Alex started speaking in a low voice, "I want to do this right. I don't want to assume anything, but I think you like me, or at least I hope you do. And, well..." He took a deep breath and looked down. I rubbed small circles onto his hand, waiting for him to continue. "Will you be my girlfriend?" he finally asked, hanging his head as he said the words.

"Fuck, Alex! You scared me for a moment there. I thought you were breaking up with me," I said with a nervous laugh. No one had ever asked me to be their girlfriend before, but if anyone was going to ask, I was glad it was Alex. I guess I thought we were already together. "Yes, Alex. I will," I said quietly, keeping my voice low and looking at him through my lashes.

His head shot up, and his face lit up with an excited smile stretching from ear to ear. "You will?!" he exclaimed, causing a couple walking by to turn their heads and look at us.

"Yes, but now be quiet, or you'll scare the fish," I said in a teasing tone. Alex leaned forward to press his lips to mine, cutting off any other remarks I might have made. His lips were soft, and his tongue danced with mine for, in my opinion, too brief of a time.

This was turning out to be one of the best dates I had ever been on, or at least, the only real date I had been on. We finished up our date and went back to his car, holding hands the entire time. The drive back to my apartment was quiet, and I felt nauseous with all the butterflies in my stomach. Alex pulled up to my parking space and ran a nervous hand through his dark hair that reminded me of someone else—someone with silver hair instead of black.

"Do you want me to stay tonight?" he asked.

Pretending to think about it, I tapped my finger against my lips and hummed a little. "I don't know," I teased. "Okay, I guess you can stay!" I laughed, poking him in the ribs.

As we walked inside, I felt my phone vibrating in my jacket pocket. I took it out and saw that I had a message from an unknown number.

UNKNOWN: Did you enjoy the aquarium? You look stunning in that dress.

A tremor took over my hand as I read the message, almost causing me to drop the phone. I couldn't believe what I was reading. It couldn't be happening. Covering my head with my hands as I crouched down in the entryway of my apartment.

"What's wrong, beautiful? Is everyone okay?" Alex asked, his voice sounding like he was speaking underwater. I felt his hands on mine, bringing them away from my head. He gently gripped my chin and tilted my face to look at him. "You're safe," he said softly. "No one can hurt you here."

Still unable to speak, I just nodded my head, refusing to let the tears fall. Alex led me to sit on the bed and helped me remove my shoes and jacket. When I was settled, he took my phone from me to read the message. I saw his eyes move across the screen, and his grip on my phone tightened as he gritted his teeth. A string of angry Spanish left his lips in a mumble. He seemed angry, and seeing him like that triggered something in me.

"Get up, Mel! Are you going to let some jerk ruin your life?" I shouted, standing up and ripping the phone from Alex's hands and throwing it on the floor. "I'm not letting that sicko take anything else from me." I pulled Alex to me and kissed him fiercely, letting him feel the passion and love I felt for him. Our tongues clashed in a collision of teeth. This kiss was nothing like the ones we had shared before. It was brutal as I tried to erase the feeling of Harvey's touch from my skin.

My hands roamed over his body, seeking out the buttons of his shirt. I tore at them with urgency, eager to feel the hard muscles underneath. A soft moan escaped my lips as my hands traveled lower, fumbling with his belt. I could feel him harden beneath my touch, and he let out a growl as I explored him through the fabric.

Suddenly, he pulled back, halting my actions. He took his hand to my face and guided my gaze to meet his. "Are you sure?" he asked, ready to stop if I gave the slightest indication.

"Yes," I replied, my voice rough with desire, "Please," I begged for him to touch me, to help me feel something good. The sound of my pleading broke the hold he had on himself, and he pulled me back into a kiss. I grabbed at the edges of his shirt, pulling it off of him. His hands were gentle, each touch a question. He lowered the thin straps of my dress, and it fell, exposing my nipples.

He looked at me and said, "You're a goddess, Mel." He then began kissing down my neck, lower and lower, until his tongue met my nipple, swirling around it in a delicious rhythm. I was panting, my head thrown back as I wrapped my leg around him, pressing my heat against him. Feeling his hardness, I rubbed myself against him greedily, desperate for some friction.

Cupping my ass, he lifted me up and carried me to the bed, where he hovered over me, staring at me like I was the most beautiful thing in the world. At that moment, I felt like I was worth something. I slipped off my dress, leaving it in a crumpled heap at the end of the bed, and reached for his belt. I was pulling him back on top of me in nothing but my pink lace panties. His hands found mine to stop me again. Letting out a growl of frustration, I looked up at him.

"Not yet," he murmured as he resumed his journey of kisses down my body. He took his time with each of my breasts, showering them with attention until he reached the most intimate part of me. I could feel his hot breath on the thin material of my lingerie, causing me to squirm with anticipation.

"Please, please," I whimpered, urging him on. He obliged, pushing the material aside and groaning in approval at what he found. His tongue began to swirl and tease, nibbling at my sensitive skin and driving me closer to the brink. He knew just what he was doing as he took my clit between his lips and gently sucked.

Just as I felt myself breaking apart, he pushed two fingers inside me, causing a scream of ecstasy to leave my lips as waves of pleasure crashed through me. He continued to pump his fingers inside me, rubbing against a spot I didn't know existed. "So beautiful." He said against the flesh of my stomach.

He moved back up my body, leaving a trail of warm kisses in his wake. Our eyes met as our lips melted in a soft, lingering kiss. I could taste myself on his lips, and it made me want to return the favor. I tried to reach for him, eager to continue our lovemaking, but he stopped me, holding my hands in his.

"Let's save the rest for another night," he whispered tenderly, pushing my pink hair away from my face.

"I don't want to wait for another night," I eagerly whispered. I reached for him again and slid my hands down under his pants to tease him, gently gliding my hands in his inner thighs and lowering myself as I wrapped my hands around his impressive length. He didn't protest as I removed his pants and boxers, sliding my hands to feel every peak and ridge of his abdomen. Bringing him to my lips, I tasted the salty bead of liquid at his tip.

Using my tongue, I licked him from root to tip before wrapping my lips around the head of his cock. He let out a rough moan, bringing his hands to my hand, gripping tight but comfortable. He lowered my head, guiding my movements in the way that he liked, bringing him to the back of my throat over and over again. Just when he couldn't take anymore, he pulled me up and started kissing me, his tongue eager to find mine. I began pressing myself against him, separated only by my thin, wet panties.

"I think I might love you," he whispered to me between the kisses. He was so close to where I wanted him, and he lined up with me perfectly. If only we would go forward that extra step.

I pushed myself up to look into his eyes. "I think I might love you too," I told him honestly as I moved myself to drag my panties down, tossing them to the floor without care. I positioned myself over him and guided him in as he sank into me, inch after delicious inch. I moaned into his ear as I felt him pushing into me eagerly. We began to move together in a rhythm that brought me to cry in pleasure while he panted in ecstasy. Nothing had ever felt this good before, and his cock pounded into me over and over. I could feel my body reaching new peaks.

Lips crashing together in haste to taste his tongue against mine, I brought the seam of my lips to his, and I ground my clit against him. I felt like I was burning alive—like I could never get enough of this. His hands wouldn't stop like he wanted to feel all of me. His hands ran from my breasts to my arms, to up and down my legs, to grabbing my ass and tugging me close. I found myself running my hands over his beautiful body as well. It was everything. This was everything. Then, as our pace picked up speed, I started digging my nails into the pillow under him as I reached my limit, panting.

"Come with me, Mel," he groaned. The sound of his words brought me to another high. Stars flashed behind my eyelids as he continued to move inside me, slowly dragging out my pleasure. I felt the warm spray as he filled me up with his cum. This felt so right.

Slumping against his well-muscled chest, I felt thoroughly exhausted. As I relaxed against him, he brushed his hands down my spine to send delicious tingles throughout my body.

I couldn't help but consider how this was so different from the sex I had ever had before. This passion I felt, the desire for his body, was unlike anything I've had before. I wanted all of him to be a part of me. I wanted this feeling forever. I didn't feel desperate for a shower like with the men before, desperate to wash them off of me. *Is this love?* I questioned, never having experienced it before. *Yes.* As this truth rang through me, I felt content and sated.

Before I could fall asleep, I got up to prepare for bed. I knew that if I went to sleep without removing my makeup and brushing my teeth, it would be detrimental to my skin the next day. So I hopped up to do just that, giving Alex one last kiss on his flushed cheek. When I returned to the room, I found Alex fast asleep on my bed, looking relaxed and at peace.

I turned off the light, crawled into bed beside him, and put my head on his chest, listening to the steady beat of his heart. He instinctively wrapped his arm around me, holding me close. My heart was so full of hope and love. This... this was what had been missing my whole life. I closed my eyes, taking deep breaths as the sound of his heartbeat lulled me into a deep, peaceful slumber.

Chapter 22

Telaria

The fragrant aroma of flowers permeated every corner of the city, even in its poorest slums. It was a mystery why the rulers of the city would choose this as the only aroma to permeate the air. As Klein and Mystic sat in the inn waiting for their meal, Klein couldn't help but ponder the outcome of their latest job. Today, they had a plan to observe the guard's rotation and put the rings given to them by the Lord of Mabon to the test. A single misstep tomorrow could mean the end of their lives, and Klein was determined to ensure that that didn't happen.

The previous night, the rings had performed flawlessly, enabling them to enter the city undetected by any wards they tested them on. Finding an inn to reside in while they plotted their heist was surprisingly easy, almost as if the city was inviting exploitation. It was even just a few blocks away from the Ostara Castle.

Their job today was to scout the city, seeking out all the possible ways in and out of its walls, as well as gather intelligence by asking around. Klein had already familiarized himself with the city's layout by spending hours pouring over maps at his desk, but seeing the city in person was always different. The city of Ostara was renowned for its skilled earthwielders, capable of changing the landscape with their magic. The walls, the plants, everything was created by their powers.

The Ostara Fae were highly sought after for their construction abilities. Their capability to create walls and structures from the very earth itself was a remarkable talent, one that was greatly coveted. However, only a few of them possessed the vast amount of power necessary to execute this feat. It typically took the collective efforts of multiple skilled earth movers working in unison to bring their creations to life. Most Fae were limited to a more modest display of their abilities, such as sprouting a single flower or shaping a single brick.

The lush greenery of Ostara was truly something to behold. The vines and roots seemed to wrap themselves around every nook and cranny, infiltrating even the indoor spaces. The shower in their room was no exception, with walls covered in a tapestry of leaves and a natural rock floor that drained the excess water back into the earth. Despite the warm water of the shower, Klein's skin still felt damp and sticky—a testament to the ever-present humidity in this corner of the world.

The inn they were staying in was a typical example of the establishments found in this city, complete with a pub that served three meals a day to its guests. After a quick shower, Klein and

Mystic headed down to the pub for breakfast, eager to gather information from the innkeeper. They found her quickly, wiping down a table with a rag.

"Good morning!" Klein smiled, trying to appear less intimidating but likely failing. The owner of the inn, a Spring Fae with golden hair and bright blue eyes, common features in these parts, approached Klein and Mystic with a warm smile. The owner was dressed in a white apron over a pale blue dress, dusted with flour. Klein had gathered that she and her husband ran the inn and didn't have any children.

"Morning, did you sleep well?" she asked, "I hope the accommodations were to your liking."

"Well enough, thank you," Klein replied. "Everything was just fine."

Mystic interjected, "Just hungry for some breakfast. What's on the menu this morning?"

The innkeeper chuckled, "Straight to the point, I like that! Here, let me show you to a table. This morning, I have eggs, potatoes, and fresh bread. Just water to drink, or feeling adventurous this morning?"

"Water is fine," Klein answered.

She led them to a clean table and went to retrieve their order.

"You could have tried being a little nicer," Klein muttered to Mystic once the innkeeper was out of earshot.

Mystic gave Klein a blank stare. "That was me being nice. I was hungry, and it was her job to bring me food, wasn't it? Besides, you weren't exactly charming her either." Mystic was never a morning person, but they needed information—and being nice wouldn't hurt.

It didn't take long for the innkeeper to come back from the kitchen with a tray in hand. "There you are. Is there anything else I can get for you two?"

"We are actually here for sightseeing," Klein said, taking the plate of scrambled eggs and potatoes covered in a generous serving of cheese. "Can you tell us anything about the city or the royalty who run it?"

The innkeeper closed her eyes, contemplating what to say. "Well, as you know, the city is run by the Ostara Court Lord and his daughter. Though, I'm afraid she hasn't been seen in many years. Word on the street is that ever since her mother died, she hasn't left her room. Most of the city is built and powered by their magic, though. As far as sights to see, there is the Great Royal Rose Garden. It's beautiful this time of year and open to the public. I'm afraid the castle itself is limited access only. You know, even the servants live there full-time and aren't allowed to leave."

"No one ever leaves?" Klein asked quizzically. "Not even the High Lord?"

"Ever since the Lady of Spring passed away twenty years ago, the castle has been kept tightly locked down. If you were hoping to meet with the Lord, I'm afraid you would be disappointed. The only time he leaves his castle is during the Spring Solstice when he has to give his blessing to the land."

"Thank you for the information and for the delicious breakfast," Klein said, finishing his meal.

"Yes, thank you," Mystic added, crumbs from the fresh-baked bread falling from her mouth.

The innkeeper left with a smile and went on to continue serving the patrons.

"See, I told you I could be nice," Mystic chuckled, taking large bites of her food. She was eating like a wild animal that morning, and all the traveling seemed to have taken a toll on her.

Klein finished his food, finding the bread to be buttery and warm, melting in his mouth. It was the best thing he had eaten in a long time. "Let's just finish up quickly and go check out those gardens," he mumbled between bites. "Clearly, you're not having any trouble eating fast."

"Har har," Mystic replied.

The city of Ostara bustled with Fae walking to and from their errands. Some of them rode large bird-like creatures, similar to the Lithan drakes, that were covered in colorful feathers of yellow, green, and blue. The buildings in the city were intricately carved with designs that would have taken centuries to complete by hand. The designs depicted scenes from the past when the gods of the Fae walked among the people and showed the gift of the crystals they had given. The gods were depicted using clear crystals, which was said to be how they appeared. The thought of a moving crystal god was unnerving for Klein. The crystals the Fae used to build churches were bad enough. Those crystals were once living, breathing Fae who sacrificed themselves for the 'greater good' of our world.

Everywhere they looked, images of the Ostara Sapphire were depicted. On signs, on buildings, even the Fae females of this city seemed to all be wearing replicas around their necks. Each of the courts used to have jewelry said to be blessed by the gods—necklaces for the seasonal courts and crowns for the courts of light and dark. Out of all the necklaces given to the Fae, the Ostara Sapphire was the only one left.

The rulers of each side of the continent, the Seelie King in the south and the Unseelie Queen in the north, both still had the crowns of black obsidian and white opal. They were probably what gave them the power to keep the rest of the courts in line. The rest of the relics were lost to the ages or stolen, much like this one would be. If the Ostara Sapphire had some great power, as they claimed, they certainly weren't using it. They probably wouldn't even notice it went missing.

Mystic put on one of the replica necklaces with a wink to Klein. Clearly, she had stolen it from one of the females they passed by in the town square. He had to admit having a replica would come in handy for the crime they were about to commit. They took their time buying new outfits and cloaks in deep colors that would give them some cover. They had kept their faces wrapped up in the Litha clothing when they entered the city to keep their distinct hair hidden, and the new navy cloaks would do the same job.

The heist was to take place the following night. Get in, get out, and never step foot in this court again. Today was all about figuring out the guards' rotation and maybe testing the rings they had to get through the wards. A walk through the rose gardens was the perfect excuse to do both.

Dressed in their new cloaks, Klein and Mystic arrived at the Great Royal Rose Garden, hidden within the heart of the city of Ostara. They had spent the morning exploring the city, and despite the sea of Fae citizens going about their daily errands, they found few answers to their questions about the goings-on of the royal court. The common folk of Ostara seemed to know little about the last twenty years of their rulers' lives, only that they were shrouded in a veil of mourning.

As they entered the gardens, the scent of flowers and pollen greeted them, filling the air with the sweet aroma of spring. However, the abundance of blooms and greenery proved to be too much for Klein's sensitive nose, causing him to sniffle and sneeze loudly. He quickly wiped away the resulting mess, trying to hide his discomfort. Despite the distraction, they pressed on, determined to complete their reconnaissance mission. The garden paths were lined with towering trees, offering them a quiet escape from the bustling city, and the colorful blooms swayed gently in the soft breeze. It was a peaceful, serene place. And for a moment, Klein was able to forget about the task at hand—that is if it wasn't for the damn pollen everywhere.

As they navigated the maze-like pathways of the garden, Klein and Mystic made it their mission to soak in every detail of their surroundings. The beauty of the blooming flowers and the enchanting aroma was inescapable, but it also had an adverse effect on Klein. The pollen was causing his eyes to become red and itchy, and he couldn't help but continue to sneeze.

"You doing okay there, brother? Your eyes look extremely red," Mystic asked, studying Klein's face with concern.

"It's nothing I can't handle. Just a little pollen in my eyes," Klein responded, trying to sound unbothered. "I might need to stop at the apothecary on the way back to the inn."

The size of the garden was massive, and it seemed as though every tree and flower in existence was present. The hedges, used to create intricate mazes, looked challenging and complicated, and Klein wished he could view them from above. But he knew that was impossible, as the guards were always present, keeping a watchful eye and ensuring no one got too close to the towering castle nearby.

The castle was a massive, gray brick structure that could house the entire city within its walls. Its walls were adorned with tooth vines, giving it a neglected appearance, at least from the outside.

As they walked through the garden, taking in all its beauty, they spent hours observing their surroundings and learning the guards' routines. They eventually grew hungry and headed back to the city to buy some food and stopped by the apothecary to get some allergy remedies for Klein. They couldn't afford to have his allergies disrupt their mission, so they made sure to take all the necessary precautions.

Stopping at a sandwich cart, they bought cucumber and cream cheese sandwiches and chatted with the male who ran the stall. He was darker-complected than most in Ostara, with brown hair and eyes, placing him from Litha.

"Did you guys already check out the gardens?" He asked them, tilting his head curiously.

Mystic answered him first. "Yes, we walked around them. They were lovely."

"That they are, lass. That they are. But if you really wanted to see them shine, you should have taken a tour during the Spring Solstice," the male gushed. "They string all sorts of amazing lights and crystals in all the trees. It makes it feel like the stars have come down from the sky."

"Oh, I'm sorry we missed it, then," Klein said, taking the sandwich the fae was handing him.

"Well, they're still worth viewing at night this time of year. There are no lights, but there are some extra special flowers throughout. They say taking your true love to look at them will seal your relationship for eternity," the stall owner said dreamily. "I sell the seeds for those flowers if you want to try growing some yourself. Only ten gold a seed, and your true love could be yours forever."

"Um, we're good. Thanks. We could use some information, though. What can you tell us about the Ostara Royals? No one seems to know anything." Mystic said, giving him a sultry smile.

The Fae looked around, seemingly checking to see if anyone else was nearby before speaking. "I'm not from here, but I've heard rumors," he said, leaning close. "I'll tell you what I know for a few gold coins."

Klein handed over the coins and gave the Fae a serious look. "This information had better be worth the gold," he growled.

"You can trust me on this," the vendor said as he eagerly rubbed his hands together after putting the gold coins into his pocket. "The Princess of Ostara was cursed when she was a young girl to spend her life in an eternal slumber. The curse stated that only death could save her. Her mother, in desperation, gave her own life in an attempt to break the curse, but unfortunately, it didn't work. The princess is still said to be in a deep sleep in her room in the north tower, surrounded by magic flowers believed to keep her alive. However, I have heard rumors that the true reason for her longevity is the necklace she wears. It is probably the only remaining ancient magic capable of keeping her from passing away."

Great, so by stealing the necklace, we might also be possibly committing murder against the Royal family, Klein thought to himself.

"Thank you for the information," Klein said, maintaining his polite demeanor. "It's been fascinating to learn about the family history."

The vendor tilted his head. "I hope you enjoy the rest of your time in Ostara," he said. "And don't forget about the limited supply of magic flower seeds I have for sale!"

After finishing their sandwiches and exploring more of the city, the siblings returned to the gardens to check on any changes to the night guard schedule. As they walked, they noticed small, glowing blue flowers throughout the garden. Although beautiful, Klein couldn't detect any magic from them. Perhaps their magical powers were only activated during the Spring solstice.

Klein and Mystic carefully observed the guards as they began to usher the remaining Fae out of the gardens and lock the gates. The Fae, who seemed unperturbed by the guards, calmly walked towards the exit while the siblings kept a low profile to avoid any suspicion. The gardens were almost empty, and the only sounds that echoed throughout the area were the faint rustling of leaves and the occasional chirping of crickets.

As they made their way back to the inn, Klein and Mystic couldn't help but reflect on the information they had gathered during their tour of the gardens—the mystery of the sleeping princess and the tale of the cursed young lady of Ostara still lingering in their minds. The siblings wondered what other secrets the city might hold, but for now, they were content with returning to their room to rest and gather their thoughts. They were looking forward to finishing the job and getting paid.

"So, do you think we have enough information to carry out the plan?" Mystic asked as she collapsed onto the soft bed.

"I think we have enough, but it never hurts to have more. We need to be quick and leave before anyone realizes who we are," Klein replied, rubbing his hands through his hair after taking off his cloak. "We're already attracting attention. I haven't seen any other Yule Fae around here."

Mystic sighed. "It's hard to believe that the princess is cursed. To sleep all day in a nice castle, servants attending to your every need—sounds more like a dream come true."

"We just have to make sure that taking the necklace won't end up killing her," Klein muttered, settling into a chair near the fireplace. "But the curse says death is the only way to break it, so maybe it's for the best. We have to be cautious, though. If anyone discovers what we're up to, we'll be in big trouble."

"You'll have to be especially careful tomorrow when you sneak into the north tower," Mystic agreed, closing her eyes as she leaned back against the pillows. "But, I have faith in us. We've tackled harder heists before. Remember that time with the goblins and the maze of death? I thought for sure we were dead." They had both decided that Klein would be the one to enter the castle, and Mystic would stand watch.

Klein let out a chuckle. "You're right. We've always gotten lucky in the end. This time will be no different."

"Luck?" Mystic scoffed, "It's called skill. We're the best thieves in Jelaria. At least, I am anyway." She gave Klein a feral grin.

"Sure, that's why they call you Kleptis." Klein deadpanned, waving her off. "Let's get some rest and be ready for tomorrow. We need to be alert and focused if we want to make this work."

Mystic stuck out her tongue and flipped him off before moving to her bed to rest for the night.

With the time for words over, the siblings settled down to get some much-needed rest—each lost in their own thoughts about the task ahead as Klein prepared to take the first watch. Despite the risks involved, they both felt a thrill of excitement at the challenge that lay ahead. They were going to succeed, no matter what challenges they faced tomorrow. Luck was on their side.

Chapter 23

Mel

It was warm under the covers, and as I snuggled deeper into my lover's arms. I felt content. I was cocooned in his warmth, with his arms holding me tight—almost tempting me to stay sleeping in bed for just a little while longer. But just as I was about to drift back into sleep, the harsh beep of the alarm clock pierced through my peaceful rest and jolted my heart back to reality. Fucking alarms ruin everything.

"Good morning, beautiful," Alex's soft voice greeted me, stirring something deep in my chest. Opening my eyes, I took in his handsome face, dark stubble lining his jaw. The warmth and comfort of being in his embrace was the best feeling in the world. The sound of the alarm ringing in the background served as a reminder that we needed to start our day. But I wasn't ready to leave his arms just yet. I turned away from him briefly to snooze the alarm, tossing my phone off the bed. *Now, it's later me's problem.*

"Good morning, handsome," I murmured, turning back to cuddle into his warm arms, resting my head on his shirtless chest. "What time do you have work today?" I asked, trying to shake off the last remnants of sleep.

"Not until twelve. I've been talking to my dad about making my schedule closer to yours so you don't have to be home alone for long. He's been understanding about the whole thing." The alarm was set to go off at nine to give us a little more time to relax. I snuggled deeper into his embrace.

"That would be nice. Then, we can always wake up together." I told him sleepily.

"I'd love that Hermosa. More than anything." Warm hands trailed down my back before circling at the base of my spine. Alex brought his chin to rest on my head. "Did you know you talk in your sleep sometimes?"

"Do I really?" I asked, embarrassed. "What did I say?"

He looked up, thinking. "Well, it was mostly gibberish, but you were talking about the flowers making you sneeze."

"Oh, that must have been when they got to Ostara..." I shook my head in confusion. "Oops, sorry. I didn't mean to let that slip. I just have really vivid dreams," I said, shaking my head again. My cheeks felt hot as all my blood rushed to my face.

"That's amazing. I wish I could remember my dreams that vividly," Alex said.

"I'm so embarrassed. I hope I didn't say anything weird." I thought about it for a minute. "Oh no, I hope I didn't keep you up all night!"

"Don't worry about it, and I didn't mind. Plus, it was kind of cute," Alex chuckled. "But, to get back to our schedule, I'll see what I can do. I want us to spend as much time together as possible." I smiled, feeling grateful for him all over again.

We spent a cozy morning talking in bed, surrounded by the comfort of our bedsheets and each other's warmth. As I opened up about my dreams, I was met with the undivided attention of my boyfriend, Alex. He listened attentively, never once interrupting me, and I couldn't help but feel grateful to have someone who takes my thoughts and feelings seriously. I went into detail about the vividness of my dreams and the emotions that came with them.

He was interested in the characters and world of Jelaria, asking for more details. He even went on to say what a great anime it would make. Alex responded with gentle touches and an understanding ear, making me feel heard and comforted. It was a beautiful moment, being able to finally let someone in on my innermost secrets and have them accept and understand me. A weight lifted off my shoulders as I confided in Alex. I couldn't be happier to have him in my life.

"How about we grab breakfast?" Alex's voice was soft as he spoke into my hair. In response, my stomach gave a loud rumble, making Alex laugh. "I think breakfast is definitely a good idea," he said, placing a kiss on my forehead before getting out of bed to get ready for the day.

Dressed for the day, I decided to wear my athletic gear, including a crop top and leggings, so that I could attend my gym class after breakfast. Meanwhile, Alex chose to wear an anime t-shirt and jeans, creating a casual yet stylish look. We agreed to go to the café down the street, as it was close by and offered a more relaxed atmosphere compared to Wacky's.

Hand in hand, we strolled towards the little cafe, the crisp winter air nipping at our noses, yet not as cold as yesterday. We wore our winter coats, but the weather started to feel like spring was on the way. Birds were singing, and the sun was shining—or at least the pigeons were cooing, and the sun was sort of shining through the smog, but you get the point. It was a pretty nice day.

Upon arrival at the little cafe, we took a seat in the back, where they had little couches set up near an electric fireplace. It was cozy, so I took off my jacket. The table had a little sign to scan with your phone for the menu.

Taking out my phone, I did as instructed and looked at what they had to offer that day. They usually had seasonal coffees and treats. "What are you going to get?" I asked Alex, who was also looking at the menu on his phone.

"Maybe the peppermint mocha and a breakfast burrito," he said, glancing up at me. "Peppermint is my favorite, and they're probably going to get rid of it after this month."

"True. To be honest, it kinda tastes like toothpaste to me," I joked as I continued to scan my phone. "But a burrito would be good." I looked through the seasonal flavors: sugar cookie, peppermint, and gingerbread. "I guess I'll try the gingerbread." I used the app to order, and they brought it to our table. It was amazing what these modern restaurants were doing now. It probably made it easier for the workers.

Using the app, I ordered my drink with almond milk and a bacon breakfast with red chili. I started to order Alex's food, too, but he stopped me. "I can get us breakfast."

"You have to let me buy things for you too. I'm supposed to be your girlfriend, right?" I told him. After a little argument, he agreed to let me pay for his food, too.

Our order came out quickly, with our coffee steaming in ceramic mugs. Taking a sip, I hummed my satisfaction. Gingerbread was a good choice. "How's yours?" I asked Alex.

"Minty fresh," he laughed. We cut into our breakfast burritos, which were smothered in chili. It amazed me that there were parts of the country that didn't know what real chili tasted like. We were so close to the border of New Mexico, home of the red and green chili. Even so, only a few restaurants carried it on their menus. It was spicy and not too hot, covered in melty cheese. The burritos were a lot bigger than I expected, and I was doubtful I would be able to finish the whole thing.

As we savored our breakfast burritos and coffee, we discussed our living situation. With Harvey still stalking me, I wasn't comfortable staying by myself. Jess simply didn't have the time to stay with me, as the club was too far away. The thought of moving in together crossed our minds, but we were unsure if it was too soon.

"I need to wash some clothes today at my place," Alex said. "Do you want me to wash yours? I know you don't have easy access to a washer at your place." The thought of him finding my wet panties made my cheeks heat up.

"No, that's okay," I replied quickly. "Do you need to get your stuff before you go to work?"

"Yeah," he said. "I'll drop you off at the gym." He smiled at me. "I'm really proud of you for sticking with it. Too bad it's a women's only gym, or I would go with you."

"Maybe I could start going to your gym once my discount membership runs out," I said, smiling back. It would be nice to work out together, especially since the few times he helped train me were incredibly helpful. I was now confident that I could fight my way out of most dangerous situations. Not that I hoped to ever be in one of those situations again.

After leaving a tip on the table, we walked back to the apartment so Alex could get his backpack. There was still plenty of time before my gym class, so it wouldn't be a problem to go back and forth.

As we stepped into the apartment, a chill ran down my spine as a gust of cold air rushed past us. My eyes immediately fixated on the open window, the curtains fluttering in the wind. Just as I reached for the light switch, I felt a cold, hard object press against my temple, making me freeze and gasp in shock.

A rough voice spoke into my ear, "Don't do anything stupid, Princess." I was being dragged against a man's body, the feeling of a gun pressing into my head. Everything inside me went numb as I froze. My mouth started to tingle, and the fear ran through the rest of my body. "Take a seat, little boy," he sneered to Alex behind me. "I'll tell you how this is going to go. You're going to let me leave with my whore, and no one has to get hurt."

My mind raced as I tried to figure out what to do. My training should have kicked in to give me a way to escape this situation, but I was frozen, barely able to breathe. I cast a pleading look to Alex, hoping he'd run. What was the point of all my self-defense training if I can't use it when it matters most? Another surge of fear coursed through me as I thought of my kitten and wondered if she got hurt.

As I locked eyes with Alex, I saw a look of resolve. He wouldn't abandon me to this monster. I forced my limbs to move—to do something, but even as I tried, my muscles seemed locked in place. If this man took me with him, there wouldn't be any hope left. He'd lock me up and throw away the key, only letting me out to force his body onto mine. Alex hadn't sat down in the chair as was demanded of him. Was he going to run?

"Hurry up, or I'll have to damage my prize!" The intruder's voice boomed with anger, droplets of saliva landing on my face as he spoke. Alex sprang into action, not heading for the chair as directed but instead rushing towards me and the man who had a gun to my head. Alex grabbed the hand that held the gun and directed it away from me with one hand while using the other to twist his wrist, causing the weapon to fall to the floor. However, his efforts were in vain as a loud shot echoed through the small apartment. The man collided into me with force, sending me tumbling to the ground. For a second, everything went white, and I was sure I had been shot.

A sharp pain shot through my skull as it collided with the bed frame, causing a sickening crack to fill the air. My head spun, and my vision blurred as nausea overwhelmed me, making it impossible for me to rise. This was so much worse.

The attacker, who I now realized was Michael, was engaged in a fierce fight with Alex, exchanging punches and kicks. As Alex and Michael engaged in a brutal exchange of blows, the sound of fists striking flesh and curses echoing through the room filled the air.

Michael swung wildly—desperation evident in his movements, but Alex was relentless, dodging each attack and striking back with precision. The two of them struggled for control, neither one giving an inch. Finally, with a surge of strength, Alex managed to disarm Michael, causing the gun to clatter to the floor. Despite the violent struggle, Alex showed no signs of slowing down, his eyes locked on his opponent as he prepared for the next round.

Michael cursed, wiping the blood from his swollen lip, sneering, "Just let me take the girl back to the club! You wouldn't believe what Harvey offered me for her return! We could split it?"

Hoping the gunshot would draw someone's attention to call 911, I lay helpless on the floor, unable to move—watching this nightmare. The gun slid across the floor, just inches from my hand. I desperately tried to reach for it, hoping to help Alex, but my body refused to listen. Charlie crawled out from under the bed, where he must have been hiding. The kitten started licking my eyelids as if begging me to get up. I was relieved to see that Michael hadn't hurt my little kitty.

The sensation of warm liquid from my nose alarmed me. As I looked at my reflection in the TV, I could see a pool of blood slowly growing around my head. *That can't be a good sign.*

The reflection flickered back and forth, alternating between my prone image and the image of pale hands reaching forward. The hands seemed to be covered in more and more blood as my own continued to leak out of me. I tried to turn my focus back to the fight, but it was so hard—my body started to feel so heavy, and my vision was getting blurry. It took a tremendous amount of effort to drag my eyes across the room. When I finally did, I was filled with pride. I saw Alex viciously kicking Michael, who had fallen to the ground and covered his head like the coward he was.

Bloody and battered, Alex came to me, and I could see his lips moving. His voice was quiet as he cried. "No. No. No! Don't leave me. Look at me, Hermosa. Help is on the way. You just need to hold on a little longer. I love you, don't go."

I tried to respond. I wanted to let him know that I wasn't giving up, that I was going to be okay, and that I loved him too—but my tongue was lead in my mouth. I was so fucking tired as bitter tears flowed down my cheeks. He started talking and shouting as he began to cradle my head in his arms. But I couldn't hear his words anymore. How strange. Tears filled his eyes as he looked at me, and I wanted to wipe them away—but I found that I was unable to move my arms. I couldn't even feel them anymore. I just wanted to touch him, just one more time. He shouted something at the door, but I was unable to make myself look to see who it was.

Despite my desire to keep looking at Alex, my eyes were drawn back to the TV. The bloody hands urging me forward and an ethereal voice—both young and old, male and female, filled my head with whispers: "It's time. Destiny awaits." *Destiny? My destiny is to be with Alex and Charlie and to make a life for myself. I finally found my place in the world. I want to live the life that I chose.* But even as I thought that I could feel my spirit leaving my body, as if I was floating up and out. The sensation of being sucked into a vortex took over.

Fighting the sensation with everything I had, I tried to stay and bring my mind back to Alex. *Please just let me stay. I don't want to leave just yet. It wasn't the best life, but it was mine.*

In this spirit form, I brushed my lips against his, my sweet love, as he held my still body. I wished for the chance to live the life I would have had with him by my side. If only we could have more time. Grief broke me apart as I pondered all that we were losing—all of our plans and future together. All because of the man whom I wished I had never met. We could have had so much more.

As a scream built in my throat, I was thrown backward into the unknown.

Chapter 24

Telaria

    Like all well-planned heists, Klein's plan was proceeding smoothly. He had analyzed the guard rotation and timed the execution perfectly. Mystic, in her snake form, was waiting to use her sleeping toxins on the guards while Klein entered the castle of Ostara, hidden by the amulet of invisibility. The amulet's power cloaked Klein, making him invisible to anyone who might see him. The map they had acquired showed precisely where the Lady of Ostara would be sleeping, and their plan was simple: slip in, grab the necklace, and slip out.

    Klein checked his pocket watch as the minutes ticked by. On schedule, the old guards began to leave, patting the new guards on the back as they took over. Mystic was waiting in the shadows, ready to strike. The guards seemed relaxed as if nothing bad could ever happen in this castle. That was their first mistake. Their second mistake was not checking their surroundings when they took up their watch. Mystic, sleek and silent, slithered among the vines hanging on the wall and attacked the first guard, biting him on the neck.

Before the second guard could cry out in alarm, Mystic had moved on to him and knocked him out. She then transformed back into her Fae form and dragged the bodies into the bushes where they wouldn't be seen. Mystic sent Klein the signal from her vantage point in the trees, with a burst of air magic tapping him on the neck three times to indicate it was time to move. Klein entered the castle through the now unguarded side entrance.

As he entered, Klein was awed by the grandeur of the castle. The walls were decorated with intricate frescoes, and the gleaming marble floors echoed his stealthy movements as he made his way to the north tower where the Lady of Ostara slept. Confident that the castle's wards wouldn't detect him, he crept slowly and cautiously—sidestepping the guards he encountered. He was determined not to make a sound, avoiding the risk of knocking out the guards and leaving behind bodies that might raise the alarm.

Klein had planned for the heist to take no more than an hour, but even that seemed like a long time given the vast area he would have to cover to reach the north tower. The castle was cold and eerie, with most of the rooms empty and the furniture covered in white sheets, like lifeless bodies. The paintings on the walls were hidden behind cloths, giving the illusion that the only occupants were the ghostly apparitions patrolling the halls. As Klein passed through a large throne room, he was startled to find one of the guards away from his post. The guard was sitting on the dais with a bottle of wine in his lap, seemingly unbothered by his lack of vigilance.

"Who's there?" The guard slurred, squinting in Klein's direction.

Checking to ensure the amulet was still working, Klein looked down to see that his body was still invisible. He was confident that the guard wouldn't be able to detect him and continued to walk through the throne room.

Suddenly, the guard stood up, waving a bottle in the air. "This is all your fault!" he yelled. "Mom was right. I should have never taken this job. I should have found a nice female and settled down, not be guarding this haunted castle like a fool." With a hiccup, the guard stumbled back down to the floor.

Klein surveyed the room, making sure he was alone. It was empty except for the guard, who had clearly had too much to drink and was talking to himself. He realized that the castle's security was lacking, and he was sure that after tonight, they would improve it—but it would be too late to stop him and his sister from stealing the crystal.

Being careful not to alert the guard, Klein snuck past him and approached the throne. Behind it was a hidden door used by servants to bring food and wine to the rulers during court sessions. But it had been many years since this door had been used. Klein pushed the wall, and the latch clicked loudly. He spun around, checking if the guard had noticed, but he was still snoring softly on the floor, wine spilling all over the dusty rug.

As Klein pushed open the door, he stepped into a dark, cobweb-filled servant's passage. The creepy crawlies seemed to be attracted to him, as he felt them gathering on his clothes, only to quickly disappear due to the power of his amulet. Though he couldn't see them, the thought of spiders crawling all over his invisible form sent shivers down his spine. With a deep breath, he shifted his eyes to his wolf form, allowing him to see clearly in the darkness. He cautiously continued down the hallway, aware of the unseen creatures around him.

He noticed that even though he was invisible, his boots were still leaving footprints. He hesitated, wondering whether he should wash them away with water magic or if that would raise more suspicion. He decided to leave the footprints, reasoning that no one had been in this passageway for years, and it was unlikely that a servant would check it now.

Following the mental map he had memorized the night before, Klein took two left turns and a right, arriving at a small door. Beyond it, he expected to find the main hall leading to the north tower. From there, it was just a few hundred steps to his goal.

As he opened the small door, he entered a bright room. It wasn't the hallway he had expected, but a small kitchen. The door opening caused a small female to jump up in fright. It was a servant who was washing dishes, the soapy suds covering her hands as they flew to her throat. Not seeing anything amiss, she began to laugh. "Damn, drafty castle!"

The kitchen was much better taken care of than any of the other areas of the castle. Each surface shone with pristine cleanliness. Klein was careful not to make any more noise and left the door open. After wiping her hands, the servant girl closed it shut, getting so close to Klein that he could feel her breath. Her brow furrowed as if she could see him there, but after a moment, she returned to her dishes. He was going to have to be careful on the way out and avoid this room altogether.

The door he needed to go through next was heavy and wooden, hopefully leading to the main hall. There was no way to do that without alerting the servant. Making a quick decision, Klein hit the female on the back of her neck, knocking her out cold. He caught her as she slumped forward and placed her on the floor. She wouldn't be out for long, but without Mystic to knock her out with venom, there was no way to predict when she would wake up. As gently as he could, Klein put her in a small pantry and placed a stool under the handle. Someone would find her in the morning, and she would be just fine.

The door creaked loudly, and Klein winced. At first, no one said anything, so he assumed the hallway was clear of guards, but as he started creeping into the hall, he saw a guard standing at the end. The man was wearing thick leather armor, durable without being restrictive. A helmet partially covered his head, exposing the lower half and revealing a strong jaw and blonde stubble.

"Is that you, Linda? Done for the night already?" The guard chuckled. "Linda? Is everything alright?" He frowned when the servant girl didn't respond to his call. They must have been friends. The guard rushed down the hall and came face to face with Klein, blinking rapidly. "You're not Linda."

Klein realized he was no longer invisible and looked down at himself. "Well, shit. You caught me," he said. "That's a first."

He quickly tried to knock out the guard, as he had done with the servant girl, but his neck was too thick with muscle, making it difficult to reach the nerves. Grunting, the guard pulled out his sword and prepared to attack. Klein managed to dodge the first slice, but the blade still cut through some of his shirt, sending it fluttering behind him. He put some distance between them and used his speed to pull out his daggers, aiming for incapacitation, not murder. He couldn't leave a trail of bodies behind on this mission, as it would only make the rest of the guards work harder to catch him later.

"If anything happened to Linda, I swear, I'll skip the trial and end you right here and now. Who would blame me for killing thieving Yule-scum like you!" The guard growled, charging at Klein. He seemed either too angry or too foolish to alert the other guards, but there could be one close enough that had already heard the commotion.

Klein didn't have time to think about that. He needed to knock out the guard and move quickly to the top of the tower. The time for subtlety had ended; now that they knew someone was in the castle, this hallway could be swarming with guards in mere minutes.

The guard's heavy boots clanged against the stone floor as he raised his blade and swung. Klein crossed his daggers to block the blow, using the guard's weight against him to twist the sword down. This move threw the guard off balance, giving Klein the opportunity to bring his foot up in an arch, aiming for the enemy's head. It hit with devastating force, landing with a satisfying crunch. Something was definitely broken. Klein hoped it wasn't the poor man's spine.

The guard crumpled to the ground, no longer a problem. Klein leaned down to check if he was still breathing. It was shallow and labored, but he wasn't dead... yet. The blow had broken something vital in the guard's neck, and Klein was sure that if help didn't come soon, the guard wouldn't make it through the night.

One complication after another.

"I don't have time for this..." Klein grumbled under his breath as he made the quick decision to leave the guard where he lay, sprinting up the hall to the staircase. The stairs seemed endless as he took flight after flight, his muscles burning with each step. Despite the exertion, he pushed on, driven by the feeling in his chest that everything he had ever sought was just a few steps away. He couldn't afford to stop now.

As he got closer, the air grew heavy with anticipation. He could feel an unseen presence watching his every move. Finally, he saw the double doors carved with roses and thorns. The golden doorknob glinted in the soft light filtering through a small window, beckoning him forward. He reached for the handle, only to find it locked. Of course, it wouldn't be easy, he thought.

Klein didn't waste time fiddling with his lock-picking tools. Instead, he summoned a blast of ice magic, causing the door knob to explode in a shower of frozen fragments. The doors swung open with a creak, revealing the room beyond. It was fit for a princess, with ornate furnishings and delicate tapestries hanging from the walls.

When he stepped inside, the lights suddenly began flashing a dangerous red tone, signaling an alarm. The physical alarms, along with the magic wards, had been triggered. There was no longer any doubt; they knew he was here. But Klein didn't hesitate, driven by his need to reach his goal and claim his fortune and freedom.

Chapter 25

Telaria

Breaking into the Spring Court castle should have been a simple task for Klein and Mystic. However, as soon as Klein entered the room of the slumbering princess, he triggered an alarm system that he had never encountered before. Most Fae relied on magic wards to protect their treasure, but with the introduction of electricity, they had begun experimenting with other forms of protection. With every second that passed, Klein felt that fate was turning against him and that the gods were laughing at him.

Klein reached for the necklace, ready to take it from the princess's neck, but something stopped him. A deep pulling sensation in his gut as he gazed upon the princess's face. She seemed so familiar to him, yet that wasn't possible. There was no way he would have encountered the heir of Ostara before. Her strawberry blonde curls framed her peaceful features, and her skin—which should have been golden, was pale from lack of sun exposure. Despite this, a smattering of freckles dotted her cheeks. She slept, unaware of the situation around her, with her hands crossed over her chest in a prayer-like pose.

Klein tried to reach for the blue-stoned necklace, his fingers barely touching it, when the princess suddenly sat up, screaming and crying in devastation.

When Klein's vision was momentarily obscured by the bright white light that radiated from one of the princess's eyes, he instinctively raised his hands to shield himself. The sudden loss of his amulet left him vulnerable, and he was in need of a new plan. The only escape he could think of was to jump out of the window despite the danger of the fall. Mystic was waiting outside, and she would catch him if necessary.

With the princess now awake, he knew that there was no chance of him leaving with the necklace. The guards were probably on their way to this room right now.

As his vision cleared, Klein was struck by the sight of the princess, who was in tears. The sounds she was making were gut-wrenching and evoked a deep sense of empathy within him. He was desperate to help her, to do anything to ease her pain. He shouldn't be feeling any of this. He had a job to complete. But as he reached for the necklace one last time, with the intention of knocking her out, their eyes met. One eye was a sparkling blue, and the other was glowing yellow. With a single word, she froze him in his tracks.

"Klein?" she said, her voice barely above a whisper.

He was frozen, unable to move, as if an ancient force was holding him in place. *How does she know my name?* He thought to himself. It was the name of a lost Fae, a thief and a liar, but from her lips, it was like a plea that he wanted to answer. Something inside him was pulling tight, like an iron rope tying him to the princess. He felt his feet turn to lead, and he knew that if he didn't move, he would be caught by the guards and thrown into the dungeon.

Klein could hear the faint footsteps of the guards as they ran up the stairs, but he was paralyzed by the bond that had formed between him and the princess. It was as if he was under a spell and unable to break free. With each passing moment, he felt the fear of his impending capture grow stronger. It was too late to turn back, but he was faced with a difficult decision: follow his instincts and run, or stay and face the consequences of his actions.

"Why am I here? I'm dead!" The princess cried out, gasping for air. "This isn't real. None of this is real!" She shook her head, mumbling to herself. "Not real. Not real..."

Klein struggled to find the words to answer her, but he desperately wanted to ease her pain. He was unable to do anything but stare at her as she spoke, but with a burst of magic, he splashed water on his face to break out of his stupor. The cold water helped clear his mind a little, and he finally found his voice. "How..." But before he could speak, the guards burst into the room, making any words he had useless.

One word repeated in his head. *Mine... Mine... MINE!*

No, never mine. The gods would never grant him something as special as a mate bond. He didn't deserve it—didn't deserve her.

This feeling that was building within him could only mean one thing—that this beautiful and powerful Fae was meant to be his mate. But how was that possible? He had heard of this happening to other Fae, although it was exceedingly rare. He felt a mental connection being triggered by his proximity to her, and he realized that she must be feeling something similar. How else could she know his name?

It was pointless to fight the guards, and they easily overpowered him, bringing him to his knees. As they placed iron manacles on his wrist, draining his magic, he couldn't help but feel a sense of hopelessness wash over him. He had just found his mate, only for it to be taken away just as quickly. It seemed like the gods were watching and laughing at his fate.

But as the guards started to drag him away, the princess reached out her hands to him. "Stop! Don't hurt him!" she cried out, trying to get out of bed. Her muscles failed her, and she crashed to the ground with a scream. Klein wanted to help her, but the guards forced him down. The sight of another's hands on her sent a wave of rage through him, and a roar escaped his lips as he tried to break free from the iron manacles. He had to help her.

"Enough of that!" a guard growled, bringing the pommel of his sword down on Klein's head. Everything went black as he fell into unconsciousness.

The only certainty was that Klein would be dead by morning.

Shattered Crystal

Written by M. T. Syler

Book One of the Crystal Fae

Letter From the Author

Wow, we did it! Congratulations on successfully completing the first book of the Crystal Fae series! Are you excited about what's going to happen next? I'm truly grateful to have shared this writing journey with you. To be honest, when I started writing this book, I had no idea what I was getting myself into or the sheer amount of work it would take to finish it, but I'm so glad it did it! If you enjoyed it, please leave me a review and let me know! Book 2, Broken Gates, is already in progress.

I want to extend a special thanks to Melissa for her tireless editing efforts, which significantly improved the readability of the book. Additionally, a big thank you goes to my husband, who's always been supportive of my ideas, no matter how crazy they may seem. And, of course, my mom has been my unwavering rock throughout this entire process.

Last but not least, I want to thank Valene and Mary for reading through the book and providing valuable feedback that confirmed Mel's story was worth telling and that the revisions were worth it to get it to where it is now.

M.T. Syler

Made in the USA
Columbia, SC
20 August 2024

2abfcb36-b491-425a-aa14-5d205814f46dR01